Ambergris

Briony Collins

BARNARD
PUBLISHING LTD.

Also by Briony Collins

<u>*Poetry*</u>
Blame it on Me
Whisper Network (with Caleb Nichols)
The Birds, The Rabbits, The Trees
cactus land
I Know Where the Pelicans Go
Wyoming

<u>*Short Fiction*</u>
All That Glisters

For the best boys a girl could grow up with:

Cale, Finn, and Foxx

Ambergris

HENRY

As **hard as** he tried, Henry Belvidere couldn't recall where he was or how he got there. The first thing he remembered at the beach was looking for his oxygen tank. He couldn't leave home without it, but it wasn't here. The last thing he remembered before waking up was bringing Madeline coffee in bed. She smelled like the eucalyptus soap in the bathroom. Henry hoped he wasn't dead.

He sat and scooped up a handful of sand, letting it run through his fingers. Some grains stuck under his nails, and he swore. He watched his hands stretch and barely recognised them. His fingertips were nicked with a hundred, tiny white scars from decades of splinters — evidence of the forty-three years he'd spent working at Dixon's Lumber before he retired. Down the side of his left thumb, between freckles and age spots, was a longer, redder scar. Henry stroked the lines on his palms with hardened fingers. It looked like his flesh was cracking, made up of different pieces instead of one unending wrap of skin.

It felt like only recently his hands belonged to a young boy. They weren't soft and smooth like other children's, but instead suffered just as many cuts and scrapes as when he took up lumbering. The scratches he got when he was young were different to these in one important detail: as a man, Henry handled the real world. As a boy, his sole line of work was in shaping the imaginary. With one touch a tree could be transformed into a mighty monster, whose almond-shaped leaves became thousands of eyes that blinked in the wind. He ran from it to the garden wall, which was his medieval castle. Moss grew between the slabs and stained his palms green – the same colour as the blood of the monster Henry slew. At ten years old, he was Midas; every golden opportunity lay at his fingertips with all of the glory and none of the consequences.

Henry grabbed another handful of sand and let it flow out of his grasp again, aware that he didn't have the same hold on the world as he did in childhood. In any other scenario, the beach might have been a magnificent place. The sea's white horses galloped onto the shore that swooped up into the dunes behind him. The golden hills met an oasis of greenery where birds dipped into the thickets of trees. Clouds smoked in a sky that was the colour of Madeline's eyes.

He thought it was strange that he remembered playing along the garden wall fifty-seven years ago, but had no recollection of how he came to be on this beach alone. He brushed his hands clean on his trousers and lifted his shoes off his feet. Peeling back each sock and rolling them into a ball, he wedged them in the left shoe. Leaving his loafers, Henry pulled himself onto his feet and shambled to the sea, wheezing without his oxygen tank. He couldn't go far without it. Turning up the bottoms of his trousers, he stepped forwards and let the water ripple over his feet. Each breath he took whistled in his lungs. He stroked the red scar on his thumb.

It was a childhood mishap that gave him the scar, but he remembered every detail as though he'd just lived through it. His mother was in the kitchen baking her "famous" Christmas cake. Once, when Henry enquired as to precisely how famous her cake was, he discovered that no one outside the family had even heard of it. Nevertheless, it was delicious and full of raisins, which Henry liked to poke out with his little finger and eat by themselves. The marzipan icing was the best part. It was so white that his mother could have taken snow off the lawn instead and it wouldn't have looked much different. Henry liked to hold it on his tongue and feel the sugar spread around every single tooth, the saccharine delight swirling in the cheeks of his smile.

When the cake was in the oven baking, Henry went to his bedroom. There wasn't much to do in the winter as he couldn't play outside. The weather that year was especially bad; the rain was relentless and there were storms with hail stones so large that they would have dented a car if his mother had been able to afford one. Henry was in his room for a couple of hours playing with his toy soldiers when he smelled burning. He ran into the kitchen. His eyes watered from the smoke and he was relieved that there were no flames.

"Mum!"

Henry tried to fan the air clear in front of him with his hands, but he began to cough. Without a second thought he snatched the tea towel, dashed to the oven, and yanked the door open. The cake was heavier than he realised and, in his haste, the tray banged the roof of the oven on the way out. It slipped from his grasp, the metal burning his hand on the way down the floor, where it clattered in a pile of black mush. He cried whilst he turned the oven off and opened the window, clutching his wounded hand close to his chest.

"Mum?"

He found her in the living room on the sofa. She was asleep with an empty bottle of sherry on the table by her head. Her whole body reeked of it. Henry stared at her for a few minutes. She looked almost happy as she slept. Taking the blanket off the nearby chair, he put it over her as best he could with one arm and then went back to the kitchen to take care of the mess, his hand still burning.

As Henry caressed his long-healed scar, he stared out across the sea to the horizon. He brought his hand to his chest again, the way he did when it had first been burned, and felt his heart struggle to beat. Where was his oxygen tank? He'd never find his way home without it. Madeline's face filled his vision as he thought of her with lips so close to his that he could feel the tingle of mouthwash on them. Henry thought that if he didn't figure out how to get back to her, it would be just like abandoning his family, or perhaps even worse as Henry had never intended to go anywhere in the first place.

There was no one about. He wasn't sure how long he'd been at the beach, but it must have been at least an afternoon and nobody had come along. He resolved that he was either dead or dreaming, trying to suss out which it might be with what little information he had. If he was dead, surely his heart would be the way it was before he developed emphysema. Henry knew one thing for certain; he was alone.

Suddenly, a voice:

Henry? Henry, can you hear me?

"Hello? Yes! Yes, I can hear you!" Henry called back, twisting around as best he could in the water to scan the shore for the source of the voice.

Are you sure he can hear me?

Henry recognised the voice. It was Madeline. His heart clamoured for her to continue. He wanted her to say more. Every part of him begged for her to never stop speaking. He needed her to say absolutely anything, as long as she carried on talking.

"Madeline? Darling! Where are you?" he cried out. "How is your day going? Do you know where I am? What's for dinner? Honey? Madeline? Madeline?!"

Henry?

"Madeline!"

A second voice cut through:

I think he's listening.

How do you know?

His face looks calmer when you speak, Grandma.

Henry knew the second voice too. It was his granddaughter, Lacey. He searched for her in all directions, but he couldn't see where she was either. Her stark black hair should stand out against the brightness of the beach, but there was nothing. It occurred to him that they weren't where he was at all, but somewhere else.

"Lacey! Madeline! Hello?" he tried again, but the volume was slowly going out of his voice.

For the first time in years, Henry tried to run. His feet took off before he questioned whether his lungs could take it. He wasn't going fast, but managed to jog down the stretch of the shore, having no idea where he was going. He sweated and tightened every muscle, pushing himself to the fastest speed possible, but Henry could keep it up. He panted and felt his heart straining in his chest. Stopping only when he had no other choice, Henry dropped to his knees. His eyes traced the horizon again, begging for Madeline to step out of the distance towards him.

Grandpa, please. Give us a sign.

Lacey, I don't think he can hear us.

He can! Look at his face. He really can.

No, honey. Grandpa is asleep. We should go.

"I'm not! I'm awake! I'm here."

Fine. Bye, Grandpa. I'll be back soon.

You head out, sweetie. I'll be right there.

Henry's chest heaved as tears mingled into the sweat that dripped down his face. Frantic, his neck snapped left and right as he searched for his wife. Was he sleeping like she said? In all the decades they had been married, they had never slept apart. He missed watching her next to him. Every now and then, her nose would twitch and her mouth would fall open, but she never snored. As each night passed until decades slipped away from them, her face changed and aged. She had laugh lines around her mouth and eyes, while stress left its mark on her forehead. When they met, she had curly blonde hair, but now it looked like dove feathers. As he longed to pull her close, he could smell the eucalyptus soap; wisps of her sweetness flowed into the air around him. Hairs rose on his neck when he felt her breath in his ear. She was right next to him.

Henry? I don't know if you can really hear me. Seems like another doctor's lie. I just – oh, this is stupid. I know I'm just talking to myself. Maybe I am mad… If there's a chance you can hear me, just hurry up, Henry. I need you to wake up.

When she stopped speaking, her presence evaporated with

her voice. Henry sat with his legs out, feeling heavy and stuck. He was unable to catch his breath and unsure he ever would. The truth dawned on him like a present being unwrapped – a terrible, frightening present; at first it was revealed slowly and with caution, but when Henry began to figure it out, the mystery ripped itself into reality. He wasn't dead or alive. He wasn't awake or asleep. Henry Belvidere was somewhere in between, falling into oblivion from a hospital bed.

MADELINE

adeline stroked Henry's cheek and kissed his forehead. For a second, she lingered close to his face, half-expecting him to kiss her back. Standing upright, she saw his pillows were flat and made a mental note to bring him some fatter ones from home. The nurse – whatever her name was – seemed too run off her feet to bother with the comfort of patients who might never wake up. Madeline pulled his duvet up higher and slipped her fingers into the palm of his hand. It felt cold, and she recoiled like she was touching death, before lifting her eyes to the face of her husband again. She wondered if he heard anything she said or felt when she touched him. If there was even a chance he felt the draught in the hospital room, Madeline couldn't bear it. She slipped her cardigan off her shoulders and placed it over him, tucking his hands into the sleeves to warm them. On her way out of the room, she turned off the light and pulled the door shut as quietly as she could.

Lacey was sitting at the end of a row of plastic chairs a little way down the corridor. Her dark, black hair hung limp around her withdrawn stare. She scuffed her shoes against the tiled floor, shuddered when they squeaked, but continued anyway. Some music group Madeline had never heard of posed on her t-shirt. When Lacey saw her grandmother staring at her, she sat up straight and smiled, but the expression looked pained. Madeline drew in a sharp breath and began the long walk to her only granddaughter, twenty feet away.

"Ready to go?" she asked Lacey.

"Yeah."

"Got your coat and everything?"

Lacey nodded and patted the jacket beside her.

"Right, let's go get Kyle then."

Lacey sighed as though fetching her brother was the absolute last thing in the world she would ever want to do, and then hauled herself onto her feet. Madeline wasn't sure whether to put her arm around her granddaughter or not. It was so hard to tell what she needed anymore. It was easier when she was born. Lacey would wake up at night as a pink, wriggling stranger, and cry until she was fed and comforted. That's all a baby really needs: food, warmth, and a little love. Not to downplay the roughness of fresh parenthood or the special powers some babies have to scream and scream and scream, but...teenagers were, in some ways, much harder. A newborn baby's entire world was a few inches from its face. Everything else beyond that didn't exist yet. Lacey was fourteen now and realising that the world extended to places she would never see. In light of everything that happened in the past couple of weeks, Lacey must have felt so small and hollow. Madeline thought she did anyway, because that's how she felt herself.

Outside, the snow that was fresh when they arrived turned to grey sludge in the car park. Madeline watched water bleed out of the dirty clumps that she deliberately squashed under her feet. She felt the cold seep in through a hole in her shoe that she didn't know was there, but carried on flattening all the lumps anyway. The skies were grey and she knew they held more bad weather in them. She needed to get back home to the farm to start dinner and light the wood stove, so they would be ready when Ned came home.

As they approached the car, Madeline noticed the passenger side wing mirror was folded in – someone had hit it pulling out of the parked space next to them. When she got closer, she saw that some of the paint had been scratched off. Swearing under her breath, Madeline popped the mirror back out aggressively, and caught Lacey raising her eyebrows. Neither of them spoke, each climbing inside the car and flinching at the slam of doors. Madeline put the heating on immediately and didn't drive off until the windows began to demist, which was when she switched the hot air off. She cracked the back windows half a centimetre to clear the glass and then pushed a button to shut them again. They buckled their seatbelts and Lacey pulled her phone out of her pocket, typing quickly before putting earbuds in and listening to music in her own world. At a red light, Madeline could hear furious drumming coming from Lacey's ears and worried the volume might be too high, but she didn't say anything. Instead, she leaned forwards and flicked on the radio, receding back into her own mind.

The country station serenaded her into a memory:

> …ain't no place like home,
> an' home is where you are,
> but since you left me all alone,
> home's never felt so far gone…

She tapped a hand to the slow tempo of the singer's crooning and her wedding band made a surprisingly loud clap against the steering wheel. She couldn't remember the last time she'd felt the joy of coming home. In the five years she'd lived at the cottage with her husband, son, and grandchildren, she had never once enjoyed returning.

Ned moved there when Karen died. She was a wonderful person. Madeline was delighted whenever she came to visit with the children. Yes, Madeline thought, that's it. The last time she felt that sense of home was the Christmas before Karen died. Lacey was nine and Kyle was three, both dressed in matching jumpers and grinning in the doorway as Madeline greeted them with the biggest hug she could. Henry took all the bags out of Karen's hands and brought them inside, before putting the kettle on for them. Ned was still in the car on his phone. Everyone was already settled and talking before he came into the house.

Without Karen, Ned struggled with the children. He got a deal on the cottage; it was rent-free in exchange for taking care of the land and looking after the holiday home next door, which belonged to the landlady. When Henry got sick, Madeline couldn't cope by herself either, and they moved in with their son. They had to sleep in Ned's bed while he took the sofa at first, because the cottage only had two bedrooms. Eventually, Ned turned the enclosed porch into a third bedroom and his parents were able to sleep there instead.

Some days, Madeline resented being sixty-six and sleeping in the porch of her son's home – a home that he didn't even own – but there was no way she could go out on her own now. She glanced over to Lacey, who was staring out of the window. Her blinks were long, as though she might fall asleep at any second, and her head moved more than it should over the bumps on the road, like her neck couldn't hold up the weight of her thoughts. Madeline pressed her lips together and flicked the radio off, knowing she had to say something, but not knowing what.

"What do you want for dinner tonight?" was all Madeline came up with. Lacey didn't respond.

"Any thoughts on dinner?"

"Huh?" Lacey said, pulling out one earbud.

"Dinner?" Madeline tried again.

"What about it?"

"What do you want?"

"Don't care," she said, putting her earbud back in her ear.

Madeline tried to picture her kitchen inventory, concocting a meal in her mind. She might not know how to reach Lacey, but she could at least feed her. Maybe Kyle would want something specific, she thought, as they turned onto the right street to pick him up. Though, knowing him, it would just be pizza again.

This was the kind of street Madeline imaged her grandchildren growing up on. Each home was a replica of the one that came before it, and all of them were perfect. Some might think it was boring to have every house look the same, but Madeline found it comforting. A person didn't just live in a neighbourhood like this; they belonged to it, which meant fitting in with friends and family. All the snow from the pavements was shovelled out of the way. In the summer, the grass was manicured as local teenagers would mow lawns for money. All was idyllic, right down to the smell of the street, which wasn't of anything at all. Beats the smell of cow shit, Madeline thought as she pulled up the driveway at Kyle's friend's house. She didn't know much about the boy Kyle called his best friend, but he appeared well-groomed and far more polite than any other eight-year-old she had ever known. His house smelled of wood chips and biscuits.

Kyle was waiting in the front window and Madeline saw him call over his shoulder as he disappeared back behind the curtains, reappearing at the front door. He ran over to the truck and slipped, falling flat onto his backside. Lacey laughed. Madeline waited to see if he would cry before getting out of the car. Kyle stood up, said something angrily to the patch of ice, and then brushed himself off in a way that nobody ever did outside of films and television. He grabbed the handle of the back right car door and tugged it open, crawled up into the seat, closed the door, and snapped his seatbelt in place.

"Aren't you forgetting something?" Madeline asked.

"Ah, crap! My bag!"

"Hey, hey. Language."

"Crap ain't a bad word," Lacey said, and for the first time Madeline realised she could hear over her music after all.

"It isn't a bad word. And it is," Madeline replied.

Kyle looked confused as his eyes went from his grandmother to his sister and back again.

"Manners are important, okay?" Madeline said. "Speaking properly is too."

"What?" Lacey said, pointing to her earbuds.

"Right," Madeline muttered, just wanting to get home. "I'll go get your bag. You two stay here."

She pulled the zip of her coat as high as it would go and buried her mouth in the collar that now covered it. Her breath came back hot and humid on her lips and the tip of her nose, spreading up to her cheeks. It warmed her a little as she got out of the car and went to ring the doorbell. The friend's father answered, and it occurred to Madeline that she'd never met him before.

"Yes?" he said.

"Hi, sorry to bother you. I'm Kyle's grandma. He's left his bag here."

"Ah, of course! Pleasure to meet you, Mrs Belvidere. Austin!" he called to his son. "Where's Kyle's bag?"

"Dining room table!" came a faint shout from upstairs.

"One moment," he said, returning a few seconds later with Kyle's lime green rucksack. "This thing looks radioactive," he chuckled.

"It's Kyle's favourite colour. It was a fight talking him down from having his whole half of the bedroom painted with it too. He shares with his sister, you see, and I don't think she was impressed with the proposal."

"They do have some funny ideas when they're young. Well, Kyle is a great kid. Really good to see Austin making friends with the right people."

"Thank you. Austin is lovely too," Madeline said, having never met Austin and without knowing anything about him.

"Kind of you to say! You know, every Wednesday night we have a family dinner. Buoys our spirits for the second half of the week. We're doing fajitas next. You should come. Bring Kyle and…uh…sorry, his sister's name has totally slipped my mind!"

"Lacey."

"Yeah, Lacey. Their father too, if he can make it. It would be wonderful to get to know each other better, now the kids are so close." He put his hand on the door frame and leaned forwards, a huge grin taking up half his face.

"Well, I really shouldn't –" she began to say.

"I'm sure Kyle and Austin would love it," he interrupted.

"I was actually –"

"And Lacey too," he paused delicately. "Kyle mentioned what happened in passing. About his grandpa. It might be nice for them…not to presume anything, of course."

Seeing that she wasn't going to get out of this – very irritating – conversation without agreeing, and not wanting to talk about Henry any more, Madeline nodded her head.

"Excellent! Wednesday at seven. We'll see you then." He passed Kyle's bag to Madeline.

"Oh – how rude of me – my name is Jac, by the way."

"Thank you, Jac."

Madeline gripped the strap of Kyle's rucksack tightly as Jac closed the door with a smile. She shook her head and turned back to head towards the car. Lacey was staring straight ahead and Kyle was watching intently. Nothing escaped him. He banged on the window and pointed to the ice. Madeline smiled and waved, side-stepping around the slippery patch and making it back to the car without falling over. She passed Kyle's bag to him and began the drive back to the cottage.

"We're having dinner with them on Wednesday," she said.

"Really? Awesome!" Kyle grinned.

"All of us?" Lacey asked.

"All of us."

Lacey rolled her eyes and turned up her music. Madeline wasn't going to lecture her for being ungrateful or rude. Truth be told, Madeline wished she had the guts to roll her eyes in front of Jac and walk away. She knew he was just being charitable, but when did she become charity? Was she not coping as well as she thought she was? Could the world see something she couldn't? Madeline had children to protect now. She checked her watch. She'd have to make something quick for dinner, so Ned wouldn't be upset that it wasn't ready when he got home.

Kyle began to tell her the details of every second he spent with Austin while she nodded and smiled at him in the rearview mirror, but she didn't hear a word he said. Her eyes brimmed with tears as she played along, but everything she did was a lie. She was acting with every breath. Her grandchildren had no idea why Henry went missing, or why he was found three days later in a coma. Her hands tightened on the steering wheel. Her knuckles turned white. Her breath quickened as she pulled up to the cottage.

LACEY

The next day at school, Lacey tried to slip Anna some notes as her friend hadn't done any of the reading. There would be no chance to catch Anna up before Mr Golding began the lesson, but maybe they would help if he called on her to answer a question. During class, Lacey couldn't have been any further away from her best friend; she was Belvidere and sat in the front row, but Anna was Wilson and took her seat right at the back by Williams and Yellowbrooke. Wishing her friend was as interested in English as she was, Lacey dropped into her chair and pulled out her copy of *Romeo and Juliet*, loaded with notes and annotations.

Mr Golding strode into the room in exactly five steps, stopped – feet together – and placed his briefcase down completely parallel to the edge of his spotless desk. He opened the case and pulled out his copy of the text, which was dog-eared, and flipped through it. While he read a few passages, he ran a thumb and forefinger across his thick moustache, starting at the centre and pushing out in opposite directions. When the bell went to signal the start of the class, he snapped the book shut and clutched it to his chest while he took attendance, knowing the names from memory and marking them on a sticky note stuck over the blurb of Shakespeare's classic.

He was an excellent teacher, and it came across as deeply devoted to his students, but hard to please. He seemed to take exceptional pride in his work. Lacey showed up to every lesson on time, if not early, with all her notes prepared and questions to ask, waiting for the moment when his attention would turn to her.

"Right, class. How did we get on with R and J?" he began, after attendance was noted.

A murmur of mixed responses spread through the class. Lacey sat up straight and made sure her pencil case was aligned perfectly with her notebook. Mr Golding's eyes traced the faces of the class – some confused, some content, and the rest far away.

"Perhaps the question to ask is: who read it?"

This time, no one said anything. Some faces even looked down to avoid eye contact. Lacey couldn't see what Anna was doing, but she didn't want to turn and look in case it gave her away. Mr Golding, sighing into the silence, fetched a bone-like piece of chalk from a plastic tub in his briefcase and went over to the blackboard, which he insisted on using over the technologically superior digital whiteboard.

"Let's break it down then. Where does it take place?"

Verona, everyone muttered, unsynchronised.

"'In fair Verona where we lay our scene...' Good. Good. And what are the names of the families?"

The Montagues and the Capulets.

"'Two households, both alike in dignity...' Excellent. See, some of you do know something. But what other forces are at play here?"

"..."

"Anyone?"

"..."

"How about authority? Fran?"

Francesca Groves rolled her eyes lazily away from the

window to the front of the room, where Mr Golding waited.

"The prince," she said.

"Great! Yes. Anyone else? Martin? C'mon Marty, I know you know…"

"The church?" Marty guessed.

"Absolutely. You see, we have these two families pitted against each other, for no significant reason. Now they're caught in a blood-feud that is terrorising the streets of Verona. Of course the prince gets involved, but then we have Friar Laurence who comes to the aid of our Romeo and Juliet. What did we think about our friend the Friar? Lacey?"

Lacey sat upright when he said her name, which surprised her because she thought she was sitting as straight as she could before. She cleared her throat to buy a little time, but most of her thoughts clarified themselves as she started to speak.

"I-I suppose…"

"No, no, no. Don't suppose. Know."

"Right, okay. Well, he is called upon to help them, but in a way, he ends up doing the most damage. More than anyone else in the play," Lacey said.

"Fantastic. Tell me more."

"I guess – I mean, I know he's the one who gives Juliet the sleeping potion and marries them behind everyone's backs."

"And why was that wrong?"

"You said he was authority. That means he needs to be reliable."

"But wasn't he?" Mr Golding dug further. "He was the only one that would unite Romeo and Juliet. He was helping them to be together. Being a reliable friend."

"Yeah…" Lacey trailed off.

"No, not 'yeah.' You don't agree with that, do you? Tell me what you really think."

Lacey hesitated. She trusted that Mr Golding was earnest in his interest in what she thought, but something about the book wasn't sitting right with her anymore.

"He shouldn't have done it. None of it. It was all wrong," she said after a few moments.

"Why?"

"Sometimes not helping your friend is what's really best for them. Especially if you've got power. Sometimes you have to stand up to them. Tell them things they don't want to hear," Lacey explained. Was she regretting lending her notes to Anna, or was her discomfort coming from somewhere else? Somewhere deeper?

"But the Friar believed he was doing the right thing."

"Doesn't matter how good his intentions were. If you do something bad, your reasons don't justify it. Bad is bad. He had a choice."

Mr Golding raised his eyebrows and stepped back. The room was so quiet when they stopped talking that Lacey was immediately embarrassed. He had a way for making Lacey feel like she was the only person in the room, and she forgot what she was saying or how long she'd been talking.

He went over to the blackboard and wrote down the word: STAR-CROSSED.

"What does this mean? Dai?"

"Fate," came the reply.

"Exactly. Fate. So did the Friar have a choice, really? Or was everything determined for him from the very beginning?" No one answered, so he continued, "I'll tell you what, Friar Laurence has always been my favourite character in the play. Perhaps you think it's all boring and absurd. How could these two teenagers fall in love in a matter of days? How could they live and fight and die in mere pages? Maybe you actually find it moving.

"There are a lot of ways that the events in Verona can be learned from, even today. I'm sure many of you have experienced things in your lives that are better kept in fiction. But I want you to think about fate and choices. Are you star-crossed?"

"No," said Lacey, without raising her hand.

"How do you know?"

"I don't."

"Then why do you think that?"

"Because I have to believe it. Thinking of living a life already…scripted. It's twisted."

"And what is life, if not twisted?" Mr Golding replied, with a soft smile.

The classroom had come to life and frozen. Every student that began the lesson unfocused or daydreaming was now present, listening intently and thinking. No one moved as the words fell around them and all the different meanings revealed themselves in the silence. Grandpa's sleeping face flashed between Lacey's blinks and she had to grip her desk to steady her breathing.

"It's something to think about. Something I think about anyway. I don't believe there's a right or wrong answer. The point is, you don't know what's going to happen, so you might as well try your best and shoot for what you want."

"Like Romeo and Juliet did? Look where that got them," someone called out.

"Well," Mr Golding smiled again, "they also made some pretty stupid choices now, didn't they? You can't cheat death. You can't hide from love. You can't run forever, live a different life behind people's backs, or sell out your friends. Figure out who you want to be and stand by that. Hold onto your convictions. Whatever the outcome, never regret being yourself.

"Now, let's open our books to look at Mercutio's 'Queen Mab' monologue. Anna, what is a monologue…"

For the first time since Lacey met him, Mr Golding's voice faded into the background. Her spine relaxed and she sunk back into her chair. She opened her book up to the monologue, which was barely legible under the scribbles of annotations and markings. The book lay on her desk as flat as the words that fell around her. Lacey needed to think.

The class carried on without her as she made herself into a student-puppet; she turned to the right pages, nodded at the correct times, and moved her eyes around the room to avoid looking like a daydreamer, but Lacey wasn't there anymore. She didn't come back to the classroom until the bell went, signalling the end of class.

As she packed her belongings into her bag and slipped her jacket on, Mr Golding called her name and asked her to stay behind for a couple of minutes. Anna stared as she left the room, curious about what they would discuss. When everyone had exited, Lacey made her way over to Mr Golding's immaculate desk. He sat in his chair and leaned back in it until it creaked. Gesturing that she should sit in the nearest chair too, he had an expression on his face that Lacey knew meant he was thinking about something difficult.

"How did you find the class today?" he asked.

"Good."

"Do you like Shakespeare?"

Lacey bit her lip and considered her response carefully. "Sometimes," she settled on.

"Why only sometimes?"

"Mostly it's great, but then there are bits that get on my nerves."

"Perhaps those are the best bits though. The ones that get an emotional reaction out of you. The bits that make you think." Lacey didn't reply, so he carried on, "I've been teaching for a long time. A little over a decade. And your insights are not typical of a fourteen-year-old. You're very perceptive for your age. There's an advanced English class at the school which you didn't apply to take this year. Why didn't you?"

"I don't know."

"With how far ahead of your classmates you are, I could move you into that class if you wanted. It would open up the option of a higher-level GCSE exam, which would look better on your CV. Have you thought about what you might want to do after school?"

"Not really."

"Well, whatever you do, that's your business, but this class will help you get more out of life, Lacey. You and I share the same beliefs about literature, don't we? I know I have to teach stuffy old classics by dead white men, but these are also records of human thoughts and teachings for life. If you're good at it, you should pursue it. Don't do it for me or a university. Do it for yourself though, Lacey. You need to get more out of your education. You're more than capable of excelling in the advanced class."

"Okay, well maybe I could..."

"You absolutely could! You can go away and think about it if you like, and feel free to say no, but if you want to give it a shot just let me know."

Lacey felt a headache coming on. Her palms began to sweat as she fidgeted in the hard plastic chair. The thought of moving into a more interesting and challenging class was exciting, and she was desperate to jump at the opportunity, but Lacey couldn't hide the fact that her nerves were getting to her. School was the only part of her life that was still stable. Did she really want to disrupt that if this new class didn't work out?

"You could always come to a couple to see what it's like, rather than committing right away," Mr Golding said.

"That sounds better."

"Good. I'll let Miss Hayes know and perhaps you could attend her classes next week? If you like them, we can switch you there properly. I'd just need your dad to sign off on it and meet with both myself and Miss Hayes."

"My dad?"

"We can't just change up your classes without letting a parent know."

"What about my grandma?"

"It needs to be whoever your legal guardian is."

"Is that all?" Lacey asked, standing to leave.

"Yes. Head on to your next class. I'll see you tomorrow," he said.

Lacey rushed out the room without saying goodbye, but could tell by the way Mr Golding looked at her that he knew something was wrong. She felt powerless knowing she'd never get her dad to come in and sort out moving her to an advanced class. It was her grandma that dealt with everything like that. Dad didn't have the time. At least, according to him, he didn't. Anna was waiting outside the room for her.

"You okay?" Anna asked.

"Yeah, I'm good."

"You sure? You look a bit off."

"I'm fine. Honest. I just don't want to be late to class."

They walked in silence to Cymraeg, Lacey simultaneously hating the distance she'd put between her and her best friend and feeling safer alone in her own mind.

MADELINE

She touched her face with her fingertips. They felt cool even though she just got out of the shower. Looking in the mirror, she traced trickles of sweat and water down her cheeks to her chest. Wiping away the condensation that obscured her reflection, she stared at herself. She didn't remember looking this way. Her hair was white and feathery, unlike the blonde ringlets she had when she was younger. Skin rippled around her eyes in wrinkles. Madeline picked up her toothbrush and examined the frayed bristles. Time for a new one, she thought, before coating it in toothpaste.

Crisp and sharp flavours flushed through her mouth and she immediately scrunched up her nose. For as long as she could remember, mint made her sneeze. She wasn't allergic to it, but something about the burning coldness made her nose tickle. When she was a child, Harvey Cragg would chase her around the schoolyard with mint leaves from his mother's kitchen. Mad Maddy, he called her, while he held her down and made her sneeze herself dizzy.

Madeline faintly shuddered whilst white foam leaked out of the corners of her mouth. With the back of a hand, she wiped away the bubbling toothpaste. Finishing up, she rinsed her face with cool water and picked up a towel to dry her face, but stopped to stroke the skin across her naked stomach. Her body dipped and undulated with life – life she had both lived herself and given to others. She ran her shaking hands over herself. Her body had felt empty for years. It had been decades since Ned was born, but she still missed the fullness she felt when she was pregnant with him. Even though their rooms were next to each other in the cottage, he was so distant. It exacerbated the lifelessness of her breasts and the hollowness of her womb.

Her pyjamas hung on the towel rack, cooling themselves on the chrome rail. She struggled to recall the days when she had central heating. Lacey gave the pyjamas to her last Christmas. They didn't suit Madeline at all (long gone were the days when she could pull off violent pink and their stiletto shoe pattern), but she wore them to please her granddaughter. Madeline's fingers trembled a little as she fastened the buttons. At least the pyjamas would warm as she wore them. Winter was creeping its way across the valley again, and the lonely wood stove in the living area spread little heat to the rest of the cottage.

She didn't mind living on the farm and she couldn't complain that they could stay there rent-free. There was plenty of room outside for the grandchildren to play, but Lacey had grown out of games and Kyle found he had little to do all alone. Madeline hung up her damp towel and looked out of the window to the mountains their home nestled against. In any other life, she might consider herself lucky to live in the only occupied home along Glyn Uchaf with her whole family surrounding her.

Ned banged on the door. She jumped and the boyish chants of Mad Maddy echoed around her head once more. She knew she had to confront him soon. It was the best thing to do for Henry, and she knew she needed to put him first now. Better late than never. Pressing her lips into a smile, she turned the handle.

Her son was standing with his hands on his hips, left foot tapping impatiently and shaking his head. At one point, Ned was handsome, but time had been cruel to him. Eyes jutted from a piggy pink face and years of drinking tumbled over his belt in one large, round belly. He used to cut his hair short to make the grey ones harder to spot, but now it was the brown hairs that were difficult to see against the dull, nickel-coloured bristles that stuck straight out from the top of his head. Madeline never saw herself in him, but there were still traces of Henry hiding in Ned's face, like his treacle black eyes and the way his mouth only curved on one side when he smiled.

He wasn't smiling now. Ned put a hand around each of his mother's arms and pulled her out of the bathroom. His fat fingers wrapped around her skinny arms so they met his thumbs on the other side. When he dragged her out, Madeline's neck bent backwards. It hurt, but she didn't make a sound, holding her wince inside her mouth to let out later in her pillow, long after everyone else went to bed.

Madeline didn't blink as the door slammed in her face. She worried that it may have woken Kyle or Lacey, so she tip-toed towards their bedroom to check. Not wanting to go inside in case Ned came back out and made a fuss, Madeline listened for a few moments by their door instead. Their breathing was long and deep, full of sniffles and whispers, and she knew they were dreaming. She pulled their door shut and went into her own room, where she sat on the edge of the bed.

The lamp on the bedside table cast long shadows that moved if she blinked too quickly. One of the floorboards under her foot was coming up and when she pushed it back down it groaned. She used her big toenail to flick paint away that was flaking up from the loose board. The floorboards had been painted dark brown to try and make them look better, but instead they were now shabby and peculiar-looking. Ned never sealed the paint, so it flaked off when scuffed and scratched, leaving it patchy and uncomfortable to walk on in bare feet. Madeline knew Henry would have done a better job, but Ned wouldn't hear of it.

"Dad, I've got it, okay?" he said to Henry.

"Sure – I don't doubt it – but I'm trying to help."

"I don't need help."

"Suit yourself."

Henry stood up and went to the kitchen to help Madeline with lunch. He walked up behind her quietly, so she wouldn't hear him. When he put his arms around Madeline's waist and pulled her into a hug from behind, she jumped and then settled her head against his chest. He rocked her from side-to-side while she sunk a knife into the carrots, metal hitting wood with a *snap, snap, snap*. Henry kissed the back of her neck and Madeline was taken back thirty years. She looked over to Ned, who was now two years old and wearing a green onesie covered in dinosaurs. He looked up from his toy fire truck to smile at his parents. With a gleeful "Mama", he yelped and carried on playing. Madeline blinked and Ned was back to normal, sanding down the cottage floors.

"Fucking stupid things," he muttered, wiping sweat from his brow with a dirty sleeve.

Henry's arms no longer felt comforting and Madeline leaned forwards again with a sigh, slicing through the carrots and blinking with each smack of the knife on the board. Sensing her discomfort, Henry pulled away, giving her one last kiss before going to make some coffee. Madeline rolled her eyes – she hated when he had coffee with lunch – but didn't speak. Henry made two cups, both black, and brought one over to Ned.

"No," Ned said, shaking his head.

"Go on, you need a break," Henry replied, still holding the coffee out to him.

"I said no."

"Ned…"

"No," Ned swatted the mug away, knocking it and spilling some on the floorboards where he was standing. "Fuck! Dad! Look what you've done."

"Can't sand wet wood. Looks like you can take a break now after all."

"Don't be an idiot."

Madeline looked around her empty bedroom and shivered. That day felt so far away, but it had been longer still since Ned looked at her with the love he had for her when he was two. Still pushing the floorboard with her foot, she winced as a sharp pain stabbed her toe. Madeline bent down and turned the sole of her foot up to face her. She was expecting a small splinter, but saw a piece of wood as long as her thumb nail sticking out of her flesh. It was hard bending down fully to pull it out. Turning to ask Henry for help, she stopped short when she remembered he wasn't next to her, but in the hospital. His name lingered unspoken on her lips as she struggled to reach it. Eventually, she locked a forefinger and thumb securely around the wood and tugged it out. Madeline stretched out and watched a droplet of blood welt up from the tiny wound and drip down onto the paint below. She stood up, lifting her toes and walking on the palm of her foot only, and hobbled over to the door.

Opening it slowly, she saw that Ned was still in the bathroom. She wanted a piece of toilet paper to wipe the blood up. Upon seeing the bathroom was still occupied, Madeline closed the door and walked properly on her feet back to bed, a trail of bloody toe prints following her. As she slipped in between the sheets, a little blood streaked across them. Madeline held her breath as she heard Ned open the bathroom door. The hinges groaned and his feet were heavy. She reached over to the bedside table and turned off the lamp with a click. The footsteps stopped outside her door. Madeline stared up at the black ceiling with her lips clamped shut. After what felt like minutes but could only have been seconds, she felt his presence disappear and his feet could be heard padding to his bedroom. The door shut and Madeline breathed again.

She pulled her duvet up higher around her chest. The bed was cold without Henry to share it. Madeline wondered if perhaps she really was Mad Maddy after all. Sometimes she forgot where she was or even her age. Sixty-six years had vanished before her eyes and it wasn't until she gazed at herself with confusion in the mirror that she saw time slip away.

ELEN

Elen **stared at** her computer screen as vacant as the black rectangle in front of her. She pushed the button to turn the bloody machine on and frowned as it whirred to life. Last night, she submitted her police report to Chief Inspector Richardson and, judging from his text to her this morning, he was not happy. She rubbed her eyes, forgetting that this morning she managed to put on make-up for once, and immediately grimaced. Pulling her bag from the floor onto her lap, she fished around inside it for a mirror, but couldn't find one. Eventually, she settled for the front-facing camera on her phone. She was taken aback for a moment by her image, raccoon-like and startled. Elen snorted at herself and grabbed a tissue to wipe away the smudged mascara, but couldn't get it off dry. She leaned back in her chair to look out the door and, seeing that no one was about, she spat a small amount of saliva into the tissue. Now armed with spittle, she wiped away the black mess around her eyes.

She closed the camera on her phone and went to put it down, but it buzzed and lit up while still in her hand. Elen turned it around and saw that Richardson had sent her another message: *10:30. Don't forget.* She switched her phone off entirely and dropped it into her handbag, which she zipped up all the way, dumped on the floor, and kicked under her desk. She knew exactly what he wanted to discuss – the Belvidere case. Now that her computer seemed awake enough to use, she closed three pop-ups, and opened her notes on the case to refresh herself before the meeting. As she read the file on Henry Belvidere, something felt amiss. If someone she loved had disappeared she knew she'd spare no time in calling the police. Neither Madeline nor Ned Belvidere – Henry's wife and son – made any such report. Her first impressions of them didn't necessarily pique her suspicions.

Ned had come across sincere in his concern for his father. At no point did he give away any hints that he might know more than he was saying. Elen had made a note of his appearance and demeanour in her little pad that she always kept with a pen in her pocket. Fumbling around for it, she pulled it out to reread what she had written:

> Ned Belvidere (no middle name), 47.
> Employed at Littlebrooks supermarket – mostly
>   night shifts.
> Madeline (mother), Henry (father), Lacey (daughter),
>   Kyle (son).
> Last saw Henry 3 days prior to disappearance.
> Calm & well-spoken.
> Claims to know nothing.
> Didn't report b/c Henry often went on fishing trips.

Elen had sat across from Ned at her desk and discussed the events with him. Ned's grey hair had clashed against his red face, and Elen remembered thinking he looked like a cartoon with his huge black eyes set in a scarlet circle.

It was Madeline that Elen had been uncomfortable around. Henry's wife looked permanently unsettled, as though her own skin repulsed her, and had said very few words. In all her years as an officer, Elen had become good at reading body language. She had to be able to predict the future; Elen needed to know what a person was going to do before they did it. When she had read Madeline, all she had seen was confusion. Ned's mother had sat angled away from him, arms unfolded but wrapped tightly around her abdomen, as if she had been holding something inside her. In many ways, Elen had seen her own mother, small as a dormouse but full of potential for bravery. If Madeline knew something, Elen would find out soon enough.

She snapped her notepad shut and slid it back into her pocket, avoiding the computer screen as she spun around in her chair to face the window. The weather had been particularly cold that winter, but humidity still hung in the air, almost as tangible as wet laundry over a line. Elen shrugged off her blazer and scratched her armpit, itchy from a fresh shave. The office felt smaller today than it had in the six months since she'd moved in here from her cubicle in the main room. It was supposed to be a perk of her promotion to detective, but the room was far too quiet. She began to drum her pen on the edge of the desk. Without noticing, ink welled up out of the ballpoint and its black blood leaked out.

"Shit," she groaned, pushing her chair away from the spill before it dripped off the desk and ruined her trousers.

"Been here five minutes and you're already making a mess," a voice said from the doorway.

Elen swivelled around to see Dan carrying a stack of folders to his desk that was stationed opposite hers. She didn't mind sharing with him and he made a good partner, but Dan couldn't be any more different from her. He placed the folders down carefully and removed his jacket, drooping it over the back of his chair and brushing the creases out of it. He sat down slowly, pushing back from the desk to put his briefcase on his lap and open it, pulling out a fountain pen, legal pad, and handkerchief. Closing the briefcase with a snap of each clasp, he then opened his desk's bottom drawer which he kept empty, specifically reserved for his bag. Dan picked up the handkerchief by one corner, shook it out, and leaned over to pass it to Ellen.

"For the ink," he said.

"It'll be ruined."

"Yes. It will. But better my hankie than your trousers."

"Thanks."

Dan nodded and switched on his computer while Elen mopped up the ink, throwing the ruined handkerchief in the bin when she was done. She examined her hands and saw that a large black spot of ink had dried on her right thumb. Licking her other thumb, she tried to rub it off, but it was no use. Elen made a fist and tucked her stained thumb away underneath her fingers. Dan looked up at her as he waited for his computer to warm up and raised his eyebrows.

"What?" Elen asked.

"An attempt at make-up?"

"Yeah. So?"

"So who's that for?"

"Me. I felt like wearing it."

"Elen."

"Fine, I have a meeting with Richardson. He texted me this morning. He told me at the Christmas party I look nice with a splash on."

"You're not…you don't want…"

"No! Nothing like that. I'm just nervous. I want him to have a good impression of me still, I guess," Elen confessed.

"Nervous? About what?"

"These fucking Belvideres. I know something is amiss. Richardson needs convincing though."

Chief Inspector Marcus Richardson was all about the statistics. He had the best numbers in Powys County and he had every intention of keeping it that way. There was no evidence at present that Henry Belvidere's coma was anything more than a tragic accident. Ned's story held up and no family member said a word to contradict it.

Richardson was happy to take it as the truth and mark down another case as closed if it boosted his ranking.

"You're a good detective, El. Richardson knows that. No use speculating until you talk to him. When's the meeting?" Dan asked.

"Forty-five minutes."

"Plenty of time to collect your thoughts."

Elen nodded and gathered her opinions together in a mental note. If there was something the family was hiding, what was it and what proof did she have? She dragged her fingers through her hair and then pulled it back into a ponytail. She kicked her shoes off under her desk and wriggled her toes until they clicked and relaxed. She opened her emails on her computer and saw that she had five unread. One caught her eye. It was from her dad, sent late last night without a subject line. Elen opened it up and read:

> Dear Elen,
> Just wanted to get in touch to say we hope you are
>   well.
> Please call whenever you're free. Your mother is
>   getting worse. She's asking for you.
> Love,
> Dad.

She sat and stared at the words until they didn't look real anymore. Elen looked out the window again and watched the world live and move while she sat still in her desk chair. The pavement was split in two by a median of grass that sparkled from a recent snow. The pavement was completely free from litter unlike outside her flat building on the other side of town. A red Ford Fiesta was parked illegally outside her window and she rolled her eyes at the irony. There were so many places to break the law, but right outside a police station was perhaps the stupidest one. A traffic officer made his way to it in a green hi-vis jacket, armed with a pad of unused parking tickets. He frowned at the car and whipped a pen out of his breast pocket, filling out one of the forms and slipping it under one of the windshield wipers. Before he moved on, he caught Elen's eye in the window and waved to her. She waved back, forced a smile, and then reigned her attention back into her office, resolving to call her father after work.

Slipping her shoes back on, she pulled her bag onto her lap again and opened it, taking out her phone. She switched it back on and laid it on her desk, waiting for it to buzz with another message from Richardson to cancel the meeting. Hanging her head when no such text came through, she pocketed the phone and opened her desk drawer for an unbroken pen and slipped it in her jacket next to her notepad. Elen used her fingers to rub underneath her eyes in case there was any excess mascara and then she made sure her ponytail was smoothed out.

"You okay?" Dan asked.

"Yeah."

"Nerves?"

"Something like that."

"Get yourself a coffee. Take a walk, El. Head to the kitchen. Waiting in this office will do you no favours."

Elen stood up and buttoned her jacket, straightening it and smoothing out any creases. She left the office and walked down the corridor past the cubicle space towards the kitchen. Someone new was sitting at her old desk now. She didn't know all the officers by name anymore since the new ones were hired and she hadn't had the chance to work with them all yet. Her old desk was in a corner cubicle by the window, looking out onto the same street as her office did now. When she looked out onto the same view she had ever since she had finished training seven years ago, she couldn't help but wonder if the step up the career ladder was as significant as Richardson made it seem.

The kitchen was also too familiar. The mugs were in a

cupboard above the sink. The kettle was a temperamental nuisance – sometimes it turned off before the water was properly boiled and other times the button got jammed and it had to be turned off at the mains. Elen got out her favourite mug, which was plain blue and a little larger than the others. She saw that Richardson's mug was still in the cupboard unused. He had a special black one only for himself. This meant he hadn't had a coffee this morning. Elen put extra water in the kettle and grabbed the instant coffee, putting a spoonful in her mug and another in Richardson's. They both took their coffee the same: black, no sugar. At home, Elen liked a splash of milk, but at work she didn't bother – not since a couple of years ago when she didn't notice the milk in the fridge had gone off until she was sick after drinking it.

The kettle decided it was going to be cooperative this morning as it boiled the water, going off with a click at the right time. Elen poured enough into each mug and stirred them. A little from hers spilled onto the counter. She went to grab a paper towel, but there weren't any. It was time to head into Richardson's office anyway. Instead, she held the drinks away from her and made her way over to his room in the corner. She knocked on the door with her elbow and read the name plate: Chief Inspector Marcus Richardson.

His office was separated from the cubicles by two walls of windows. He kept the blinds up so that he could look up from his desk periodically to scan his workforce and make sure everyone was doing their jobs. He called out for Elen to come in and she used the crook of her arm to lower the handle and open the door. Richardson leaned back in his chair and smiled when he saw the coffee. He pushed two coasters forwards for Elen, who put them down before closing the door. He gestured for her to take a seat opposite him. Elen looked around. While his office was normally neat, books from his shelves were on the floor and his desk was in disarray. His jacket that ordinarily hung on the coat stand by the door was crumpled at its base on the floor, as if he went to hang it up and missed, but cared too little to pick it up.

"Elen Parry…what are we going to do with you?" he said after a pause.

"Boss?"

"These Belvideres really have captured your imagination, haven't they?"

"Less imagination, more instinct."

"I see," he said, taking a sip of coffee. "This is good, thanks. No one else here makes a brew this strong. Your coffee is like shock therapy, Parry, but that's the way I like it."

Elen didn't say anything, but smiled and took her own coffee in her hands, sipping it slowly. She looked over the rim of the cup at Richardson, who was looking around at the cubicles beyond his windows. The light caught his face in a way the made his jawline appear clenched, his nose sharp, and his cheek bones cutting. Elen blinked and looked away, overlapping her hands around the mug to hold them still. She pressed her lips together to even out the lipstick she wasn't used to wearing.

"What is it about them?" Richardson asked.

"Them?"

"The Belvideres. What is it about this case that you can't move on from?"

"Move on? It's not closed yet."

"No, not yet. But that's the issue, isn't it? Something is stopping you from closing it. Ned Belvidere's story matches everything we know and Henry's behaviour wasn't out of the ordinary prior to him being found. The only witness is Henry himself, who is a little…indisposed at the moment. I need to know what's going through your head, Parry."

She wondered if there was a way to explain her feelings without sounding insane. He looked at her so expectantly that she couldn't bear it. Elen looked down into the black coffee and watched her own reflection stare back up at her. She didn't look like she normally did. Her unruly frizzy hair was pulled back and tidy. Her naked, bare face was now shaded and sculpted with make-up. She took another gulp of coffee to disrupt her reflection and met Richardson's stare. Licking her lips, she thought about her next words carefully.

"Something about their demeanour doesn't fit the situation," she said.

"Specifically?"

"Madeline Belvidere."

"What about her?"

"If my husband – if I had a husband – went missing, I'd report it. I'd expect him not to go on trips without telling me or without any communication. And when I found him in hospital, I'd certainly show a little more emotion than she did."

"None of this is evidence, Parry."

"I know that."

"So what do you want me to do?" he asked. "We've got a quarterly review coming up. We've got quotas to meet and reports to submit. I need you focused on more important cases. Ones that aren't so open and shut. You're one of my best detectives."

"Exactly." Elen jumped in "One of the best means I've earned your trust. I don't need long. Just let me talk to Madeline. Let me go back to the hospital. I won't prioritise it over my other cases. All I need is your permission to keep digging for a couple more weeks. If I find nothing, I'll drop it. You have my word. But I can't let it go knowing it might not be over…Boss."

She added the 'Boss' – a term she knew he found amusing – when she saw Richardson raise his eyebrows, but she knew he was considering it. He leaned back and tapped his right foot as he always did when he was contemplating something important. Elen finished her coffee at the same time as he did, and they both watched each other think.

"Alright," he said, a few moments later, "you have two weeks. You turn up something tangible by then and we'll talk about it. But if you have nothing more within the next ten working days, you drop it, okay? There will still be enough time for this to count towards our percentage of cases closed for next month's review. I want to make something very clear though, DC; if this impacts the rest of your caseload in any negative manner, you're off the case. Understand?"

She stood up to go, taking both empty mugs in one hand and turning towards the door. As she made her exit, Richardson called after her:

"One more thing," he said.

"Boss?"

"I appreciate the coffee."

She nodded with a faint smile. On her way back to the kitchen, she thought she felt the eyes of everyone staring at her from their cubicles but, when she glanced over to them, no one was paying her any attention at all. She turned on the hot tap in the sink and squirted some washing up liquid onto a sponge. When she finished cleaning her mug, she lifted up Richardson's to scrub. She forgot that there were no tea towels around and shook the excess water from her fingers before patting them dry on her trousers. She wanted to do Richardson proud, but to do so she needed to be right about this. Elen knew she could spare no time in continuing her investigation and decided what she had to do next. It was time to go back to the hospital to speak to the doctors again. Elen needed to see Henry Belvidere.

HENRY

He didn't know how much time had passed since Madeline's voice had faded away. He thought he had been there long enough for days to have come and gone, but there was no way of knowing. The sun didn't rise or set. The weather never changed. Henry stared out at the waves that crested and crashed on the shore, each one identical to the last. He found a rock that was flat enough to sit on and perched there, facing out towards the sea, and wondering if there was a hell worse than incessant boredom. Somewhere from the trees behind him, Henry could hear a faint beeping, which he decided must be a heart rate monitor. He didn't go and investigate the sound for two reasons. First, if he got lost in the trees, he might never find his way out and it seemed safer to stay on the beach. It was unlikely he'd see anybody on the beach, but the smallest spark of hope was enough to keep him from straying too far. Second, he liked to think it was his heartbeat and didn't want to discover it was something else entirely. As long as he could hear it, Henry knew he wasn't dead. It was steady and strong. On this island full of isolation and oddities, he took comfort in the regularity of his own breathing, however weak it might be.

He drew reassurance from each sharp breath now as he watched the sea roll up the beach, though it didn't appear to have a tide at all. Fifty feet away he had drawn a large X over the spot where he heard Madeline's voice. He sat and watched it, waiting for her to come back, but in all the time – however much that was – since he first sat on the rock, nobody came. He looked down at his bare feet and laughed to himself when he considered taking a walk for his health. Picking up his shoes and emptying sand from them, he pulled them back on after his socks, and stood up slowly. A walk certainly wouldn't cause any harm, as long as he kept the X within eyesight. It might not have made the slightest bit of difference, but it made him feel a little better believing there was a spot on this strange island that may be important. The thought that he could be lying to himself was quickly brushed aside as he made his way over to the spot.

Henry made a point to stop walking well before he reached the X to not to interrupt its lines by scuffing the sand around it. Closing his eyes, he froze in place and listened. Madeline had been right here. He knew it. He hadn't seen her. There had been no way of talking to her. He had no way of proving she was ever on the island with him, but Henry knew it. Her whispering had been so close to his ear that he had felt the hairs on his neck move. Henry sighed. He had smelled her soap. With his eyes still shut he leaned forwards to inhale the memory of her. He lost his balance and opened his eyes to catch his footing before he ruined the X Madeline wasn't there now and had left no sign she'd visit again.

Deciding he would feel better if he marked the spot with something more visible, Henry made his way into the trees. When he was a few feet into them, he looked around and realised something odd. The trees didn't belong on an island. They were the kind that belonged in forests and were out of place next to the sand and sea. Henry plucked a leaf from one of them and held it up to the sunlight that filtered down through the branches. He recognised it as a leaf from an oak and smiled faintly at the way it caught the light. It almost looked like it was glowing. Instead of dropping the leaf, he tucked it into his pocket and carried on walking, being careful not to go too deep into the trees for fear of losing the beach. The ground was soft under his feet and, when he looked down, he saw that it was covered in reddening pine needles.

He shrugged off his jacket and tied it into a sling, which he began to fill with the pine needles. When he couldn't possibly carry any more, Henry returned to the X and filled its shallow trenches with them. It took two more trips to gather enough needles to complete it, but when he was done, Henry wiped his brow and went back to the rock to sit down. Now the X was vibrant and red, standing out like a cross on a treasure map. That was when he heard her.

It wasn't Madeline. It wasn't a voice he'd ever heard before. She sounded both brazen and soft at the same time, as though she masked her tenderness with ferocity. He knew there was no point in calling out and yet he tensed every part of his body, suppressing the urge to ask who was there.

Henry. Henry Belvidere. What are we going to do with you?

She wasn't really talking to him. Henry knew that people had a very different tone when they were speaking to someone versus about them. He gritted his teeth together. This strange woman was in the same room as he was and standing right next to him, but she used him as a subject and, until he woke up, that was all he was. He shivered under the blaze of the sun.

Quite a looker for sixty-seven.

A second voice broke through the sky:

Can I help you?

Hi. I'm DC Parry. I have a few follow-up questions about Henry.

Questions? Everything you need to know is on the chart. Until he wakes up, there's really nothing more we can tell you.

Perhaps. When was he checked in here?

Just after 2pm. Eight days ago.

Tell me about his wounds.

A few bruises and scrapes. Nothing critical on his body, but his head was in bad shape. We feared brain damage but found no signs of it during our scans.

Bad shape? How so?

It looked like he was struck on his right temple with something heavy and round.

Henry put a hand up to his head and felt around, but there was no bump. He didn't feel any pain or seem to have an injury. If he was in such a terrible state that the doctors worried he had brain damage, surely he should be able to feel something? And what did the doctor mean by struck? Struck like an accident or deliberately?

Struck? On purpose or accidentally?

It's hard to tell. There was so much rain that night. A branch could have easily dropped on his head, but judging from the placement of the blow, it's not beyond contestation that someone may have done this to him. Whatever happened, he's just lucky the tide was going out.

On the horizon, for the first time, Henry thought he saw a cloud. It was hard to make out at first; he had to squint and shade his eyes to be able to see beyond his nose, but the longer he stared the more he was certain. There was definitely a cloud up there. The sky had been nothing but blue for the duration of his stay on the beach. Henry took his shoes off again and lined them up neatly next to the rock. He pulled his socks off one by one, rolled them up, and tucked them into each empty shoe away from the sand. Plunging his feet into the beach, he filtered sand through his toes. It occurred to him, somewhere between the doctor's words and the hot grit under his toenails, that they had used the word *tide*. The smell of seaweed began to sicken him, and the open plains of the shore suffocated him. Henry was on a beach when he got hurt.

> *Is there a way of proving it was deliberate?*

> *Unless he wakes up or someone comes forwards as a witness…no. I'm afraid not.*

> *Have the family been back to visit?*

> *Yes. His wife and granddaughter.*

They had been here. Henry found slight relief in the knowledge that Madeline and Lacey really were next to him not so long ago. He knew that they would come back soon and talk to him. Henry eyeballed the cloud as he thought about his wife and hoped it didn't come any closer. He looked back over to the red pine needles laid out in the X he'd drawn with his heel, and wished there was a way to say something back.

> *No proof it wasn't an accident. Do they have anything useful they can tell me at all? Let's check your chart again.*

By the way the detective was talking, he could tell she was alone again. He felt a draught and when she next spoke her voice came from underneath his feet. She was at the bottom of the bed and somewhere underground at the same time. Henry laughed and then caught himself. It was both silly and scary, and he didn't know how to handle that.

> *Hold on. This says…you were on an oxygen tank? Issues with your lungs…*

She trailed off and suddenly began to speak again very loudly. Henry could hear a faint voice, heavy with an electric fuzz, and knew she was on the phone.

> *Dan? Hey, could…no, yeah, everything's fine…great…could you do me a favour? Pull up the file on Henry Belvidere. Was there an oxygen tank with him, or anywhere else on the scene? It's…chart says nasal cannula…shit…okay, thanks. I'll explain later. Bye.*

Her shoes were heavy on their way out of the door and they squeaked on the floor. Did they find his tank after all? Maybe that's why he didn't have one on the beach; he was already hooked up to one in the real world. Henry tried to remember where it could have gone. It was a bulky silver canister and there was no way it could have been misplaced. The nearest beach was almost two hours away from home by car. He couldn't imagine leaving on a trip that long without his life support. This could mean one of two things: either it was still on the beach – the real beach – somewhere, or what happened to him was no accident. Had someone set out to harm Henry, they wouldn't care about his oxygen supply. Henry dug his feet so far into the sand that they disappeared, and considered the possibilities as he watched the cloud drift closer.

MADELINE

"**C**ome in, come in!" Jac beamed, opening up the front door wide and inviting Madeline, Lacey, and Kyle into his home. "Please, let me take your coats."

Madeline ushered Lacey and Kyle inside and the three of them handed over their outerwear, leaving their shoes by the door as they went into the living room. Madeline was struck by how much warmer Jac's house was than the cottage. Her socks sank into the carpet and she realised she hadn't felt anything but hard, splintered wood under her feet in years. From the kitchen, she could smell the spices of the fajitas and could tell immediately that the meal was being prepared from scratch.

It was clear that everything in the living room was bought brand new. The sectional sofa in the corner was in perfect condition and she couldn't see a single spill or scratch. The sofa back at the cottage wasn't even second hand – probably more like third or fourth – and one of the seat cushions had to be flipped over because there was a large stain on one side of it. When Madeline sat down on Jac's sofa, she felt like it was absorbing her entire body. She wanted to lie all the way back but, in the interests of being polite, she resisted all her urges and stayed sitting upright. She wriggled her toes on the floor and even they felt warm and happy.

"Austin is up in his room. Kyle, why don't you go see him?" Jac said, and Kyle bolted off to see his friend.

Jac's wife came into the room carrying a large bowl full of Bombay mix and put it down on the coffee table. She was wearing high-waisted jeans and a button-up white blouse that somehow made her look both dressed up and ready to work at the same time. Everything about her was modest and gentle in a way that made Madeline grit her teeth when she smiled at her.

"Hi, I'm Bronwen. It's so lovely to have you here for dinner," she said.

"Thank you. I hope we're not causing any trouble –" Madeline began, but Bronwen waved the rest of her words away.

"No trouble at all. We don't have people over anywhere near as much as we would like. Austin just hasn't clicked with anyone the way he did with your Kyle."

"I could say the same about Kyle. Austin seems to be his only friend in the world."

"Better a single outstanding friend than five mediocre ones," Jac said.

Madeline picked up the bowl of Bombay mix and held it out to Lacey, who took a handful. Madeline took some for herself and then put the bowl back down. She didn't particularly want any, but always felt obliged to accept the hospitality of others. Lacey, on the other hand, shovelled the entire handful into her mouth at once, and it was gone before the bottom of the bowl touched the table. Lacey leaned forwards, clearly wanting to have more, but feeling too timid to reach out for a second helping. Madeline put her hand on Lacey's knee to tell her to be patient.

"Kyle tells me you live on a farm," Jac said.

"We do. It's not our farm, but we have a cottage on the land," Madeline said.

"A cottage? Kyle, Lacey, their father, and grandparents…is it not too small for five people?"

"Jac," Bronwen whispered and elbowed him.

"Sorry, I mean that it must be lovely to enjoy the land with your whole family."

"It is," Madeline replied, drily.

She folded her hands in her lap and pressed her lips together. Bronwen smiled and put her arm around Jac, rubbing his arm a little too aggressively. Lacey raised her eyebrows. Nobody spoke. The ticking of the clock on the wall became louder and drew Madeline's eyes to it. The clock was wooden and appeared to be handmade. At the point where all the hands were joined together there was a little silver crucifix with the figure of Jesus Christ on it. The cross was no larger than a couple of inches and caught the ceiling light from certain angles. Bronwen caught Madeline staring up at it and smiled.

"Austin made that in his Design and Technology class last year. Of course, he had a little help with it, but we think it turned out nicely. Makes for a good ornament," she said.

"It's certainly unique," Madeline said.

"Yes. The crucifix was from a necklace I had that had broken. The metal loop that held it to the chain snapped. Very unfortunate. I really liked it. But Austin made it so I could still see it every day. So I could still see Him."

"That was very thoughtful of him."

"He's a thoughtful boy. We have the 'think before you speak' rule enforced in this house," Bronwen laughed. "I think he's done well for himself so far. As has Kyle, I'm sure. And what about you, Lacey? What class do you like best in school?"

"English," Lacey said.

"More of a reader or a writer?"

"At the moment, a reader. But I like to write too."

"That's excellent. In time, I'm sure you'll get more opportunities to explore it."

Madeline heard them continue to chatter, but didn't really listen. Instead, her focus was still on the crucifix clock. She could feel the eyes of Christ boring into her soul. He stared through her, as though he saw every cell in her body and found then full of darkness. Silver blood trickled down his forehead where his thorny crown pierced him and Madeline felt her own head begin to burn. She wrung her hands together to avoid touching her face, even though she felt like blood was trailing down her forehead too. Religion didn't do her much good, and neither would losing her mind as a guest in someone else's home. Perhaps giving her soul to a deity would bring her some reassurance, but she needed much more than that right now.

Her thoughts drifted away from religion to Henry. She dropped her gaze from the figure of Christ. Madeline swore to herself that if God existed, Henry would be here right now instead of her. He would have done a better job too. Henry and Jac would be laughing and joking like they had been friends for years. Bronwen would fall in love with his soft eyes and endless stories. Austin and Kyle wouldn't be upstairs, but instead they would be seated at Henry's feet joining in. Madeline picked the bowl up again and passed it to Lacey. Henry would be so much better.

"Why don't I finish cooking while you three natter," Jac said. "Would you excuse me?"

He went into the kitchen, leaving Bronwen, Madeline, and Lacey together on the sofa. Lacey scooped out a large handful of snacks and handed the bowl to Bronwen, who asked for it. They weren't alone for long as soon the thundering of Kyle and Austin's feet came down the stairs, and they appeared in the living room, grinning.

"And what have you boys been up to?" Bronwen asked.

"Making a fort!" Kyle said.

"A fort? Out of what? Your bed stuff?" Bronwen continued when they both nodded. "That's cool! Are you having fun?"

"Yeah! Kyle is good at making forts. He says he's got a

proper one at his house," Austin said.

"Is that true?" he asked Madeline.

"It is. It's on a little stream behind the house and it's made out of wood," she answered.

"Can I come over one day to play in it with Kyle?"

"Well," Madeline hesitated, answering only when she saw the pleading look on her grandson's face, "of course you can."

"Dinner's ready!" Jac called from the kitchen.

Everyone followed Austin into the dining room and found a seat around the table. Jac brought in bowls full of tortillas, peppers, chicken, and sour cream, placing them in the centre for family and guests alike to help themselves. The table was laid far too well for something as messy and informal as fajitas, and the white tablecloth made Madeline nervous. Plates were passed around until everyone had taken their share. Madeline watched Kyle and Lacey put the mix of vegetables and chicken in the centre of their wraps and fold them into neat rectangles. She tried to imitate what they did, but didn't seem to do it as well as her grandchildren.

"It's a shame Ned couldn't make it," Jac said a few minutes into the meal.

"He has work," Madeline replied.

"At this time?"

"He's covering a late shift. Starts at five in the evening and finishes about midnight."

"Sounds exhausting," Jac said, swallowing a mouthful of food and taking a sip of water from his glass.

"Where does he work?" Bronwen asked

"Littlebrooks."

"Ah," Jac said, unsure of how to continue.

"What about you? What do you do for a living?" Madeline asked, giving him an out.

"I'm an accountant. Sounds boring, I know, but it's not so bad. Gets the bills paid at any rate!" he smiled, showing a small piece of green bell pepper skin lodged between his two front teeth.

Madeline thought about how this life was different from her own. All she'd ever known was hands: hands-on work and hand-me-downs. Nothing was expensive in the cottage. Even her clothes were all sale items. She didn't think she owned anything that was full price or brand new. Sometimes, she didn't even bother locking the door to the cottage because it was so far from everything and nothing in it was worth stealing.

She looked around at the dining room and marvelled at it as she ate. On the far wall, there was a large glass cabinet full of plates propped up as decorations. Madeline couldn't imagine owning so many plates and never using them. One caught her eye in the centre of the top shelf. It wasn't white like the others, but dark blue. An image was painted on it in silver paint, so that the brush strokes speckled like stars in the sky. It depicted a piece of land shaped like a diamond, not attached to any world but floating by itself, with a small home on top. Madeline recognised the shape and design of the picture to be Jac and Bronwen's house, but the building and land around it and been cleaved out of the neighbourhood and existed on its own, like a separate planet. Jac caught her staring at it.

"One of Bronwen's creations. We used to have a kiln in the garage. Austin gets his creativity from her," he said.

"Your house? Why is it cut off like that?" Lacey asked.

"Not cut off. Free. This is our space that we own and enjoy. It fits in with all the other houses on our street, looks the same on the outside, but on the inside it's special. It's ours," Bronwen said, smiling.

Madeline didn't comment on it. She thought about the cottage in the middle of nowhere. The nearest house to it was their landlady's – Beatrice Wallace's – holiday home, which was empty apart from the weeks surrounding the middle of summer and Christmas. The closest place other people could be found was the post office that was three miles away. If some omnipotent being, if Jesus Christ himself, came and cut into the land around the cottage and lifted it away like a slice of cake, nobody would notice. Beatrice would be the first to know and it would still take her a few months to discover the pit where the cottage used to be when she arrived for one of her stays in her house down the road. As far as Madeline was concerned, the cottage could be demolished by some unnatural force tomorrow and not a soul would know.

Perhaps it wouldn't be such a bad thing to be floating around in space on her own planet. She'd still have the pond next to the cottage, where they kept the old canoe upside-down. Of course, there was a wasp's nest in it now, which Ned promised to clear out weeks ago. Once that was gone, she could flip it over and sit in it to really feel like she was floating. The pond itself was awful. Algae grew over it in a thick layer of slime. Fortunately, it was populated by dozens of dragonflies to eat the midges. It was too dirty for fish to live in it. Madeline knew she wouldn't care. She'd be happy to sit out with the dragonflies and float her afternoons away.

If the land was cut away from Earth, she was sure some of the trees would be taken too. Maybe even the ones around the back of the cottage that hid Kyle's fort. At night, if she kept her bedroom window open, she could hear the stream whispering away to her, and she always found herself tempted to pull on her shoes and sneak outside to it. There was a small parting in the trees just beyond the washing line with a little path down to the side of the water. Kyle's fort had been built on a wooden palette over the stream, secured in place by ropes, nails, and rocks. Inside, he'd decorated it with his best drawings and kept a blanket in a plastic box with a lid for when he wanted to sit in it on colder days. The stream itself was full of tiny fish and frogs. Madeline thought that if her home was displaced from Earth, the stream would be what she missed the most.

She couldn't stop imagining the cottage like the house on

the plate. Bronwen said it was separate because it was special, but Madeline knew she would never own a home again. The cottage belonged to Beatrice. If she ever wanted it back, she could take it without a moment's notice, and then where would Madeline go with her family? The thought of floating away in it, beyond the reach of anybody else, seemed ideal. As much as she couldn't stand the wood stove, the cramped bedroom in the converted porch, and the smell of the cow farm, the thought of having nothing at all was far, far worse. Everything she had done to this point was for the good of her family.

LACEY

More than anything, Lacey wanted to be in her bed asleep. Instead, she was up early on a Saturday in Beatrice's empty house next door, cleaning in preparation for her Christmas visit. The wooden boards of the front porch cried under Lacey's feet as she searched for the key to the front door. Columns held up the roof which had shed so many tiles in the storm that Lacey wondered how there could be any left. The pillars brought a regality to the old house that seemed out of place against the splintered floorboards and flaking paint. She frowned as she stretched up to the wall light and stuck her hand into the upturned shade. As she fished for the spare key, a tickle spread up to her wrist. Slowly, she pulled away to see a spider creeping up her arm, triggering each hair like a tripwire. She jerked back when she saw it. It dropped onto the deck with the keys. Before she could blink, it scurried into a gap between two dried up plant pots that were too sheltered to catch the rain. Lacey scrunched her nose, picked up the keys, and unlocked the door.

A cold gust of air hit her face as she stepped inside and she zipped her coat up two more centimeters, as if that would make a difference. The living room was exactly as

Beatrice had left it when she had gone back to Scotland six months ago. Papers were scattered across the oak desk in a trail that ended in the wastepaper basket next to the chair. Lacey immediately started tidying away all the loose paper into the bin. She was sure it wasn't all rubbish, but it wasn't her job to sort out the mail. It wasn't even her duty to clean Beatrice's holiday home in the first place, but her father would never do it. As she dusted the desk, the swords above the fireplace caught Lacey's eye.

They were family heirlooms from some old war, initially used to defend Scotland and now coated in dust and hanging like trophies in the decrepit farm house. Both were identical and crossed over each other the way swords are on pirate flags. Underneath, a musket ramrod hung parallel to the mantelpiece. It was long and metal, with an end shaped like a tulip. Lacey decided it was almost pretty, until she thought about the petals of the rod pushing cloth and bullets down the barrel of a gun.

Across the room from the fireplace, stairs clung to the wall. Above them, long dresses hung with bonnets above them like apparitions from the eighteenth century. She understood why Beatrice would want to keep so many historical items, but Lacey couldn't figure out why they would be used as decorations. In this house, treasures of the 1700s were displayed as mundanely as framed photos of Beatrice's border collie. It was stranger still that Beatrice would put them on show in her second home of all places, as if she not only came here to come to a different country, but to escape to another time.

Lacey pulled a cloth out of her pocket and began to wipe down the windowsill by the desk, knocking the shells of long-dead insects onto the floor by her feet. She stepped on one accidentally and it crunched and cracked like a dried leaf. The dust piled up on the cloth until she couldn't see the fabric through it. Lacey sighed and went to the kitchen to wash it off.

The water to the house and cottage came from a well, apparently, although Lacey had never seen a well on the property. She knew it couldn't be like the one she imagined – a stone circle and a bucket on a rope – but that was the only image she had to associate with wells. The water came out of the tap freezing cold and it stung Lacey's skin. She knew it would take ages to warm up when the pipes were cold, so she gritted her teeth and washed the cloth as quickly as she could. She'd have to wash the cloth another dozen times just cleaning the living room alone. There seemed to be something about old houses that attracted dust, as if it was produced in corners and poured out of the crevices.

Back in the living room, Lacey wiped the mantle down and stared up at the swords. What would it feel like to swing one? Nobody else was in the house. She dropped the wet cloth onto the floorboards and dried her hands on her jeans, leaving dirty streaks from her fingers across the denim. Reaching up slowly, Lacey grasped the handle of a sword and lifted it off its hooks as carefully as she could. The hilt was smooth and Lacey gasped to find it warm instead of cold like everything else in the house. She pulled it down in front of her eyes and figured the sword was longer than her arm even if she stretched. She turned to face the dress and bonnet that hung on the wall by the stairs and brought the blade up to her eye-level and parallel to the floor to strike. Lacey wasn't really going to swing – she didn't trust herself – but as she held it up she felt as though it would lunge without her. It was heavier than she expected, so she sat down on the sofa and rested it on her lap, running her fingers along the flat metal cheek.

"Who owned you? Who wielded you and who did you kill?"

When she put it back, the sofa shifted a little on the wooden floor as she stood up. It groaned as it scraped the boards. Lacey lowered the sword back onto its hooks above the fireplace and turned around to see something poking out from underneath the sofa. She put her hands firmly on the back of the sofa and pushed it further, revealing a small, dead mouse.

It was curled up in a ball, as though it had fallen asleep trying to stay warm. Its grey fur still appeared soft, though Lacey could tell by its face that it had been dead for a while. The mouse's eyes were just two lines in it face where its top lids met the bottom ones and they looked almost glued together. Lacey didn't squirm. She knelt down next to it and studied the way it appeared to be drying out. Mice weren't scary. The shock of one dashing past might make her jump, but it was never fear. This one seemed almost happy. Perhaps life in Powys for a mouse was hard. There were too many dangers to count.

The front door opened and slammed, and Lacey bolted upright. Her father walked in and stared at her. His eyes dropped to her jeans which were covered in dirt.

"Should have worn your old ones," he said.

"I couldn't find them."

"Now you've ruined those."

"It'll wash out."

"Clean them yourself. Don't give them to Grandma."

"Okay."

Ned grunted and put down a bag of tools he was carrying. Lacey picked up the cloth and laid it over the mouse. She picked it up through the cloth and wrapped it up. The mouse was stiff. Feeling the cold, wet cloth and knowing she held a dead creature in her hand, Lacey's heart began to beat faster. Ned watched her as she stared at the bundle in her palm.

"What's that?"

"I found a dead mouse under the sofa," she confessed.

"Throw it outside. In the bushes somewhere."

"I thought I'd bury it."

"Why bother? It'll rot the same. Just dump it somewhere."

"But I —"

"Throw it," he said, narrowing his eyes.

Lacey adjusted her coat and opened the back door in the kitchen. It was a long walk to the bushes at the back of the garden. The air was still and so bitter that it stung her nose. Snow clung crisp and white to every stem and leaf. Lacey pulled back her arm, ready to throw the mouse away, but couldn't. She crouched below the bushes and tried to dig into the ground, but it was frozen solid. Finding a nearby stick, she began to pick away at the earth until there was a hole big enough to place the mouse in, but before she could Ned pulled Lacey to her feet.

"Hey. What did I say?"

"Sorry, I just thought –"

"I know what you thought. It's just a mouse for Christ's sake. Here," he said, and knocked the mouse free from her hands.

It fell to the ground. Ned lifted one of his heavy work boots and effortlessly crushed the mouse under his weight. Lacey heard the grind of its bones and closed her eyes when she saw its flattened remains pressed into the soil. She looked up at her father and saw the faintest smile trace his lips.

ELEN

Elen watched Dan as he drove down the motorway. As he moved his hands on the steering wheel, his leather gloves creaked. Elen studied his face and watched his eyes flick up and down, tracking the lines on the road that disappeared beneath them. She stared a little too long and he caught her.

"What?" he asked.

"Nothing."

"Elen."

"Thanks for coming with me. I know Richardson is still not sure about all this."

"It's what partners are for, right?" he smiled, before immediately frowning at the car ahead. "You know you don't have much to go on still. A missing oxygen tank isn't hard evidence by any means."

"I just have a feeling."

"A feeling?"

"I can't switch my instincts off, Dan."

"Yeah," he paused. "I really want you to be right."

"Me too. I've been going through everything I've learned about the Belvideres so far and nothing stands out. But that's sort of the point. If something like that happened in my family nothing would be so…plain," she said, half to herself.

Dan laughed and nodded, reaching down to the cup holder for his travel mug full of coffee. He took a long, irritating sip and continued to grin.

"What?" Elen demanded again.

"You're fun to work with. Okay, I'll bite. Tell me what you mean."

"Hmmm," Elen grumbled, but continued anyway, "Henry went away – an elderly man dependent on an oxygen tank – on a fishing trip. Alone. I doubt that his family would let him go without worrying. But when he didn't come home…there was no report. No search for him. How? How could anyone let that happen to a family member?"

"Not all families are the same. Perhaps they don't love him. Nobody has to love anyone."

Elen clasped her hands together and looked out of the side window. She rubbed her thumbs over her other fingers and caught the edge of some nail polish that was peeling up. It was dark blue, the colour that her father said he liked on her several months ago. Elen grabbed it between her other nails and began pulling it off. It came away in one piece, like pulling off a scab to an old wound.

"No. Maybe they just don't love him," she said at last. "Still doesn't explain why he would go to a random bloody beach if he was on a fishing trip though, does it?"

Dan shrugged and kept driving. She rummaged in her bag by her feet for her phone. It didn't have any messages on it. Elen didn't know what she expected, but she always hoped there would be something there. She knew she had to call her family soon. Her father's email to her still echoed around in the back of her mind. *Your mother is getting worse.* Was she guilty of denying her family love in the same manner that the Belvideres might have denied Henry? Would she only be calling home to alleviate her guilt? Elen turned her phone off and slipped it back into her bag.

Tonight, she'd go visit her parents.

"You look worried," Dan said.

"I'm okay."

"El, I've known you long enough now to be able to tell when you're lying."

"Yeah. It's one of the things I hate most about you," she muttered.

"Sucks for you. What's up?"

Elen started chewing the inside of her cheek. They were almost at the Belvideres' cottage, and she needed to keep her emotions in line. She looked out of the window as she spoke.

"…Dad says my mother…isn't getting better."

"I'm sorry," Dan said, after a moment.

"It's been coming for a long time."

"If there's anything I can —"

"Thanks."

The car pulled off the main road onto a gravel driveway. Heavy rain had caused huge divots and potholes that threw Dan and Elen off their seats when the car hit them. Elen reached up to her neck and pulled the seatbelt away from her skin to stop it from being rubbed raw. Dan slowed down to five miles per hour, but they were still shaken about violently.

"Christ, how long is this road?" Elen asked.

"Map says about a mile."

"A mile? They live in the middle of nowhere."

"You already knew they lived on a farm."

"I did, but somehow I thought it would be different to this."

"Different how?" Dan laughed. "More quaint? More functional? You haven't been to a proper farm before, have you?"

"Is it so obvious? It's all trees and obstacles."

Dan continued to drive. "Ah! Look, we're coming up to something now. A house? Looks empty."

"They live next door."

They finally arrived at the Belvideres' residence and parked their car around the side of the cottage, next to a pond swarming with dragonflies. Elen and Dan got out of the car, closing their doors and staring at the cottage. The front door wasn't anywhere that she could see. They made their way around the cottage and found a door at the side. Elen took in a lungful of cold air and knocked.

Madeline answered the door wearing jeans and a jumper that was far too large for her. Her eyes widened a little when she saw the detectives, but she pushed the door aside without speaking and gestured that they should enter. Elen and Dan sat down on the sofa. Elen noticed that there was a large scratch down one of the arms and the material around the damage was fraying. Madeline went over to the wood stove and loaded a couple more logs into it to burn, then came to sit with the detectives.

"Mrs Belvidere, I just had some follow up questions I'd like to ask you," Elen began.

"Please. Continue."

"I went back to the hospital yesterday. Henry is still stable and doing well." Madeline didn't respond, so Elen prompted again. "I hope you are doing well too."

"Ask me what you want to ask," Madeline said curtly.

Elen glanced over at Dan, who nodded once, indicating that they needed to press ahead through the discomfort.

"Henry has a heart condition, yes?" Elen asked.

"Yes."

"He's on an oxygen tank?"

"Yes."

"How long can he go without it?"

"Sometimes a few hours, though it really depends on what he's doing." Madeline frowned at Dan while he took notes of the conversation.

"But no more than a few hours?"

"No."

"And you say he was on a fishing trip when he went missing?"

Madeline hesitated and replied, "Ned said that. Yes."

"Is that true?"

"Yes," she answered, this time without hesitating.

"He often took these trips alone?"

"Yes."

"And these trips lasted…how long?"

"A couple of days. A weekend," Madeline shrugged.

"How long was he going for this time?"

"I – I don't know."

"Did he often go without his oxygen tank?"

"Withou –"

"No tank was found on the scene. He wouldn't leave without it, would he?"

Madeline stopped replying. As the pace of the questions ramped up, her pauses and stumbles became more pronounced. Of course, Elen knew that this was often a natural response to the pressure of having to answer rapid fire questions, but there was more to it. It was her best bet at getting Madeline to trip up.

"So you don't know how long he was going for and he didn't have his life support with him, but you never tried to contact him?" Elen pushed.

"What is this?" Madeline asked sharply. "Perhaps it's best you leave."

"We could finish this discussion at the station if you like, Mrs Belvidere. Did you try to contact him?"

"…No."

Elen leaned back a little. Dan was writing in his notebook. Madeline stood up and clasped her hands together, making her way over to the kettle. The living space was small and open plan, with the kitchen and dining table on one end, and the sofa and wood stove on the other. She brought the kettle to the sink and filled it with water, then put it back to turn it on.

"Drink?" she asked.

"No, thank you."

"None for me either," Dan said, gesturing to his travel mug which he had brought in with him.

Madeline nodded and pulled a single mug down from the shelf. As she grabbed it, her hand shook, and her wedding ring clinked against the ceramic handle. Elen heard the sound and watched as Madeline made herself a herbal tea of some kind.

"Where is your son? Ned?" Elen asked.

"He's working."

"He works weekends then?"

Madeline didn't respond. She stirred the tea bag around in the hot water, then lifted it up and squeezed it out with the tea spoon.

"The children?" Elen continued.

"At friends' houses."

"How do you spend your time alone?"

Madeline was making her way back to the sofa with her tea, but stopped slightly en route, as though she hadn't expected a question like that. "There's always something to do. Even when the garden is frozen over for the winter."

"Yes. You must stay so busy out here," Elen nodded, looking out of the window. "Do you mind if we take a look around?"

"Yes, I mind. You don't have a warrant."

"Mrs Belvi –"

"This is my home," Madeline snapped. "I've answered all your questions. I think it's time you left now."

"She's right, Elen. We should head off," Dan said.

Elen felt his hand on her shoulder tugging her back slightly. "Thank you for your time, Mrs Belvidere. We'll be in touch," she said.

Back in the car, Elen grabbed her phone and turned it back on. It wasn't much, but she was certain Madeline was lying to her. The oxygen tank had to be somewhere in that cottage, but she didn't have enough to get a warrant yet. Her phone didn't have any messages at all. Another realisation hit her, and she grabbed Dan's arm.

"Dan!" she said.

"What?"

"We've been asking the wrong questions."

"What do you mean?"

"We've been so concerned with why Henry was on the beach that we didn't ask how he got there. There's a car in front of ours…and Ned probably has one. How else would he get to work?" Elen pulled out her notebook and began to scribble as they spoke.

"Carpool? But we can find out if he has a car easily enough," Dan said.

"Right. So either Henry has his own car, which means it's somewhere around the beach…"

"Possibly containing his oxygen tank."

"Yes, which would mean I've been wrong," she paused, "or he could have got public transport there."

"There might be a record of that and there are CCTV cameras all over. We'd have a good shot at tracking that."

"But there's one more possibility," Elen said. "What if Henry was driven to the beach and left there? Without his tank?"

"It could have been left behind in the car accidentally."

"Then why would no one return it? And wouldn't Henry be more careful if he depended on it? Something isn't adding up here. I need to find out what happened, Dan."

Elen began writing a list of what she had to do. Even though she was leaving the cottage with more questions than she had when she arrived, she knew the questions were better ones, and that made her smile. She breathed deeply, and wondered if she should be smug or straightforward with Richardson if she managed to pull together some hard evidence soon.

MADELINE

Madeline closed the door behind the detectives and wished she had the courage to slam it. She stood with her hand gripping the handle for a few seconds afterwards, not being able to let go. Her cup of tea was on the floor next to where she had been seated on the sofa. She settled on peppermint tea because it was supposed to help with nausea. Madeline brought it into her bedroom and put it on her bedside table. She propped up her pillows and sat down on the bed, leaning against the headboard with her legs out straight. Staring out of the window opposite, Madeline knew it wouldn't be long before Ned and Lacey were back from Beatrice's house next door. She felt guilty for lying to the police, but what else could she do? She had to protect her family and that meant not letting anybody get too close.

She laid a hand on Henry's pillow. It had been cold for many nights now. Madeline picked it up and clasped it to her chest to warm it. Burying her face into the pillow, she inhaled, and tears blurred her eyes when she smelled him. It was sweet and heavy, scented like apple shampoo, but missing something. The pillow didn't have the tickling of his hair or the softness of his skin. Madeline put it back, not wanting to wear out the smell. She took her mug of tea in both hands and held it under her nose. The scent of mint made her sneeze, as per usual. It struck her as odd that suddenly every smell was important to her. Smells were traces. They were memories. Madeline sneezed again and once more her thoughts drifted back to Harvey Cragg who had called her mad until she cried. One time, her mother found her after school hiding behind the bins outside the dinner hall.

"What are you doing?" her mother asked.

"Shh!"

"Madeline."

"Has he gone?" she whispered.

"Has who gone? There's nobody here."

"Promise?"

"I promise. School is over. Everyone else has gone home."

"Okay," Madeline sniffled and came out.

Her mother took her hand, and they began to walk home together. About ten minutes from home, past the Perkins' house that grew honeysuckle in the front yard, Madeline squeezed her mother's hand sharply.

"Am I mad?" she asked.

"Of course not, sweetie. Why? Who said you were?" Her mother stopped walking and knelt down so they were face-to-face.

"Harvey Cragg," she sniffled.

"Well, he's a stupid boy."

"Bethan says her mam told her boys chase you when they like you."

"Boys who terrorise you are not ones you should be spending time with. What does Harvey do?" She was stroking Madeline's arms and pushed a blonde ringlet out of her face.

"He takes mint leaves from his mam's kitchen and makes me sneeze until I go dizzy. I don't like it. He calls me Mad Maddy."

Madeline couldn't remember what happened after that. She remembered that Harvey had stopped chasing her and always assumed her mother had said something, but was never sure what. She wished she had the chance to ask her mother about it before she died, but that was decades ago now and Madeline would never get the chance. There were many questions she would like to ask now, but what happened to Harvey was always top of the list. She didn't know why it bothered her so much. What did it matter what was said to a little boy over sixty years ago? Even so, it was his taunts that bounced around inside her head now as she wondered if she was really losing her mind after all. Had she finally become Mad Maddy?

She laughed softly to herself and sipped her tea. Through the window, she could see the path to Kyle's fort between the trees and remembered that Austin wanted to come over one day to play in it. Fortunately, whilst it was winter, she could say it was too cold for that, but when summer came it would be hard to keep him away. She didn't mind that Kyle had him as a friend. Actually, Madeline quite liked Austin, but there was something about his parents that grated on her. They were so friendly and charitable, but how could Madeline let them into their lives when they were so desperate to help? They'd know something was wrong. They'd be able to see it and stick their noses in where they shouldn't.

When she put her mug back down, she pulled out the drawer in the bedside table and took out a photo frame with a picture of Henry in it. It was taken on Ned's last day of high school. Henry's pride glittered in his eyes, and he looked so handsome in his suit, which he insisted on wearing for the picture. Madeline remembered that he spent an hour that morning ironing every crease out of his clothes. She kissed a finger and stroked Henry's photograph with it.

Madeline nearly dropped the frame when she heard the

door slam. She shoved the picture back in the drawer and closed it as quietly as she could. Taking her empty mug, she got up and made her way to the other room, where she found Ned putting his toolkit in the cupboard under the sink. Lacey was already in her room with the door closed. Madeline strained a smile when she saw her son, knowing she'd have to tell him what happened while he was out.

"Ned?" she began softly.

"What?"

"…Detectives Parry and Blackwood were here this afternoon."

"When?" Ned froze, as one hundred percent of his attention turned to Madeline.

"About half an hour ago. I told them everyone else was out."

"Which was true," he said.

"I said you were at work."

"And if they check with my manager?"

"…I didn't think about that," Madeline said, taking a small step back.

"Maybe you should think more in the future then."

"I'm sorry."

"Whatever," Ned muttered, closing the cupboard and standing up. He was so tall. "What did they ask?"

"They seemed…fixated…on your father's oxygen tank."

"What about it?"

Madeline gave him a wide berth as she passed him to wash her mug in the kitchen sink. She tried to sound casual as she asked, "Did you take it with you? When you took him to the beach?"

"Of course I didn't."

"That's the problem," she said, continuing to keep her eyes on the sponge, which was squeaking against the soapy mug. "He wouldn't leave without it."

"Are…are you saying this is on me?" Ned's voice was quiet and steady. "That if we get caught this is my fault?"

"No, no, I wouldn't say anything like that," Madeline said, turning off the tap and drying her hands, turning her body to him but keeping her gaze elsewhere.

"But you'd think it, wouldn't you, Mum? You'd think the worst of me."

"Never –" She looked up at him.

"I did what I did for the good of this family, as you fucking well know!"

Ned grabbed his keys off the table and walked out, slamming the door behind him. Madeline wiped her eyes with her sleeve. When she finished, she jumped. Lacey was peering out of her bedroom door. When they heard Ned's tyres on the gravel fade out, Lacey walked into the kitchen.

"What did Dad mean? What did he do?" she asked, her voice quivering.

"Nothing, sweetie."

"I'm not a kid anymore. I'm not stupid."

"I never said you were either," Madeline sighed.

"So don't lie to me."

"Lacey, I – I've had a very hard day. Please, trust me. There is nothing going on."

Madeline folded the tea towel and hung it over the handle of the oven. She put the clean mug away and went to the fridge to start preparing dinner. Lacey watched her with her mouth open and her hands on her hips.

"Then why were the police here? Why were they looking for Grandpa's oxygen tank? And why is it still in the wardrobe?"

"You found it?" Madeline stopped.

"You hid it?"

"Go back to your room, Lacey. I'll call you when dinner is ready."

"But Grandma –"

"Back to your room."

Lacey backed up when Madeline hissed at her. She stormed to her room and shut the door. How many more doors would be slammed in Madeline's face today? She checked her watch. It was almost 5.30pm. It didn't seem likely that Ned or Lacey would want to eat, and Kyle really was at a friend's house. That one detail wasn't a lie. Nonetheless, preparing dinner would give her something to do. She grabbed everything she needed from the fridge to make a stew. It was something hearty, but it would freeze if no one came to eat any tonight.

Madeline sunk a knife into the mushrooms and began slicing them. The knife snapped against the chopping board each time it cut clean through. At first, she worked slowly. She knew she messed up and gave DC Parry too much information. She thought about the young detective and wasn't filled with distaste as she expected she would be. The truth was Madeline liked Elen Parry. She saw her as strong and capable – the sort of woman Madeline wished she was now. She didn't need to be young again. She just needed to have courage. Madeline finished chopping the mushrooms aggressively and then switched over to the carrots.

How could a person be expected to keep so much? Madeline kept her family and this cottage in reasonable order. She kept herself well enough. Now she was lumbered with keeping secrets which she felt pressing her to death. She sliced into the carrots and gritted her teeth. What was the right thing to do? Maybe she didn't have any good options. 'Good' and 'right' might not even be real. Madeline certainly didn't feel that she was either of those.

She brought the knife down faster than she ever had and sliced the smallest tip off a finger. It was only a graze – the tiniest amount of skin – but blood welted in the wound and welled up, spilling over the lips of the cut and staining the bamboo chopping board. Madeline didn't wince. She held her breath. Wrapping her bleeding finger in her other palm, she squeezed it, and blood oozed between all her fingers. She needed a towel. Releasing her hand to grab one, she stopped. Both her hands were entirely red and streaming.

She felt faint. Without her blood, she would die. Some of her blood was in her. Some was in her grandchildren. The rest was in Ned. Tears dropped from her eyes onto her hands. Madeline was trapped and bound by her blood. It was because of her loyalty to her family that she couldn't do anything.

Madeline went into the bathroom to wash her hands and stared at herself in the mirror. She lifted her hands to her face and, before she knew what she was doing, she wiped fresh blood across her cheeks. She painted herself in her own blood until she was a nightmarish, crimson demon. For the first time in a long time, she recognised her reflection. Ned took Henry to that beach, but her cowardice put him in his coma. Her inability to speak was what doomed her husband, when their son took him away to die.

HENRY

Rain smacked against the leaves above Henry's head as he tried to shelter from the shower. Something about the fact that it was raining at the beach made it seem far worse than it was because, unlike a storm at the farm, the beach was supposed to be a sunny place. Henry looked out at the sea that swirled and spat up the shoreline. If misery had a colour, it would be what the sea was now – a frothing grey bile. He huddled closer to the tree, putting his arm around the trunk to pull himself further towards it. As he reached his hand behind the tree, he felt something strange in the bark. Using his fingers to feel, he realised that there were scratches in the trunk that connected like a carving. Still crouching, Henry staggered around the base of the tree to see what had been etched into the bark.

He held the tree in both hands, gazing at the carving as rain trickled down his face and dripped off his nose. Slowly, he stroked the marking with a thumb, feeling the roughness of the bark and the smoothness uncovered beneath it. Henry laid his head against it, feeling the complete curve of his skull as he rocked his forehead left and right over the carving. HMN, it said in a small asymmetric heart. Henry

Madeline Ned. Henry pressed his lips against the letters and felt his Cupid's bow line up with the M.

He recognised why the trees were the wrong kind for the beach. He looked up at the tree he held and fell backwards, the water from the ground unable to soak into his trousers because they had already absorbed all the rain that they could. His clothes clung to him like another layer of skin, and he undid a couple of shirt buttons to stop from suffocating. This was the tree that had grown in the garden of his old house, before he and Madeline had moved in with Ned at the cottage. It was the tree he had seen every morning for thirty years as he made coffee by the kitchen window. At night, when he had held Ned up to count the stars, bouncing him gently to sleep, he had watched its hand-like branches wave to him and his baby. On Ned's first day of school, he had cried because his life was changing and Henry had taken out his pocket knife, carving a piece of them somewhere that would last for years.

Henry rested his cheek against the initials and closed his eyes. The leaves sheltered him a little, but rain still filtered through the branches down onto him. The drops should have been cold on his face, but he could barely feel them as his face was so numb and wet. The first bolt of lightning cracked. Henry could see it through his shut eyelids because they flashed bright red. A burst of thunder bellowed across the horizon to him several seconds later, but he didn't open his eyes. He listened to it growl overhead. Covering his face with his hands, he felt bits of bark that stuck to his fingers rub over his cheeks.

Grandpa?

"Lacey?"

I miss you.

"I miss you too."

I don't know what's happening.

"Me either. I wish I could tell you. I wish it hadn't been so long since I saw your face."

Nobody will tell me anything. They're treating me like I'm stupid. I'm not stupid. I know something's wrong.

Henry wrapped his arms around himself in a hug and tipped his head back against the tree. He and Lacey were so synchronised in their worry that, for a moment, it felt like a real conversation. He could smell the rain and felt like he was back at the farm. Wriggling his toes in his shoes, he could feel the deck in front of the cottage beneath his feet. Lacey whispered right next to him. He stroked his back with his hands that reached around his own torso, and she was hugging him. Her head pressed into his chest and he could smell apple in her hair.

"Give me all your questions."

Why won't anyone talk to me?

"Maybe no one else knows what is happening either."

I know they're hiding something. They know exactly what they're doing.

"Lacey, I —"

Why won't you wake up, Grandpa? Why won't you come home? I know you can hear me, but it's not the same. Telling you now isn't the same as seeing you smile and say you're proud or get mad and shout. Please wake up and shout at me.

"Shout? Never."

Mr Golding wants to put me in Advanced English. You'd like that. You could help me. Like when we were reading Treasure Island *last year. Remember? We sat out in Kyle's fort and pretended we were really there in it – you were Long John Silver – all of it. You made me read it to you. What if I get put in the special class and you don't wake up? Who will I read to? Dad doesn't care. Kyle gets too distracted…*

"What about Grandma?"

…and Grandma just seems so far away now. When I talk to her, it's like she's not even there. Sometimes I wonder where she's gone. Maybe she's with you.

Henry let go of himself and opened his eyes. Madeline was not here. She hadn't visited him in the hospital for days. He tipped his head back and watched the rain fall down to him, washing through his hair. A drop hit him directly in the eye and he jerked back, hitting his head on the tree. He drew his attention back to the carving, realising that it wasn't complete. Hunting around for a stone, he found one a few feet away. He began altering the etching as Lacey carried on talking.

Sometimes I wish I was older. Then I could do more. I could move out and get a job. I could find my own flat somewhere. I'd take you with me. When you wake up, we'd go to my place and it would be ours. You'd never get hurt again. Or maybe it would be better to be younger. Kyle doesn't seem to care about any of this. I don't think he can. I hate being fourteen. I hate being too old to ignore this and young enough to be ignored. It's dumb, but I'm not. You never made me feel dumb.

HMNLK, the carving said when Henry was done. He placed his entire palm over it and tried to push all his love and hope through his arm into the tree. Lacey was next to his head, whispering into his ear between the crackling of the rain. Lightning crashed through the sky again and the thunder was only milliseconds behind.

I know you can hear me. Your face looks softer when I talk. But you can't talk to me. You can't say anything. I feel bad, but I also think that's what I need. I have to tell you something, Grandpa. I have to tell someone. Dad is getting worse. He swore at Grandma again. Last time you were there to help her, but this time... And we were in Beatrice's house – me and him – cleaning. I found a mouse curled up under the couch. It looked like it was sleeping, but I knew it was dead. He stomped on it, Grandpa. He mashed it up and I can't stop thinking about it.

Henry drew in his breath and held it in his throat, releasing it in a gasp after he swallowed. The hand he laid carefully over the carving balled up into a fist. He pounded it against the tree over the N until his hand hurt. A knuckle caught a piece of bark sticking out and cut him. Henry watched the blood bubble out of the tear in his skin before immediately washing away in the rain. A dull ache began to settle behind his eyes. It was exhausting being there. He rubbed his temples as blood mingled with the water droplets and pattered down onto his shoulder. He closed his eyes – lightning made his lids flash red again – and opened them.

He was bone dry. The beach, which had been in the heart of a storm milliseconds before, was sunny and warm. Everything was just as it had been when he first woke up there. He brought his wounded hand down in front of his face to study it and...nothing. Only the long-healed scars of his lumbering past marked it. He could still smell apple, so he knew Lacey was nearby. Henry felt a hand on his shoulder. He turned to see who was there. As he turned, he blinked. The sky cracked into rain again and thunder roared.

"Lacey?" he called, but no one was behind him.

I had a dream that I was the mouse and he stepped on me. I felt all my bones crunching and then I woke up.

His head felt warm for the first time since the rain started. He looked down and saw three drops of blood hit his arm. It tried to cling to the arm hair as the rain diluted it. This blood was different to the cut on his hand. It was thicker. Redder. Henry felt the top of his head and, when he pulled his fingers away, he saw that his entire hand was covered in blood. He pushed his hair apart, trying to wash his scalp with the rain.

Grandma doesn't do anything. She won't say what needs to be said. She won't stand up to Dad.

Henry began to feel dizzy. He felt the hand on his shoulder return and this time when he spun around, he made sure not to blink. The beach continued to spin after he stopped, and he was sure he was going to vomit or pass out – perhaps both. He held his eyes open so wide that they burned. He refused to shut them even when he was surprised to find Ned standing there. He looked down at his father and his lips curled back over his teeth. They were as white as the lightning bolts. The wind picked up and branches shook violently above them. Henry looked away when he heard a crack, and Ned disappeared.

A branch broke free. It hurtled towards him. When it hit him, the world fell silent. It hit the gash on top of his head and the pain seared over his entire body. He felt like he was being electrocuted – or what he imagined being electrocuted might feel like. Never had he been so aware of every nerve in his body, as though each microscopic receptacle in his body had a needle jammed into it. Every tiny stab of pain was totally separate from the others, but there were so many that his entire body felt like it was on fire, searing with the heat of unbearable pain. He cried out.

I need to go. I'm not even supposed to be here now. I got the bus over, which took ages… I just felt like I had to come by myself. I'll be back soon, Grandpa. I love you.

Henry felt her disappear as he slumped to the ground and writhed in agony. After an uncertain amount of time, which was too long in any case, he had enough strength to flounder on his front until he could move out from under the trees. He crawled and felt his way around until he came across a natural trench that would give him shelter and keep him away from any more falling branches. Shivering, he fought the involuntary contractions in his body and sat up, pulling his knees towards his torso so he was huddled into a small ball.

Lightning flashed and lit up the island for the last time. A figure was crawling out of the sea. He was a silhouette at first – the blank space of a man – but as he staggered closer, details of him filled the shadow. Ned. He was as white as death and his eyes blazed with fire. He lumbered forwards, dragging his feet through the wet sand and leaving behind long trails instead of footprints. Henry hunkered down inside the trench, tense and prepared for the worst, but relaxed slightly when he realised that Ned's attention wasn't on him. It was on the tree. Ned continued to half-drag his feet and half-skate on the sand until he reached it. Then, he raised his arms and Henry noticed that he'd been so focused on Ned's movements that he hadn't seen the axe.

"No!" Henry shouted, as Ned motioned to cut down the tree.

Ned froze and turned to face his father. He flashed his signature crooked smile and lowered his head slightly, almost as if he was bowing. Then he brought the axe down on the trunk again and again, until he split the tree across the carving of the letters. As it fell, the heart cracked in half, and the tops of the letters toppled with the tree. When it hit the ground, Henry swore he could feel the earth below him shake. In that second, his memory flooded back to him. Henry remembered how he ended up here, beached on the shores of his own mind.

LACEY

Lacey clasped her hands together to stop them from shaking as she stood outside Miss Hayes's classroom, staring at her second-hand copy of *The Strange Case of Dr Jekyll and Mr Hyde*. She swallowed and sucked in her breath as she stroked the cover, turning it over in her hands and admiring the embossed title. Opening the book and leafing through it, she traced her notes and annotations with her fingers. She closed it and gripped the book along the spine, squeezing it until her knuckles were close to rupturing her skin. Today was the first day in the Advanced English class, after the pushing of Mr Golding.

Someone tapped her on the shoulder, and she turned around. It was Ezra Danforth, clutching a brand-new copy of *Jekyll and Hyde*, smiling at her. Lacey put her one free hand in her pocket, pulled it out, rubbed her neck, and then put it on her hip. What did she normally do with her hands? She couldn't remember. Lacey settled on fiddling with her necklace – a pink heart charm on a silver chain – while she thought about what she could possibly say to Ezra, or what he might want.

"Hey," he said.

"Hi."

"Hayes says you're joining our class."

"Yeah. Well, not really. Not yet. Just trying it out this week."

"But you're definitely getting in, right? You're smart. Everyone knows you're Golding's pet," he said, grinning.

"I am not his pet." Lacey stuck her chin out.

"I didn't mean it like that..." Ezra held up a hand in a peacekeeping gesture.

"Then how did you mean it?"

"...just that...that...you're smart."

"You already said that."

Ezra paused for a moment and then nodded to himself. "You're also kinda scary," he said.

"Scary?"

"You need to chill out."

Lacey let go of her necklace, put her book into her bag, and zipped it up in one swift, annoyed motion. Ezra raised his eyebrows and laughed. She turned her back to him to walk into the classroom and find a seat, but he jogged beside her and kept up with her strides.

"So what did you think of it?" he asked, sitting in the seat in front of her and turning around to lean on the bag of his chair while he talked.

"Think of what?"

"*J and H*. Did you like it?"

"I guess. I don't know. I didn't really read it," she shrugged.

"That's a lie."

"It is not."

"Is so. I saw the way you were holding it before." He narrowed his eyes. "I know you loved it."

"Then why ask?" Lacey said, opening her bag again and getting out her notebook and pencil case.

"It's rude to assume."

"It's not assumptive if you know."

"It's assumptive if I don't ask, whether I think I know or

not."

Lacey sighed. "I have no idea how to talk to you, Ezra."

"You're not the first person to tell me that," he said, grinning again. "But it's not difficult, really. Just tell me if you loved it. If you loved *Jekyll and Hyde.*"

"Fine. I loved it."

"So did I," he said, and turned away from her to face the front of class.

Other students filed through the door to Room 207 unenthusiastically. Lacey leaned forward and saw that Ezra's book was also full of annotations, and couldn't help but smile. Their seats were by the wall, which had a window and a radiator, so she could be warm and still have a view if the class was boring. She'd heard that the price for the honour of putting higher-level GCSEs on her CV would be insufferable and tedious lessons. Ezra was fumbling around in his rucksack for something. He grinned in satisfaction when he pulled out a half-chewed pen, which he immediately put in his mouth. Lacey opened up her notebook to refresh herself on her thoughts and Ezra sat absently gnawing on his pen.

Miss Hayes came into the room last, her mustard yellow skirt swishing against her knees. She didn't make eye contact with any of the students until she had organised herself and pulled out all the materials she needed to teach the lesson. When she took the class attendance, she smiled at Lacey and made an additional note of her name after introducing her to the class.

"Alright, *Jekyll and Hyde*…thoughts?" she began.

I liked it.

Me too.

Nah, it was boring.

Students offered up their half-hearted opinions while Lacey tried to form her own thoughts in her head. She watched as Ezra leaned forwards and flipped through his book to a specific page, and then laid his pen down in the centre of the novella. His eyes darted over several notes he had made around the margins.

"It surprised me," he said.

"Surprised you how?" Miss Hayes asked.

"I thought I'd feel bad for Jekyll and feel nothing for Hyde, but it was the other way around."

Lacey pulled her brows together, unsure of where Ezra could be going with this. If there was one thing she got from the text, it was that she didn't feel the slightest bit of empathy for that freak.

"You felt bad for Hyde?" Miss Hayes asked.

"Yeah. Sort of. Like when we read *Frankenstein*. Are these guys monsters for acting the only way they know how?" Ezra said.

"Good question. Let's talk about that. Everyone, with someone sitting near you, discuss this point. Is Hyde responsible for his actions? If so, how much?"

Lacey looked up to see Ezra was already facing her. Out of the corner of her eye, she saw Miss Hayes watching her, and could tell by the way the teacher's neck craned she was listening too. Ezra put his pen back in his mouth and closed his book, waiting for Lacey to go first.

"Okay," she began, "I don't think anything Hyde does can be excused. He murdered a guy and..."

"Sure, but only because of Jekyll's abuse of him. I mean, if you spend your whole life living one way, how do you know anything else? Stuff is only bad when people around you say it is."

"Abuse?" Lacey was incredulous. "Hyde was made up of all the worst parts of Jekyll. He was evil. And there's the other thing. He didn't know this for his 'whole life.' He'd been alive longer than that. In Jekyll."

"Addicted to the potion, abandoned, mistreated by everyone..." Ezra counted on his fingers as he listed. "Sounds like abuse. Mistreatment at the least."

"That's no reason to kill."

"What about a depraved-heart murder?"

"A what?"

"It's a thing in the US," Ezra explained. "A person can make another person kill by treating them with so much indifference that they have no respect for human life."

"How do you know that?" Lacey shook her head.

"Doesn't matter."

"It does if you're sympathising with Hyde. He's a monster, Ezra. The bad guy."

"And are things ever so black and white?"

"I've never heard of depraved-heart murders in my life," Lacey said, crossing her arms across her chest and staring at him.

"Now you have."

"And you think Jekyll is guilty of one?"

"Yeah. He is responsible for the murder because he messed up with Hyde."

Annoyingly, Lacey was beginning to understand his point. He brought up *Frankenstein* right away to cement his arguments before he'd even begun. In fact, it wasn't much of an argument at all. Frankenstein's monster wasn't the bad guy. All the smarty-pants scholars said as much. She was clutching at straws.

"But it's still done through Hyde. Through his body and his actions. He didn't have to act on his anger," Lacey said.

"And how could you know?"

"What?"

"You. Lacey Gwendolyn Belvidere. How could you know what it was like to feel that way?"

"That's not my middle name," she muttered.

"What is it then?"

"Don't have one."

"Noted," Ezra said, smiling in a way that made Lacey want to...want to what? Slap him? Maybe.

"Whatever," she said, trying to skirt around her own uncertainty. "How could you know how he felt?"

"I don't. Speculation." He shrugged again.

Lacey was about to protest how awful and confusing Ezra was to talk to once more when Miss Hayes, who had obviously been listening to them, stopped the discussions to continue teaching. Lacey snapped her book shut and leaned all the way back in her chair, folding her arms. It wasn't that she disliked Ezra. He could be weird and annoying, yes, but he was clever and he had eyes that reminded her of the mountains she could see from her and Kyle's bedroom window – all the greens and browns a person could imagine. She blinked and switched her attention to the view from the classroom window, not wanting to spend another second on Ezra.

The sky was the same colour as Lacey's cat, Squid, who had passed away almost four years ago. The clouds were heavy with snow, but when she gazed up at them, she didn't think that they would be cold. They looked as soft as Squid and warm; if she ran her fingers through them, they would tickle her like fur. She thought about Squid and clasped her necklace in her hand again, remembering how he would paw at it and get his claws tangled in the chain.

Squid had been a house-cat. He would have been safe in the land around the cottage, but there were wild animals and creatures everywhere. If they wouldn't have got him, he would have got them. Lacey's grandma had read an article in the newspaper once about how cats were killing off huge numbers of birds. No, it was far better to have kept Squid within the walls of the cottage.

During the last winter he was alive, he escaped one night. He followed Lacey everywhere, including to the bathroom. Somewhere along the twenty-foot stumble in the dark from her bedroom to the bathroom, Squid disappeared. Lacey searched for him and realised that the front door was open. They lived so far away from anyone that sometimes they forgot to lock the door. If it wasn't closed properly and the wind was strong enough, it would open easily. She dashed outside without putting her shoes on, not thinking that there might be stinging nettles, bugs, or animal droppings on the ground. Lacey moved swiftly around the cottage, squinting and using nothing but the moonlight to see. She called for Squid, but didn't find him.

The wind picked up and made it sound like the world was whispering to her. The moon was full and glinted off the slope of the roof. The stream around the back of the cottage sounded closer than normal. Lacey became aware that she was outside alone. A wisp of hair blew over her ear and crept against her neck like a bug. She scratched where it tickled her and left three red trails on the skin under her nails. Her toes were so white in the moonlight that they looked like they were made of porcelain. She felt delicate and wrapped her arms around her body, covered by nothing more than an over-sized t-shirt.

In her mind, she knew she was safe. There was nothing out of the ordinary, but something about her loneliness made her heart thud in her throat and she felt her blood in her ears. Lacey began to run back to the cottage, her panic rising the faster she went. Inside, she immediately felt calmer. The ticking of the clock on the wall measured her pulse as it returned to normal. Squid was out there somewhere, but Lacey wouldn't find him and, more importantly, she couldn't. It was too dark for her eyes, and she felt too fleshy and soft among the animals that came out at night. She was entirely naked next to whatever beasts lurked there. Squid stood a better chance on his own. Lacey left the front door open for him to return and went back to bed.

A muffled meow woke her up a few hours later. Before she was fully alert, she half-consciously found herself surprised that the gentle sound woke her up at all. She felt Squid jump up on the bed and heard the same, unusual call. That was when she felt it. A warm, wet thing dropped on her chest. Squid nuzzled against her cheek in the dark and left her face feeling damp. Lacey stretched over to turn the lamp beside her on, and gasped when she saw a dead mouse roll down her pyjama top. She reached down the neck hole to fish it out and flinched at how limp the corpse was in her hand. Squid stared at her, purring and proud. He had gone out at the first opportunity and immediately went to hunting for food. When he found some, he grabbed it and brought it right back to Lacey. He was respectful and fended for her, whom he must have considered family. She smiled and scratched under his chin, right where he loved to be rubbed, and lifted the mouse up. Squid enjoyed the attention, but never forgot where the mouse was at all times. He was fixated on it, as if there was nothing more important in the world than his kill and Lacey's sustenance.

Lacey picked him up with the mouse and carried them to the bathroom, where she shut the door. She took a cotton ball from the cupboard and wet it under warm water, before using it to clean the blood off Squid's face. She got a second one and wiped her own cheeks, then wrapped the mouse up in toilet paper and placed it in the bin, making sure to thank her boy well. She'd throw it outside in the morning. She cuddled him all the way back to the bedroom, shutting the front door and then hers on the way. Eventually, Squid stopped searching for the mouse and settled down in her arms to sleep.

"Lacey?" Miss Hayes asked. "Are you paying attention?"

Lacey jolted in her chair and her attention was snapped back to the classroom. "Yes," she said.

"You seemed deep in thought."

"No."

"Are you sure about that?" Miss Hayes was standing with her arms crossed.

"Yes. Well, no. I was just thinking about what Ezra said in our discussion," Lacey said, hoping that if she began talking, eventually her mouth would form a passable excuse for her daydreaming.

"And what was that?"

"Jekyll was guilty of a depraved-heart murder, because he created Hyde and therefore he created his circumstances."

"Do you agree?"

Lacey scratched her head, trying to focus on the question and not on the mental whiplash inside her mind. "I didn't think I did," she said.

"What does that mean?"

"I was thinking about my cat. Squid," she confessed. "He died. But, when he was alive, he would go hunting whenever he got the chance. One night he killed a mouse and brought it inside. Woke me up and dropped it right down my shirt." She paused, and the pieces finally connected. "But it wasn't wrong, was it? It was food. For me. It was nature. Maybe Hyde isn't just the bad guy. I mean, I can't excuse what he did, but if he was made up of all the negative parts of Jekyll, then wasn't it in his nature? Even though he must be punished, we can still understand why he did what he did."

Lacey looked over at Ezra, who smiled at her and nodded. She saw what he was trying to get at, but even as the words left her mouth, something about them still unsettled her. When the bell for the end of class rang, she packed up her belongings in a daze and walked off, forgetting about Ezra completely until he ran up next to her and tapped her shoulder.

"Hey! What's the rush?" he asked, panting slightly.

"Sorry. I was thinking."

"You think a lot, huh?"

"Only because you talk a lot," she said, turning right and going out of the double doors to the playground.

"I don't normally."

"I find that hard to believe."

"No, it's true. I don't," he said. "But you make me want to

talk."

"Oh boy. What did I do wrong?" she said, striding across the tarmac towards the opposite building for her Cymraeg class.

"I'm trying to have a moment, you know."

"A moment?"

"Yeah. Talk about feelings, or whatever," he muttered.

Lacey stopped walking so quickly that he continued for two more paces before realising she wasn't right next to him anymore. She gawped at him, slowly coming to terms with the strange territory she was now in.

"Feelings?" she repeated.

"Shit. I guess I can't go back now. Point of no return and all." Ezra was looking down at his shoes, kicking a nearby piece of dislodged tarmac across the playground, somewhat sheepishly.

"Ezra, what the hell are you talking about?"

"I like you," he said quietly.

"You like me," she repeated with significantly more volume.

"Shh! Hey, sorry, I shouldn't have said anything."

"...no, it's okay...I just...I'm surprised." Lacey muddled through her words and began waking again.

"Good surprised or bad surprised?" he asked, following her.

"Bit of both?"

"Ooof...honest."

"Like you are?"

"What's that supposed to mean?" he sniped.

"I mean it. You're pretty upfront about things. I'm not used to it. I don't know how to talk to you sometimes," she said, and now it was her turn to shrug.

"You just need a bit of practice, Lace. You free Saturday?"

"I...I think I'm going to see my grandpa again."

"The one in hospital?"

"How did you —" she began, but he cut her off.

"Word gets around. Let me know."

"…I…I will. Thanks."

Lacey walked away bright red and confused. Was that normally how people were asked on a date? Was it a date? She didn't know where they would go, what they would do, what time they'd meet… All she had was 'Saturday'. She thought she liked him. He was certainly good-looking. At least it was Monday, which left her plenty of time to consider it. She touched her heart necklace again and squeezed it between her thumb and finger until it was warm.

ELEN

Elen held her pen in front of her face, bringing the nib right up to her eye and staring at it intensely. What would happen if she jammed it into her eye? Would it be more or less painful than filling out this paperwork for Richardson? She decided the answer was undoubtedly less, but used the pen to fill in the form rather than maim herself anyway, cursing herself for doing her job. She'd spent all morning getting them done for the end of the day but, as her lunch hour approached, Elen found herself getting distracted. When she reached the bottom of the page, she dropped the pen and tipped her head back, counting the ceiling tiles and cracking her knuckles.

"Am I interrupting?" Richardson said, putting his head around the door.

Elen jerked forwards and slammed her hand on the desk to steady herself. She cleared her throat and stood up.

"No, no. Just doing the paperwork for the car theft on Ffordd Parc."

"Care for a break? It's almost your lunch hour, right?"

"Uh, yeah. Where to?" she said, taking a small step back to match how stunned she must have sounded.

"That green building," Richardson said, scratching his

head. "The café who make those killer paninis Dan keeps showing up with."

"I think it's just called Cegin."

"Oh, well that's…obvious," he laughed. "I had a craving. Unless you want something else?"

"It sounds great. Let me grab my purse."

She walked a pace behind him to rake her fingers through her frazzled hair and put on some lip balm. It was no secret that she wasn't the best at taking care of herself. He turned around just as she was rubbing her lips together and smiled. Before they went outside, she pulled her jacket on and zipped it up all the way. It was overcast, and there was a cold wind in the air. The café was only down the road. Richardson held the door open for her and made sure it was shut securely behind them before they began walking.

"How are you?" he asked.

"I'm good. You?"

"I've been meaning to talk to you," he said, and she noted that he didn't answer her question.

"You have?"

"Yeah. About the Belvideres."

"Oh. Yeah."

"Unless you don't want to do that now," he said, holding his hands up. "It's a lunch break, I get it."

"No, no. Nothing like that. Carry on," she said, forcing a smile.

It wasn't a lie – it really wasn't anything like that – but she knew how he felt about the case and didn't want to have a disagreement. She needed to tread carefully to keep the investigation going with the Chief Inspector's support.

"You know I believe you, right? The more I think about it, the more I'm sure you're on to something," he said.

She couldn't hide the surprise on her face. He believed her?

"But the thing I can't figure out is why this means so much to you," he continued.

"What do you mean?"

"You know what I mean."

"No. I don't," she said.

"Elen...detectives... they – we – don't get this invested in cases like this. Not so emotionally anyway. At least, not where we can help it and not without a good reason," he said.

They came up to the café, but he stopped outside. It was clear he wasn't asking everything he wanted to, which frustrated Elen, but at the same time she didn't want him to ask, because she didn't want to answer. She sighed.

"This is my job. My work is important to me," she said after a long silence.

"There's more to it than that."

He went inside the café without waiting for her response, so she rolled her eyes at the back of his head and followed him. They ordered their paninis and a black coffee each, all 'to-go'. Taking their food across the street to the park, they found a bench to sit on. She put her coffee cup on the ground and ate her panini slowly, hoping that as long as she was chewing, she wouldn't have to talk.

"I'm not grilling you as your boss," he said, as he swallowed his last bite.

"Then who are you?" She half-laughed.

"A friend." She didn't reply. "I just want to know, El. Why do you get so defensive about the Belvideres? What's going on?"

"That's private, Richardson."

"I told you, I'm not here as your boss. It's Marcus. Tell me. You can trust me."

She looked at him and admired his face. His eyes were as grey as the sky and his bare face was concealed behind the beginnings of a dark, bristly beard. Looking closer, she saw that there was circles underneath his eyes and his tie wasn't fastened properly, but instead hung a little looser than normal. How could she be expected to confide in him – no matter how much she wanted to – when there was some pain he was also concealing? She turned to say as much to him, but as she did her foot knocked over the coffee on the ground and it spilled over her boots.

"Shit," she said, forgetting her composure.

"Here, let me."

Richardson took the napkin that had been wrapped around his now-consumed panini and knelt down to wipe the coffee off her boot. Elen watched him, thinking it was strange that she was looking down at the top of his head, because he was so tall. He stood and picked up his coffee.

"Have mine," he said.

"I couldn't. It's yours."

"Please. I've been drinking too much caffeine lately anyway."

"Not been sleeping well?"

He looked down at her and frowned briefly, before his face softened into acceptance.

"Something like that," he said. "Take it."

They didn't say much for most of the walk back to the station. Elen clung to his coffee and brought it so close to her chest that she could feel the warmth on her skin through her jacket. He walked next to her, slowing down when she did and letting her take the lead crossing the roads. She could tell him what she was thinking, but didn't want him to pity her, and assumed that was why he didn't tell her anything either. When she sipped the coffee, it was warm on her lips and she could feel it trailing hot down inside her to her stomach, burning her inside out.

Outside the station, Richardson jogged ahead a couple of paces to open the door for her, but kept his hand on the handle for a moment before she could walk through. He looked at her for a few seconds and Elen could see what he was thinking by the expression on his face.

"Look, you don't have to tell me what's happening. When we go inside, I'm your Chief Inspector again, but I'll never force you to tell me. That's not the kind of person I am and I think you know that."

Elen hesitated and clutched the coffee tighter. He stared at her so intensely that she had to look away. His eyes burned her the way the coffee did. She could tell Richardson wasn't finished, but had no idea where he was going with the conversation. If she couldn't let go of the Belvidere case, he couldn't let go of why.

"I'm going to tell you something," he said.

"What?"

"You're suspicious of everyone. You don't have to be suspicious of me. I haven't done anything, and I won't. Everything is a bit messy right now. There are some things you can't stop. No matter how hard you fight, sometimes the bad is inevitable."

Richardson let go of the door and it closed, with the two of them still standing outside. It was beginning to feel cold somehow, even though it hadn't been that bad on the walk to the café, or while they had been sitting on the bench. He turned and walked away from her for a few paces, before stopping and gazing down the road ahead.

"What are you talking about?" she asked, standing perfectly still.

"My sister...she's... Look, I'm sure you noticed how different I've been lately. My office is a mess. I can barely shave before work. I'm losing track of everything. My mind too, I think," he said, letting out a small, unconvincing laugh, before his tone dropped again. "My sister's been diagnosed with cancer. I can't investigate it. I can't make an arrest. There's no perp, no crime, no verdict. She just has it. I look around and all I see now is the whole world coming undone."

Elen walked to stand beside him. His grey eyes brimmed as he waged a war inside himself. His fists clenched and unclenched at his sides. Gently, she put a hand on his shoulder and patted him a couple of times.

"I could see it in your eyes right from the start," Richardson continued. "You care so much about Henry Belvidere and, technically speaking, you've never met him. Whatever you're feeling, it's intense. I can't figure out how I just have to sit around doing nothing for the person that means more to me than anything, and you are running yourself off your feet for a complete stranger. Then I thought I'd rather my sister was where Henry was, and I had to drink the thought out of my head."

Richardson threw back his head and grinned in such a way that Elen knew it was pure disbelief at the callousness of a grieved mind. He shook his head and wiped his eyes with the back of his left hand, rubbing the tears away.

"I'm sorry if I pushed you too hard earlier. I know whatever it is, it's personal. I'm only telling you this now to show you my intentions are good," he said.

"Only? That's the only reason?" she said, feeling a pang in her chest.

"I didn't say that right," he said. "God, what a mess. I trust you. And I do care too. I want to know you as a friend."

"I don't know you very well. Not in any real way."

"Is there a way more real than this? I've just shared with you the darkest part of my mind, the thing that haunts me every minute I'm alive. So, I would say that you know me. And I don't know you yet, beyond you being a good person – brave and kind and a bit of a mess, but just the right amount. So when you're willing to tell me more, Elen Parry, I want to listen, just as you've done for me today."

Richardson smiled and opened the door, letting her walk through. Elen was already halfway down the corridor before she realised that he hadn't followed her. She turned around and saw him through the glass door, leaning against the frame. He pulled a battered box of cigarettes from the inside pocket of his coat and lit one up, before tipping his head back and banging it lightly on the window. Elen half-wondered whether she should go back out, but decided against it, heading to her office instead.

Dan was at his desk, tearing sheets of paper out of his notebook. He didn't look up when Elen came in and dumped her bag down on her own desk. She unzipped her jacket and shrugged it off, putting it over the back of her chair. Finishing the coffee in one last swig, she threw the cup towards the bin in the corner of the room. It bounced off the rim onto the floor. Dan looked up, rolled his eyes, used his feet to push his chair over to it, put her cup in the bin, and scooted himself back to his desk.

"What did you get for lunch?" he asked, eyes back down on his notebook.

"Paninis."

"Cegin?"

"Yeah, Richardson invited me," she said casually, turning her monitor back on and preparing to dive back into her paperwork.

"Whoa. What did you talk about?"

"Small talk. Nothing important."

"Right," Dan said, shaking his head.

She knew Dan didn't believe her – it was hard lying to a detective, especially one who knew her well – but they didn't speak about it any further. Dan carried on ripping pages from his notebook and throwing them out, while Elen opened up her computer file on Henry Belvidere. She clicked through the photos of his wounds and stopped on the last one, which showed his whole face. He didn't appear asleep. His face was the colour of death – pale and lifeless under the harsh lighting in his hospital room. She zoomed in on his mouth so it was all that filled her computer screen and saw that he was almost smiling. The corner of his mouth smirked at her and she knew she had seen those lips before, but not on Henry. This was the smug expression of her mother.

Elen hadn't spoken to her mother, Beverley, for over a month, only phoning her father, Osian, to check in when he emailed her last. Her mother wasn't herself until she was asleep, and couldn't shout or curse at her family anymore. Her mother would slip into her rest and that old smirk would drift back to her face, full of all the youth and mischief she once had. Awake, Elen barely recognised her, and her mother rarely knew who her daughter was either. Whenever Elen looked at Henry in his coma, she couldn't help but see the face of someone she loved, who could no longer love her.

"What are you doing?" she asked Dan, exiting out of the photos on her screen and opening up the document of notes instead.

"I've typed all these bits onto my computer, so I don't need the paper anymore. Just throwing it out to keep my notepad fresh."

"Could you help me this afternoon?"

"Depends what it is. I've got a report to wrap up by the end of the week," he said, tearing out a final page and throwing it away, before picking at the pieces lodged in the spiral of the notebook with a thumb and forefinger.

"I have to go over security footage from the busses to make sure Henry didn't go there alone. It'll take hours. I need you to call the depot and cab services to check if he's on any of their records. Then we can at least rule out that he took public transport to get to the beach. Would eliminate the option so I could start finding out if someone else took him there," she explained.

"It sounds like you already think he had help."

"I do. The man had an oxygen tank. He wouldn't go anywhere without it."

Dan stopped and looked up. An expression crossed his face that Elen couldn't read.

"That's not strictly true," he said. "We also need to consider that he purposefully went to the beach without his life support." Elen stared at him, but he continued, "it's not impossible. And if he had help getting there that still doesn't conclusively rule out suicide, even assisted suicide. I'll make the calls for you, but make sure you're keeping your options open."

"I am, Dan."

"I'm not suggesting otherwise. Partners keep each other on track, right?"

Elen nodded to him, grateful for the assistance, and went to download the files she'd been sent by the bus depot containing all the footage for the day Henry travelled to the beach. She plugged her headphones into her computer, not because there would be any sound, but to muffle any background noise from the police station. It wasn't an especially busy place, but Elen wanted complete concentration. She opened the first file and groaned when she saw there were four hours of footage in it. She set it to play through twice as fast as the normal speed and leaned forwards. The next two hours were long and burned her eyes, but they didn't hurt her as much as the image of her mother in Henry Belvidere's stead, with a crooked smile across her thinning face.

MADELINE

She searched all** over the cottage, but Madeline couldn't find Kyle anywhere. It was beginning to get dark outside and she worried about where he might have gone. He had a habit of following his imagination, even when it took him to dangerous places. Before she panicked, Madeline pulled on her shoes and grabbed her coat, heading out to check his fort.

The snow on the ground had turned to ice that cracked under her feet. The cold air stung her throat and dried her eyes until they watered. She longed for the autumn days to return, when it was hot without humidity and dry without drought. Walking around the back of the cottage, she went along the tree line until she found the parting that marked the path to the stream. She pushed the branches aside and made her way down to the bank. In the summer after rainfall, the ground was slick with mud, but now it was frozen and hard. The water ran over huge rocks on the bed that Kyle liked to flip over to search for fish. Last spring he had found one no larger than his little finger and had asked to keep it as a pet.

"Please, Grandma!" he begged, holding up the fish in a jar

full of stream water.

"And where would you keep him?" she asked, raising an eyebrow.

"In my room."

"In yours and Lacey's room?"

"She won't mind!"

"I somehow doubt that," she laughed.

"I'll take good care of him." His bottom lip jutted out and he was staring up at her defiantly.

"Kyle, he'll be much happier out here."

He hesitated. "...will he?"

"Yes."

"But I've already given him a name!" He looked down into the jar and clutched it to his chest.

"What name?"

"Toby."

"I'll tell you what," she said, putting a hand on his shoulder and guiding him back towards the stream. "We'll name all the fish in the whole world Toby. That way, whenever you see one, it will be Toby."

"Okay, Grandma," he frowned, but let Toby go.

Madeline could hear that Kyle was inside the fort before she saw him. It was badly built, but the tarp over the roof kept all the water out and it was wind-proof. As she approached, she heard the scratching sounds of Kyle drawing. The noise of the pen scribbling violently on the paper that lay over the rough wooden floor was surprisingly loud, and she decided to call out so she didn't startle him. He poked his head out of the hole he used as a window.

He was a sweet boy. Madeline never failed to be thankful that he looked like his mother, Karen. His hair was blonde and so thick that it looked like it had the consistency of toilet brush bristles, even though it was soft to touch. Freckles sprinkled themselves over his nose and a streak of mud had dried down his left cheek. His eyes glowed like sunlight through tree sap and made her feel warmer when he looked in her direction. Everything about him reminded Madeline of her daughter-in-law as though she lived inside him and had not died years ago. When Ned looked at Kyle, she could see the pain on his face. He saw the woman he loved and would never hold again in the face of his son.

Kyle knew he looked like Karen. In the first year after her death, it had brought him comfort to know he could still see her when he looked in the mirror. The trouble was, he couldn't figure out where she'd gone, or why she wouldn't come back.

"I miss Mummy," he said one night, as Madeline tucked him into bed.

This was before they had come to live at the cottage. Ned was still in the old house with the kids, trying to work out how to make ends meets without his wife. Lacey was old enough to know what was happening, though Madeline didn't think anybody could ever fully understand death, no matter how old or wise they grew. It was different for Kyle though. Madeline pulled the duvet up to his chin and took her time choosing a bed-time story from the bookshelf, trying to buy herself time to think of what to say next.

"Do you miss her?" he whispered.

"Yes. Very much," she whispered back.

"But she's not your family."

"Family is whoever you love."

"What happened to her?" He pushed his duvet back down and sat up, and Madeline was forced to face him.

"She's passed on, honey," was the best she could do.

"My teacher says she's gone to a better place. Did she? Somewhere better than with me and Lacey?" His mouth was pulled down to one side and he was fiddling with the feet of a tattered teddy bear.

"No," she said, silently cursing his teacher. "There is nowhere better than with family. She didn't go anywhere, my love. She's still right here with you."

"I don't understand."

"Inside a person's body is a spirit. When they die, the spirit gets let out. It stays with its family, watching over them. She's watching over you."

"She can see me? Right now?" he said, his amber eyes alight.

"Yes, sweetheart. Right now."

Kyle looked around the room. "I can't see her."

"You don't have to," Madeline paused, unsure of how far she should take this. "You can feel her."

"Can she hear me?"

"She can."

"I love you, Mummy," Kyle whispered into the dark bedroom.

Madeline turned back to the bookshelf and bit her lip, breathing long and deep. She picked up a book and began to read to him, but her mind drifted back to the stories she had already told him. Did she really believe Karen was still around, looking after them? She always thought there was some truth to that, but when she saw what the death did to her grandchildren, she couldn't bring herself to believe it anymore. It sounded too good, too pure, for the evil truth of what happened to her. There was nothing reassuring about it.

She thought about this as she bent down outside Kyle's fort and peered in through the door. She saw him huddled up in his coat, trying to draw fresh pictures to put up on the walls, but he didn't have a torch and the sun was disappearing quickly. His freckled nose had turned bright red and his breath was visible in the air.

"Come on, love. Time to go inside," she said.

"One minute. I'm just finishing this."

"Do you need tape to stick it up when you're finished?"

"No. I want this one to go inside. It's for Dad."

"...I'm sure he'll like it." She frowned, rubbing her knees which were beginning to tire from crouching.

"Do you?" he asked, holding up the finished drawing.

Madeline swallowed hard. It was of the family, standing in a line outside the cottage. Lacey, Ned, and Kyle were on one side, their father towering above them. Madeline was standing on the other side alone, far from the rest of them. Henry wasn't in the drawing at all. Madeline pulled the zip further up on her coat and pressed her face into the collar that now covered her mouth. She wrapped her arms around her torso, cold from being unable to fit into Kyle's fort and longing for the warmth of another person.

"It's lovely. But where's Grandpa?" she asked.

"I don't know. I can't draw him until I know where he is," he said.

Madeline took a breath. "Come on now," she said, taking Kyle's hand to help him out and leading him back up the path to the door.

On the way inside, Madeline remembered she needed to pick up some more logs for the wood stove. She sent Kyle in to wash his hands. Opposite the cottage there was a huge tarp that covered a large pile of logs, cut to the right size with the splitter. She moved the rocks that pinned the tarp down and pulled it back, revealing the dry wood underneath. As she began to take off a few and dump them in a separate pile to bring inside, her eye caught something hiding in the crevices between the logs. Its black stare made every extremity turn to ice as it crawled out onto the open grass below.

It was the width of her palm. In fact, it was so big that she could see the individual hairs that stabbed out from its thick legs. It sat there, completely still. Normally, she didn't mind spiders, but that didn't mean she wouldn't kill the big ones. Leaving the logs, Madeline went around the side of the cottage to grab a shovel.

As she approached the spider again, she held the shovel

with both hands, pointing the metal head towards it. She managed to creep up close enough to it to bring the shovel down like a guillotine across its abdomen. She closed her eyes and cleaved the spider in half, leaving it crumpled and warped on the grass. Madeline used the shovel to scoop up the spider and throw its dead body out of sight. A thin stripe of yellow guts clung to the edge of the metal head. Wiping the evidence of the kill off the shovel onto the grass, she pinned the tarp back down and put the shovel away. Stacking the logs for the fire in her arms, Madeline scanned the area one last time before going inside.

The cottage was reasonably warm from the fire that was slowly dying. She loaded the logs into the empty metal basin they kept in the corner for firewood and opened the door of the wood stove, stashing a fresh log inside. When she finished, she went over to the kitchen to wash her hands and make dinner.

There wouldn't usually be much to eat tonight. It was the last few days of Ned's pay period and money was low. Since Ned had stormed out the other night after their argument, Madeline had frozen the stew and had made something else, so she could defrost the frozen meal in the microwave to have tonight. She pulled it out of the freezer and put it on the draining board. Making sure that everywhere else was clean first, she began to pull four bowls out of a cupboard and put the stew in the microwave to be heated. Rummaging around in another cupboard for the last of the bread, Madeline buttered a few slices for them to eat alongside the meal.

She went to the window and waited, staring across the field opposite. There was a gate on the other side that Ned had to drive through. It was about five minutes away from the cottage in the car, so Madeline knew to heat up the food when he passed it. She stared out the window until she saw his rusting, blue car appear, and then hurried into the kitchen. She turned the microwave on and called the children out of their room. Kyle sat at his place at the table while Lacey filled up four glasses with water and put them down for each person, before taking her own seat next to her brother. Madeline heard Ned's car come up the driveway and the hairs on her arms rose. The microwave beeped as Ned opened the door and she greeted him with a smile.

Ned dumped his bag on the sofa and slumped in his chair. Madeline served up the stew and brought it over, putting each plate in front of everybody starting with Ned and ending with herself. Ned didn't speak, but instead grabbed a slice of bread and began eating, dipping it into his stew and taking oversized bites. Lacey kept her gaze down on her food, pushing it around with her spoon but barely touching it. Kyle chewed happily. Madeline watched them all.

"How was work, dear?" Madeline asked Ned at last.

"Fine," he said, still chewing.

"Dad, I drew you a picture," Kyle said.

"That's great. Show me after dinner."

They carried on eating in silence for a bit. Kyle beamed at his approval. Lacey carried on pushing food around on her plate, barely eating any of it.

"What's up with you? Not like you to refuse food," Ned said to her.

"I'm not hungry," she said.

"Your grandma worked hard on this."

"No, she didn't, she just defrosted it."

"I'm sorry, are you…talking back to me?" he asked calmly, but his stare was intense.

"No."

"No?"

"No, Dad."

"Is that true, Mum?" he said, switching his attention to Madeline. "You just defrosted this?"

"I made it fresh the other night," Madeline said.

"Why not make it fresh tonight?"

"I –"

"Do I not work hard for us all every day? Do I not bring home all the money we have?" he asked, and Madeline could tell by the slight tremor in his voice that he had a bad day.

"Yes. You do. We're all very grateful, dear."

"Then why don't I deserve proper food?" he pushed his bowl away and leaned towards her.

"It is proper food. I had to freeze it because we didn't eat it the other night."

"And now you're talking back? That's where Lacey gets her bad attitude. Don't make me look bad in front of my kids, Mum. Besides, why make it earlier and then not serve it? Sounds like a waste to me."

"I'm sorry," she said, looking down.

"I deserve better, don't I?"

"Yes."

"So do my children," he said, gesturing at Lacey and Kyle with his spoon.

"Yes."

"Don't they?"

"Yes, Ned."

Madeline's spoon scraped against the plate as she ate and she could feel Ned look up at her, but she pretended not to notice, making sure to carry on more quietly. When Madeline finished eating she looked up to see that both Kyle and Ned had also finished, but Lacey still wasn't eating. She looked ill and scrunched up her nose at the stew. Ned stared at her without blinking. Madeline bit her lip, knowing if Lacey didn't finish her food she might need to shout at her, if only to save her from Ned's shouting. Lacey looked like she was trying, nibbling pieces of carrot off the tip of her spoon, but couldn't quite manage a full bite.

"What's the problem?" Ned asked.

"I'm not very hungry," she said gently.

"Been stuffing your face before dinner?"

"No, Dad. I'm just not hungry."

"We always eat at this time. You're always ready for food

now. You've been snacking again, haven't you?" he accused, then let his eyes drop to scan her body. "You'll get fat if you keep doing that."

"She's fine, Ned," Madeline said, hoping tonight he'd let it go.

"I'm just saying," he shrugged. "Nobody likes a tubby girl."

"Ned, she's not tubby!" For a moment, she forgot who she was talking to and the incredulity burst out of her.

"How long will that last if she keeps gobbling away before meals?"

"I really haven't been, Dad. I've not eaten since I had lunch with..." Lacey trailed off.

"Lunch with who?" Ned demanded.

"Anna."

"That's a lie."

"...Ezra."

"Who's Ezra? Is he your boyfriend?" Ned smirked. "I bet Ezra wouldn't want a fat girlfriend."

"Dad, stop."

"Ned!" Madeline said a little louder.

"What?" he snapped, turning back to Madeline. "You won't even feed us proper food even though I work all day for us to afford it, and even take on night shifts. And I come home to a nice family meal, only the food is shit and Lacey won't even eat!" He looked at Lacey again, his voice uncomfortably calm and his body still like a snake before it struck.

"That's why you won't eat, isn't it, Lacey? The food is shit. The food I provide for you is horrible, isn't it?"

"No, Dad."

"No?"

"It's not, I promise," Lacey looked up at him, a pleading look in her eyes.

"Then it's your grandma's cooking. Days old. Frozen and reheated like a meal-for-one. Might as well be, given nobody will eat with me. Wouldn't feed this to a fucking dog."

"Dad, I'm just not –" Lacey tried.

"It's insulting that you won't eat, Lacey. You wanna be fat? Go right ahead. Eat. Now." He barked his last order.

Lacey stared at her father, who wasn't looking at her, but made unbreakable eye contact with his mother. Madeline tried to shift her gaze away, but somehow couldn't tear her eyes from his. In her peripheral vision, she saw Kyle hang his head low as he sat perfectly still with his hands folded on his lap. Lacey was frozen too but, seeing that Ned wouldn't let her go unless she did as she was told, she began to eat.

Each spoonful made her wince. She was sharply told to stop being a baby, and the rest of her serving was consumed in silence. Madeline couldn't bear to watch her. Tears slipped down Lacey's face as she held her stomach. Her hand shook so violently that when she put the spoon in her mouth it rattled against her teeth. Each mouthful required two or three swallows to get it down. Even then, Lacey had to pause to make sure it was really going to stay down. The entire time, Ned watched Madeline. When Lacey was done, she sat forwards with her arms folded over her stomach.

"Good girl," Ned said.

"Dad, can I show you my drawing now?" Kyle said, clearly trying in his own way to help navigate the storm of his father's temper.

"Of course you can, mate. Go get it."

"Here it is!" Kyle said when he'd fetched the picture from his room.

"That's excellent! Look at us! Grandma, me, you, and your sister. You've even done her lovely black hair," he said, reaching over the table to stroke Lacey's hair as she hunched over. "You did a really great job on this, boy. We should stick it up on the fridge, so we can see this picture of us all every day."

"Not all of us," Madeline said.

Ned's attention snapped back to her, but instead of shouting he smiled. He stood up slowly, taking the drawing to the fridge and using a couple of magnets to hold it in place. Kyle beamed and went over to Ned, who put his arms around him. With his arm firmly around his son, he squinted and looked from his daughter to his mother.

"I need to go collect the post before the branch closes. Kyle, want to come?" Ned said.

"Sure, Dad!"

"We'll be back soon. Get this place cleaned up," he said to Madeline.

Ned waited for Kyle to pull his shoes on. They left together. Lacey and Madeline sat at the table until they couldn't hear his car anymore. Madeline stood up and began to collect the plates. By the time she filled the sink with hot water, Lacey still hadn't moved.

"I'm going for some fresh air," she said at last.

"But it's dark out, sweetie."

"I don't care."

"Be careful. Take the torch and wear your coat."

Lacey left, closing the cottage door quietly behind her. Madeline could always tell her granddaughter was angry when she went silent. The more Lacey tip-toed around, the more she was trying to avoid setting herself off like a bomb; one wrong move and she would explode. Madeline carried on with the cleaning. She washed the glasses one by one, then all the bowls, cutlery, and plastic food containers. She wiped the microwave and counters, tucked the chairs back under the table, and swept the room. Putting another log onto the stove she checked her watch and saw that Lacey had been gone for half an hour. Ned would be back shortly. Madeline grabbed her jacket and went outside, expecting to have a thorough search on her hands, but stopped dead in her tracks almost immediately when she saw Lacey.

Her granddaughter was kneeling in the grass by the hedges. The torch was on the ground and cast long, dark stripes of shadows from the blades of grass that blocked its light. As Madeline came closer, she saw a large pool of vomit underneath Lacey, who shook violently. Madeline put her arms around Lacey, but saw there was something strange in the vomit. The body of a spider cut in half was covered in the puke. It must have landed here after Madeline threw it earlier.

"I-I didn't see it," Lacey shivered.

"It's okay, love. Come inside. Get cleaned up."

Madeline guided her to her feet and then kicked dirt over the vomit as best she could, given the ground was hard from the cold weather. She brought Lacey back into the cottage and took her to the bathroom. Taking a make-up wipe from a packet, Madeline began to wipe Lacey's face clean. Years were added to her face as all the foundation and powder came away on the cloth. Madeline could see her scars and blemishes dotted around her chin. Wrinkles begun to carve out a path in her forehead already. Lacey suddenly looked like an older woman, sleepless and empty. When Madeline looked in her eyes, she saw the image of the spider, halved and helpless in its agony.

HENRY

The skies were blue again. Henry sat on the beach parallel to the sea, staring down the long stretch of sand as far as he could see. He replayed everything in his mind as he lay back, rocking his head from side to side to make a little dip in the sand to cradle him. He lifted his fingers to feel his face, but everything felt normal. He was warm lying here, but knew he was really bundled up in a hospital bed. How could he be in two places at once? It wasn't possible. Everything here felt so tangible, so real beyond doubt that it seemed impossible to consider them as thoughts, as daydreams at the most.

The last time he saw his family was the day it all happened, but they had also been with him here...wherever here was. He'd heard them, smelled them, even felt them. They were just as present in this world as the other, but it wasn't the same. Henry longed to look at Madeline's face again. Before they had said goodbye on the day he went missing, he had put one hand on each of her cheeks and held her up to look into her eyes. They were ageless, as bright as they had been on the day they met in Belmont Café. With her curly blonde hair and blue dress, Henry had thought she looked like Alice from *Alice's Adventures in Wonderland,*

and she had seemed just as precocious. He had loved her then as he did now. When he thought of her, it was always of that blue dress and those endless questions – the sign of an unsatisfied mind. When he held her before he left, he gave her a kiss long enough to last forever, before walking out of the front door.

Ned had told him they were going fishing for a few days together. Henry cursed himself for never being suspicious. It was the simple desire of wanting his son's approval that had fooled him. Ned had said he'd loaded his bag and oxygen tank into the car. The policewoman he'd heard in his hospital room didn't find a tank with him. Henry had the tank in the car. Ned must have taken it away. There had never been any intention of a fishing trip. They had sat in Ned's truck together like it was any other day and, as far as Henry had been concerned, it was.

"Want some music on, Dad?" Ned asked.

"Sure."

"Check the glove box. I think I still have that Frank Sinatra CD in there."

Henry reached forwards and rifled through the compartment. "Ah, yeah. Found it."

"Put it in then."

He nodded and slipped the disc into the slit between them, a relic that betrayed the age of the car, and had watched as a small screen lit up with the song title. The music began to filter in through the speakers on either side of them.

"I'm looking forwards to this trip," Henry said. "It'll be good to hit the open water with you again. How long has it been now? Five years? Six?"

"Ten."

"Ten?"

Ned didn't respond and Henry sighed. Sinatra crooned around them.

"Well, I'm glad we're not leaving it any longer. I'm sorry, Ned."

"It's okay."

"I know things have been hard for you. Especially after Karen –"

Henry cut himself short as he thought about his dead daughter-in-law. Karen had been beautiful, but not in the classical sense. She had blonde hair like Kyle, but it had been frizzy rather than sleek. It had been so thick around her shoulders, but she had hardly ever tied it up. Instead, she had let her hair blow wildly in the wind and tangle itself up. She worked as an archaeologist for the university, so there was never any point in dressing up. She'd come home caked in mud and sweat. Henry remembered that she had preferred oversized clothes that were loose around her body. She hadn't especially curvy, but instead had been so slim and straight that the large shirts she had worn made her look even thinner. Karen had been tall though and matched Ned's height, towering over most women and many men. When she had walked into a room people had taken notice, although Karen had never seen them doing so.

They tried to be patient with Ned's pain, but he was inconsolable. After she died, Henry could tell Ned didn't want to live anymore either. The only thing keeping him going was the way his family needed him, and this only led him to resent them all. Sometimes Henry would look at his son and see an actor – someone pretending to play a part, but always harbouring another side to themselves out of the spotlight.

On the beach, Henry turned his head to face the trees. The sea whispered behind him. He thought back to the previous night, when he had seen Ned tear down the tree that belonged in the garden of their old house. The whites of his eyes had caught the brief light of the moon that had filtered down through the black clouds in the sky. His jaw hung open and all his teeth had been somehow sharper than a human's. He had been wolf-like, panting and howling as he destroyed the tree. It was gone now. It was as though it never existed.

"Maybe I'm crazy. Maybe I'll be here forever," Henry said to himself, his ear filling with sand as he lay on his side and continued to think about his last trip with Ned.

His son hadn't said or done anything out of character. In fact, it was impossible for him to do so, as he had no character since Karen died. He only had two moods – angry and not angry. That day, he had seemed to be calm. They had sat listening to the Frank Sinatra CD in silence as the views of Bannau Brycheiniog blurred in the car windows. He had smiled when he thought about the two of them out on a boat together, enjoying the mingling of air and sea and reeling their dinners in, fresh and delicious. Had Henry known then, but he was the one on the hook and line. When they had arrived at the beach, Ned had parked the car and they had got out. He had helped Henry down and had taken his oxygen tank off him.

"What are you doing?" Henry asked

"Thought it would be nice for you to breathe in the beach air for a moment. Don't worry, I'll bring it down," Ned said.

"Alright. Don't forget you need to pay for parking."

"I'll do it in a minute. I'm getting the fishing gear." Ned opened the boot and began pulling equipment out and putting it on the ground.

"To bring it down and then come back? Go pay and we can carry things down together," Henry said, reaching for a bag, but Ned stopped him.

"I'd rather help you down, Dad."

"I can manage," Henry insisted.

"...okay. I'll go and pay."

"I'll wait here."

Ned looked from Henry to the beach and then nodded,

walking over to the machine and fumbling around on his phone to pay the charge. Then he came back and got the fishing equipment. They began to walk down to the beach, but stopped.

"Your oxygen tank," Ned said.

"Oh, blow," Henry said. "I though you had it for some reason. That's the problem with a bloody tin can for lungs. Alright, let's go back."

"No. No, you go to that bench." Ned nodded towards a wooden bench underneath a large tree. "I'll bring it over."

"Give me the equipment then."

"It's okay, I've got it."

"Don't be stupid. I can manage," Henry held his hands out.

"Go sit on that bench over there. I'll be right over. Go," Ned snapped.

Henry didn't see his son's logic, but thought Ned just wanted to help. He knew he wouldn't be able to carry as much as Ned anyway, but Henry still wanted to be of some use. Instead, he did as he was told and made his way down to the bench. He didn't look back. Henry stared out at the sea and waited.

About half an hour passed. He began to wheeze. The sky over the sea began to turn grey and Henry felt a storm brewing. The pressure changed in the air. What began as a gentle breeze became a sharp wind that felt like it cut Henry's skin with each gust. It was harder for him to breathe when the wind picked up. He stood up and turned around, searching for Ned, but couldn't see him. It was definitely going to rain. He began to make his way up to the car park to go back to the car. Maybe something happened. Henry needed to get to his oxygen tank soon. His chest tightened. When he reached the spot where the car should have been, his heartbeat quickened. It was empty. Ned was gone. Perhaps he needed to go somewhere.

He looked around. The first spots of rain were beginning

to fall and drip down his nose. There was no one about – the last of the beach-goers had left at the first sign of rain, and the out-of-season kiosk was boarded up. His breath whistled in his lungs. He had nowhere to go and couldn't start walking off to find help without his oxygen tank. He needed to keep his breathing as steady and restful as possible. Henry made his way back to the bench and sat down. The tree over it would give him some shelter and he could wait here until Ned returned, or until someone passed by. There was nothing else that could be done.

It was clear to Henry now, in the present state of his comatose mind that, if he had looked back, Henry might have seen Ned load the fishing equipment back into the car. He might have seen his son get back behind the wheel and start the engine. He might even have been able to watch Ned drive away, leaving Henry alone at the beach without his life support, but he hadn't looked back.

It all felt like such a long time ago. Henry didn't know how long he'd been in his coma. The sun warmed him as he sat back up and wiped the sand from his face. There were so many moments that day in which he could have done something differently and changed the course of events. If he had, he wouldn't be here alone in this strange place, caught in the memories of his pain. Henry reached up and felt his head, remembering the final piece of the puzzle. The tree he had chosen to sit under hadn't held up under the storm. A branch had cracked, fallen, and had hit him in the head. Then he woke up in this place.

He couldn't stay like this forever. He needed to get back to his family. Ned was capable of anything, but Henry wanted more than to protect his family. He had to know why

he left him at the beach. What happened and where had he gone? Surely it hadn't been deliberate, but then... Hadn't Ned come to him during the storm last night? Why else would Ned be in this coma-dream with him? With these thoughts spinning around his mind, Henry hauled himself to his feet and began walking.

Marching down the beach, he went further than he had walked in years. His entire body felt like it was on fire. His feet were scratched by sand that rubbed its way into his socks. His legs cried out for a break. His chest burned for more oxygen than he was capable of sucking into his lungs. Still, Henry soldiered on. He didn't know why, but he had to get back to that bench. It was where he said he'd wait. He was overcome with this pull to get back. If he found that bench, Henry knew he'd be able to wake up. There was nothing he wanted more in the world than to find his way back and, at last, have the truth. It was time to go home.

LACEY

Lacey waited outside Cegin for Ezra. It was their second date, the first of which only happening after a lot of thinking and deliberation. He gave her the time and place and her grandma dropped her off with a ten pound note from her personal stash that Lacey wasn't meant to know about. She still wasn't sure if she wanted to come or not, but it was too late now. Lacey was certain that the main reason she decided to see Ezra again was pure curiosity. Something about him fascinated her in a way that nobody else had ever done. She didn't even know if she liked him. When she saw him turn the corner onto the street and begin to walk towards her. She smiled before she could stop herself and he grinned back.

"You didn't go inside?" he asked.

"I've never been here before. Thought I'd wait outside."

"Wait. Never? Someone who loves books as much as you and you've never been here?"

"No. What about it?" she asked.

"Come on, I'll show you."

They went inside Cegin. Lacey was immediately taken aback by her surroundings. The entire back wall was covered in books from top to bottom, left to right. The shelves were made of oak that was a few centimetres thick and bolted to the wall. Support beams ran through them to hold up the weight of the books. There must have been thousands. The other walls were each a different shade of green with quotes from books painted all over them in various fonts. Tables and chairs were stationed around the room and on each table was a different book, picked out by an employee that week. The waiters all wore name-tags with the title of their favourite book underneath. Mared who loved *Oliver Twist* showed them to a table for two in the corner.

"This place is amazing," Lacey said.

"I'm surprised you'd never heard of it," Ezra said, pulling his chair closer to the table.

"I...I don't get out much."

"That's a shame," he said, watching Mared pour them each a glass of water. "Diolch," he said, thanking her.

"Why?" Lacey asked.

"Because I'd like to go out again."

"We've barely been out now. We've just started."

Lacey caught Mared smiling as she turned to give them a moment with the menus, leaving her suddenly feeling self-conscious.

"Maybe I'm enjoying seeing you," Ezra said.

"Already?"

"Yes, already. Shit. You're so hard to compliment." He shook his head and laughed.

"I'm sorry. I'm...not used to it, I guess."

Lacey held the menu up over her face to hide her blushing and tried to pick out what she wanted to eat. She felt her stomach over the top of her shirt and it rumbled. She peered over the top of the lists of sandwiches and salads at Ezra, who was nose-deep in his own menu. For the first time, Lacey saw that his eyes were grey, and his eyelashes were as long as hers. His hair fell into his eyes a little and he blew it up off his face until his fringe was fluffy. Lacey couldn't help but giggle and he looked up.

"What do you want to eat?" he said.

"I'm not sure. Everything looks so good."

"Everything *is* good. I come here all the time."

"On your own?" Her eyes went wide.

"Yeah, so?"

"Bit weird isn't it? Taking yourself out for lunch?"

"I don't think so," he smiled coyly, "but maybe I won't have to come here by myself anymore." Lacey nodded shyly. "If you're struggling to choose, I recommend the Pride and Breadjudice."

"The what?"

"It's a panini and it has everything on it. Plus so much cheese. Cegin have the best paninis in Wales. You're not vegan or allergic to anything, are you?" he asked, a note of concern spiking in his voice.

"No. Okay, I'll have that," Lacey nodded.

"Do you want a drink? Ooo, have a Lime and Punishment. It's a sort of lemonade. Way too much sugar in it. I guess that's the punishment."

"I might just have a water," she said, stroking the corner of the ten pound note in her pocket and looking at the £7.50 next to Pride and Breadjudice on the menu.

"Don't be silly. Here, lunch is on me today."

Lacey was startled. She hadn't said anything about money.

"Ezra, you don't –" she began.

"Please, I want to."

"Okay, sure," she nodded. "That all sounds great."

"I'll have the same."

Ezra waved to Mared who came over to take their order. Her teeth were the whitest teeth that Lacey had ever seen and they caught the light through the window. Mared wrote down what they wanted on a small notebook before heading off to the kitchen to make their drinks, her smile never dropping from her face.

When the drinks came out, Lacey stared at hers wondering exactly what a Lime and Punishment would taste like. As she took a sip, she was both surprised and disappointed that the green concoction did not, in fact, taste like lime. This made her intrigued as to what her Pride and Breadjudice would resemble. As she waited, she adjusted her shirt and tucked some loose hair behind her ear. She had made sure to wear her favourite heart charm necklace too.

They sat with their hands on the table. As he talked, Lacey nodded along, but was so focused on looking like she was paying attention that she didn't hear much of what he said. She watched his hand and wondered how he'd react if she put hers on his. Every time she laughed or repositioned, she moved her hand a few millimetres closer. He never moved away from her. By the time their food arrived at the table, their fingertips were almost touching, and Lacey felt cold as she pulled away to eat.

As she bit into the panini, her mind flashed back to dinner a couple of nights ago when her father forced her to eat the stew. When she swallowed, she could feel the food slide down her oesophagus and drop into the pit of her stomach. Even though it was just a mouthful, it felt obscenely heavy inside her. When it mixed with the nerves from the date, Lacey's stomach flipped and she bit down on her lip. She took another small bite and chewed it for far too long, swallowing only when it was almost entirely a liquid. She winced as it went down her throat, her father's words ringing in her head: Ezra wouldn't want a fat girlfriend.

"Something wrong?" Ezra asked.

"No, no." She waved the question away.

"Are you not enjoying it?"

"I am."

"Are you not hungry?"

"I'm fine."

"Did I do something to upset you?" His tone was gentle

and almost pathetic against the harshness in her voice.

"No. Ezra, I'm okay. Really," she said, feeling a twinge of guilt.

Ezra sat back in his chair and frowned at her, as though he was trying to read her mind and, even though Lacey knew he couldn't possibly know what she was thinking, she felt like her mind was naked. *You'll get fat.* She looked down at her body and saw all the lumps and bumps that she knew should be there but somehow felt disgusting. She felt Ezra's grey eyes dissecting her. *Nobody likes a tubby girl.* A group of girls she recognised from school walked in and the bell above the door jingled. They looked over and saw Lacey sitting with Ezra and giggled. Her stomach turned again.

"Excuse me," she said and started to walk to the loo.

"Lacey, are you okay?" He reached across the table for her. "Did I –"

She couldn't hear him. When she reached the loo she was relieved to find it had been one room with a toilet that locked rather than multiple cubicles. Grateful for the privacy, she bolted the door and stared at herself in the mirror. She poked at herself and didn't think she looked bad in her shirt, but it was loose and shapeless. Turning to face sideways-on, Lacey lifted her shift over her stomach and grimaced. She pinched her belly and sucked it in.

Lacey thought back to the stew and the way her body had purged itself afterwards. What she remembered the most vividly was that the grass was cold under her knees as she dropped on all fours to retch. Later on, when her grandma had held her in her arms, Lacey's entire stomach had ached and burned from the intensity. The night air had frozen her face until she couldn't feel anything else. When she looked at herself in the mirror now, she still couldn't tell how she felt about anything or if she even felt at all. She was letting Ezra down.

She rummaged around in her handbag for her face powder and put more on her nose before heading back out to the table. Ezra was staring out of the window, not eating his panini. When he saw Lacey coming back over, he looked hopeful and concerned at the same time.

"You aren't eating?" she asked.

"I am. You were taking a while, so I stopped to wait for you." He looked away as she sat down, almost like he was trying to offer her privacy, even here. "You know, if something is wrong you can tell me."

"I'm okay."

Ezra finished his panini while Lacey picked at hers. She pulled the tomato out of it and nibbled at them until they were gone.

"Don't force yourself," he said.

"What?"

"Don't make yourself eat it if you don't want it."

"It's not that I don't want it...I...it's complicated." She trailed off in the middle of her sentence as she searched for a way to end it that would make sense.

"A panini is complicated?"

"I am."

"No argument here," Ezra smiled.

"I don't think I can eat any more. I'm not feeling well."

"Oh no. Okay, well if you're done, do you mind?" he asked, gesturing to her leftovers.

"No, go ahead," she said, sliding her plate over to his side of the table.

When her arm was all the way extended and her hand was close to him, he lifted his and laid it over hers, stroking her fingers.

"Can I get you anything else?" he asked.

"Maybe come water?" Lacey replied, staring at their hands.

Ezra called over to Mared and she returned with a large glass of water. Lacey sipped it slowly and tried to calm herself down. He finished all the food until there wasn't a scrap left and had the rest of his drink. Lacey rubbed her arms and, without speaking, Ezra took off his jacket and draped it over her shoulders, just like she'd watched a hundred times in every cheesy rom-com film. Was that really something that happened?

"...oh, I love this one," Ezra said, picking up a copy of *Of Mice and Men* from the windowsill. "So many people go on about how boring it is, but I don't think it's anything of the sort. It's so beautiful."

"Beautiful?"

"Yeah. What?" he grinned like he knew what she was going to say next.

"Never really heard a guy describe something as beautiful before."

"Don't think we can admire things like girls can?" He arched an eyebrow.

"That's not what I meant. You're just weirdly..."

"Feminine?" he finished for her. "That's because I am. At least, that's how people think of me. Brought up by a single mum with two younger sisters has that effect. But I don't see why I have to fit into anyone else's opinion of what I should be like."

"What happened to your dad?"

Ezra's pleasant expression wavered on his face for a split-second, but it was long enough for Lacey to notice.

"Sorry, that was too personal," she said.

"No, it's okay. He left when my mum was pregnant with my sisters." His tone was flat as though he'd delivered this line a thousand times before.

"Twins?"

"Yeah. Twin girls. He hated the thought," he laughed, his friendly expression back on his face.

"That's horrible!"

"That's the way it was..." he said, shrugging before changing the subject. "Want to know why I love *Of Mice and Men*? It's so bright and dark at the same time. The way Steinbeck describes the setting like this vast expanse of possibilities while the characters are living out this predetermined plot. It can only end one way. And yet the way it's told…it makes something so awful and limited so…beautiful."

"Oh yeah?" Lacey found herself amused, which surprised her. She was starting to feel better.

"Yeah… you haven't read it, have you?"

"…no," she admitted.

"Ahh, what? You should! Right, I'll bring my copy to school and you can borrow it. I don't know if you'll like it, but it's interesting. There are always two sides to a person."

"Are there two sides to you?" she asked, realising that they were still holding hands.

"Of course. I'd be lying if I said otherwise."

"And what's the other side like?"

"I don't know yet. I'm fifteen," he laughed.

When Lacey's grandmother came to pick her up half an hour later, she was sad to go. It wasn't until she saw the car pull up outside that she realised he had been distracting her from her thoughts the entire time. He went on talking until she was smiling again. His mother hadn't arrived yet, so they agreed to say goodbye at the table. Lacey stood up and he stepped towards her, lifting his arms and pulling her into a hug. For the first time during the date, she felt completely relaxed. He brought her so tightly to him that she felt small and dainty against his chest. Her anxieties left her for a few seconds, her only regret being that she couldn't spend any more time hugging him. She got into the car and her grandmother smiled at her knowingly.

"You're glowing, sweetheart," she said.

"Glowing?"

"I'm just pleased to see he makes you happy and he's brought you somewhere nice."

On the way home, Lacey rubbed the heart charm on her necklace between her finger and thumb the way she did whenever she thought about Ezra now. She leaned her head against the window and the glass was cool on her forehead. She realised she was still wearing his jacket and pulled it closer around her arms, smelling his shampoo on the collar. Her breath steamed up the window. It was getting dark outside, and she could see her own reflection as her face was lit up by other cars passing on the road. Every now and then she caught sight of her own lips in the glass and thought how pink and elegant they looked. She smiled to herself, closing her eyes and squeezing her necklace so hard that, when she took her hand away, the shape of the heart was pressed into her thumb. Bringing it to her lips when her grandmother wasn't looking, she sunk into her seat and pressed her nose further into the collar of Ezra's jacket.

ELEN

Marcus had texted again: *Lunch today?* Elen smiled and typed back: *Yep*. She was still grinning when Dan came in and put his bag down on his desk.

"You look happy," he said.

"I am. Having lunch again with Marcus."

"Marcus? This going to be a new Wednesday tradition then? Date with Richardson?"

"It's not a date. That would be…icky. No, we're just sort of…bonding, I guess. He's a friend," Elen said, swatting at him from across the room.

"I guess he'll want an update on the case, too," Dan sighed.

He pulled his notebook and pen out of his bag, then put the bag in the bottom drawer of his desk. Elen watched him, sipping a coffee. She adored Dan for how by-the-book he was, especially because it was a book that he wrote for himself, and the rules within it didn't exist anywhere else in society. He made up his own rules and rolled with them.

"I could use an update too," she said. "You finished the footage last night?"

"I did."

"And?"

"Nothing. Sorry, Elen. Anything on your files?" Dan said, dropping his jacket over the back of his chair and smoothing it out.

"Nope. I have one more to go. Figured I'd do that this morning, but so far it doesn't look good."

"The records from the bus station and taxi companies came through this morning. I picked them up on the way past the reception. Do you want me to go over them?" Dan sat down and pulled his chair closer to his desk, then switched on his computer.

"No, it's okay. I should probably do it – you've got other work to get on with. But thank you, Dan."

Elen clicked on the final file of security footage from the kiosk at the beach and opened the file. The video was five hours long and again Elen sped it up to play twice as fast. The people on the screen jerked about and looked almost inhuman as they whizzed around on camera. A figure flashed across this screen and Elen recognised him. She jumped and slammed the space bar on her keyboard to pause the video. She was too slow, and the person had already vanished from the frame. Dan jolted with fright at the sudden smashing of the space bar, and then came around to see Elen's screen as she tapped the left arrow key, rewinding the video a few frames at a time until the figure backed his way into view again.

She stared intensely at the familiar form of pixels. It was a man, very tall in stature with a solid build and dark grey hair. She played the video in normal speed and paused it again when he looked over his shoulder, his face now in full view. If there was audio, Elen was certain he'd be snarling from his expression. His lips curled up and uncovered a shock of white teeth, like a wolf.

"Hang on, is that –" Dan began.

"Ned Belvidere," Elen whispered. "He was there at the beach on the day Henry went missing. He must have brought him there."

"Keep watching," Dan said, leaning in further. "Look! Pause it again! Elen!"

"Oh my god." She watched Ned re-enter the frame.

"He's coming back. Is he leaving?"

"He paid for parking, but left less than ten minutes later," Elen said. "Henry is somewhere there off-camera. This is the moment Ned abandoned him. I know it."

Elen stared at Ned walking back across the screen towards the car park. She sat back in her chair, on which Dan leaned heavily. She sipped her coffee in silence and watched the face of Ned glower on the screen.

"Now we need to know if Henry chose to go there without his oxygen tank," Dan said.

"He didn't," Elen shook her head.

"I'm sure, but we need evidence."

"And if Henry didn't want to?"

Dan stood up and crossed his arms. "Then we're looking at a case of attempted homicide."

"Either way," Elen said, nodding, "we need to pay another visit to the Belvideres."

"You think you can get something out of Ned?"

"No. Not Ned. His mother. Madeline."

Elen spent the morning watching the rest of the footage. There was nothing else, but she had to be certain. Similarly, she didn't find anything on the bus or taxi records. Her chest felt tight and her hands were clammy even though they were freezing to the touch. Every part of her tingled. She still didn't have much, but this was her first piece of real, solid evidence. Whenever she blinked, Ned's growling face flashed on the backs of her eyelids. Her breath quickened the way it always did when she felt like she was onto something; the metallic scent of a lead ready to be pursued burned like blood in her nostrils.

When lunch came, Elen felt like all her blood was bubbling in her veins. She was desperate to tell Marcus about the footage. Marcus. In the past week, she forced herself to call him that in her head instead of Chief Inspector or Richardson. Before he gave her verbal permission to use his first name, she made a conscious effort to avoid it. There was a danger in befriending her boss. She wasn't blind; she noticed how much he was struggling. He was coming to work more dishevelled by the day. He'd explained it was because of his worries over his sister and Elen wished it was something else. It wasn't that she discouraged traits of empathy and compassion, both of which she found virtuous, but that she couldn't do anything about his grief. As her blood bubbled with excitement to see him, so too did her skin prickle with sadness that she would never be able to properly console him. Dan smiled at her as she left the office and she saw Marcus waiting for her down the hall. He didn't see her approaching at first, and was stood up peculiarly straight, looking at the wall in front of him without blinking. Elen had to call to him before he saw her.

"Marcus," she said.

"Hey, how are you today?"

"Looking forwards to a panini."

"Let's roll," he said.

Elen followed him out. The weather was beginning to change towards a glimmer of a new season. It wasn't as cold as it had been over the previous weeks and Elen could feel the air growing heavy with the dampness of the coming Welsh spring. They walked together to Cegin, where they were greeted by a waiter called Bryn, whose name-tag said his favourite book was *Slaughterhouse-Five*.

"This is different," Elen said. "Sitting in."

"It is. But I feel the need for it today. Sometimes I like to eat at the park, but I just want to chill out for an hour. That means no screaming kids playing," he smiled.

"There are so many books here. It's cool, but I never figured you were a reader."

"I am. Well, I was," Marcus said. "I don't seem to have much time for that sort of thing now. I used to read all the time. Spent every free second I had with my nose in a book. Mysteries, thrillers, horrors…that sort of thing. These days, after a shift at the station, coming home to a book about murder is that last thing I want to do to relax."

"I see what you mean, but I can't relate. I've never been big on reading."

"Why not?"

Bryn interrupted them momentarily to bring them a glass of water each and take their orders. One Green (Salad) Mile, one White Eggs and Ham, and two mugs of Black Coffee (which Elen spotted came with a note on the menu that said *Black Coffee* was the name of an Agatha Christie play, so it still counted as a pun, even if it really was…well…black coffee).

"Stories…they just aren't for me," Elen said, looking around after Bryn left. "I don't see the point in them. They're not real. Not like what we do at the station. That's real."

"But isn't that what we do? Piece together stories?"

"In a way. But when you finish a book, it doesn't do any good. Not anything measurable anyway. Finishing a case does. It makes the world a better place."

"I'll respectfully disagree with you on that one, Elen. It's all the same. The hunt for answers." He took a sip of water.

"Some answers are better than others."

"Perhaps. And what answers have you got for me?" He smiled. "Whew, what a segue!"

"Nicely done," she laughed. "Dan and I found something this morning. Video footage that places Ned Belvidere at the beach the day Henry went missing."

"That's interesting, but what does it prove?"

"Not a lot," Elen said, sitting back in her chair a little dejected.

"Right, let's go over the facts again. Tell me everything

you know in order."

"Okay," Elen said, pulling out her notebook and a pen and writing bullet points as she went. "So Henry Belvidere has emphysema. He's dependant on an oxygen tank – a nasal cannula. He can go without it for a little bit at a time, but not for very long. Ned said Henry went to the beach on a fishing trip alone, and this was later confirmed by Madeline – Henry's wife."

"But you just found evidence that Ned was on tape at the beach," Marcus said.

"Yeah. Which means that Ned was definitely lying about Henry taking off on his own. I think Madeline knew it was a lie too, but so far she hasn't given me anything concrete to prove she knew what was happening. I went to speak to her about the oxygen tank and something was off with her. The tank wasn't anywhere around, though to be fair they could have hidden it."

"So what does this mean? Go on."

"Ned brought Henry to the beach and left him without the tank. It was not an accident. Henry would die without it. Either Ned took Henry there with the intention of killing him or Henry chose to die and needed Ned's help. Whatever the case, the result would be Henry's death and Ned was involved," she finished.

"There is a slight problem, Elen."

"What?"

"The footage didn't show Ned *and* Henry, right?"

"No. Shit, of course. We can prove they were both there, but not both there together."

"Right," Marcus said, taking the notepad from Elen and looking over the bullet points.

"We need a witness that places them together at the scene at the very least."

Bryn returned from the kitchen with their coffees and food. He put them down on the table and, from the immediate silence, Elen was sure he knew he interrupted them. It must happen to him a lot, she thought. He must always be stumbling into conversations as part of his job.

"The camera showed that the kiosk desk was unmanned when Ned paid for parking," she said when Bryn had left. "There wasn't anyone around."

"Then it would appear that we've got nothing until Henry wakes up," Marcus said, taking a bite from his Green (Salad) Mile, swallowing, and then frowning. "If Henry wakes up," he corrected himself. "Until then, our case will need a little more pushing to crack."

"Our?" Elen smiled coyly.

"What can I say? You've intrigued me."

"This afternoon I'm going back to the Belvidere residence to speak to Madeline. There's something she's not telling me. Dan and I are going to talk to her again."

Marcus tucked into his salad and Elen bit into a piece of ham, enjoying the burst of sweet and savoury flavours in her cheeks as her mind reeled. She knew beyond all doubt that Ned was involved, but couldn't say how just yet. Marcus was right about needing a witness too. If she was putting together a case against Ned that she hadn't necessarily been officially assigned to work, then it had to be airtight. Elen needed to have concrete evidence before she made more aggressive inquiries, until there was no chance of her getting pulled from the case. It shouldn't happen – in fact it rarely did – but with the end of the quarter approaching and the statistics for the departments in the area being collated, Elen was sure they'd pause her investigation and redeploy her onto more easily solvable cases to boost their numbers.

Sometimes, Elen heard her own thoughts. It was like floating out of her own head and listening to them like an audiobook. They were a wild mixture of personal and professional concerns that shouldn't go together. While she watched Marcus enjoy his lunch, she simultaneously felt her growing friendship with him and the allure of the unsolved case. Her thoughts of crime and compassion became so mingled after her years on the force that it was a struggle keeping everything straight in her own head. Normally she was able to desensitise herself to the difficulties of her work. The pain Henry Belvidere must have endured hurt Elen in ways that she had never felt before, or rather had not allowed herself to feel before.

"What's wrong?" Marcus asked after he'd finished his salad.

"Remember last week, when you knew there was something off with me?" she said, after swallowing her last bite and wiping her mouth with a paper napkin.

"I remember. I told you about my sister."

"Yeah, then. It's my parents. More specifically, my mum. She…she doesn't know who I am."

"What do you mean?" Marcus was drinking his coffee but put it down when Elen explained.

"Dementia. It wasn't always this bad. At one point, it was like…like her brain had hiccups. She'd be doing something normal like the washing up and suddenly look up like she couldn't remember what was happening. I'd ask if she was okay, and she'd say she was. Then she'd carry on with the washing up. That's all it was. She would snap out of herself for a few seconds and then slip back in.

"Eventually, she'd snap out for longer, until she stopped being herself. Well, she stopped being who I knew. It was still her, but only pieces. She wasn't Mum. She was Beverley on the night of her first school disco, and she'd run around to get ready. She was Beverley who hated jazz and smashed up the stereo like that one night went she fought with her sister forty years ago. She was Beverley on the day of her wedding, waiting for Dad to sneak into her room to kiss her in her wedding dress, long before he was meant to see her. But she wasn't Mum anymore. My mother stopped being in that body altogether. I didn't know any of these other pieces of her.

"She's a stranger now. I think every time I see her, I leave some of myself behind. It kills me just a little bit each time. So I don't go and see her anymore. I'm a horrible daughter. A terrible, awful, selfish daughter. She's got almost no time left and I spend none of it with her. But every time I think of seeing her, I picture my mum. Not whoever this person is now who looks like her and sounds like her, but says all the wrong things and shouts at me for being in her house."

Elen stopped talking and looked out of the window, her eyes batting back tears. She pushed her mug away with coffee still in it, now stone-cold, and mashed her lips together to hold in all the other words she wanted to say but knew she shouldn't. Marcus beckoned Bryn over and asked for more water, and he obliged. Instead of staring at her, he looked out of the window with her, not saying anything until she felt comfortable speaking again. She took a sip of water.

"When I first saw Henry Belvidere in the hospital, I didn't see just another potential victim of a crime like I see in other people on the job. I don't mean for that to sound so cold, but I try not to care in such a personal way. I don't want to feel pain every time I start a case," she said.

"Nobody does, Elen. It's what we must do in this line of work. It's the only way to keep going."

"But why do we keep going?" She shook her head. "All this crime and violence. We see the world in a way some people just can't. Why do we keep putting ourselves through it?"

"Why do you compare Henry to your mother?" Marcus asked abruptly.

Elen was taken aback. "What's that got to do with —"

"Answer the question, Elen."

"Because he..." She thought hard. "He was someone. Someone's husband, father, and grandfather, sure, but he was also just himself. A person. Until something happened out of his control that left him a shell of the man he was. He needs help. He needs someone to fight for him. I can do something about this, but —" She cut herself off, not going to finish her sentence, but then deciding to anyway. She'd already said this much. "I can't help my own family."

"You're wrong, you know," Marcus said, finishing his coffee that was certainly too cold and rifling around in his jacket pocket. He pulled out a box of mints and ate one, before offering them to Elen, who accepted. "You can help them. Maybe your mother doesn't remember you, but if you spend time with her, you can ease your father's mind still, can't you?"

"Is it worth this much pain?" she asked, half to herself.

"Elen, look. I can't do anything for my sister, can I? I can't fight cancer any more than you can fight dementia. It kills me to see her just as much as it does when I stay away. So I see her. It hurts now, but it'll make it hurt less when she's not here anymore."

"That...that makes sense."

"So does wanting to help Henry."

Marcus paid for both the lunches, even though Elen tried to protest. In the end, he had to promise to let her pay for the next one. He held the door open for her on the way out and was endlessly polite, even though she couldn't bear to talk much more. As they walked back to the station, they passed the park. On the grass by the pavement, a little girl tripped and fell over. She began to cry as she pushed herself up and Elen gasped involuntarily when she saw the blood. The girl's mother was nearby and heard the crying. She came running over to her daughter and knelt next to her. She pulled her child onto her lap and cradled her like a baby, even though she was eight years old at least.

Elen remembered the last time her mother held her. It was just after Andrew Brace had broken up with Elen and she came straight to her parents' house while he packed up his belongings. She hadn't been able to comprehend how their whole life together could be divided into boxes and packed away like there had been nothing important about it at all. She hadn't known that memories could create an entire world and be so weightless at the same time. Elen had buried her face into her mother's shoulder, had nuzzled the bone that was sharp on her cheek, and had breathed in against the warm wool of her cardigan. Her mother had stroked Elen's tears away with fingers that smelled like the bowl of water in the kitchen that she had just been washing potatoes in. Everything about her had felt like it was made of earth. Her skin had been dark and cold, and her hair was thick and tangled. Elen had clung to her and wept until she couldn't remember Andrew's face at all.

Back at the station, Dan was gathering his notes together to head out to the Belvideres' cottage. He had that look on his face that meant she was late, but he must have seen that something was wrong, because he didn't say anything. She sat down for a minute to collect her thoughts. Before they went out to the car, Dan put his hand on her shoulder and handed her a bottle of water. Elen smiled at him and nodded. Taking a deep breath, they began the drive to see Madeline Belvidere.

In the car, Elen thought about what questions she needed to ask. All she really needed to know was what Madeline had lied about, but she knew she couldn't be that direct. Then something occurred to Elen. Madeline wasn't just Henry's wife; she was Ned's mother. She thought about the way her own mother had cuddled her fears away and how the mother at the park had cradled her daughter. An eight-year-old and a twenty-eight-year old needed a mother's comfort the same way as a baby did. Would a man approaching fifty also need to be protected in the same way? Elen couldn't imagine someone like Ned wanting any sort of comfort or hug of any kind, thinking about his snarling face on the security footage. Even so, Madeline's instinct to reach out to him might not have faded so easily. She was protecting Ned. She was trying to save her baby boy. Elen knew that it would be harder to convince Madeline to cooperate under these circumstances. All she could do was show Madeline that telling the truth was the best choice for her family. As the tyres tread down the road, Elen blinked rapidly and tried to breathe steadily. All she wanted in that moment was a kiss on the cheek from her mother.

MADELINE

Madeline saw the car pull up the driveway. She took a deep breath and looked around the cottage. Nothing was out of place, but this was a problem. It was too neat, and not in the normal way a house might be tidy. This level of cleanliness implied that there was something dirty being hidden. Panicked, Madeline knocked the cushions on the sofa over and scattered some magazines on the coffee table. She took a cup that she hadn't washed yet out of the sink and put it on the table without a coaster. In the corner of her eye, she noticed the wardrobe where she kept Henry's oxygen tank was open by a crack. She had only just shut it when there was a knock at the front door. Madeline jumped. She laid a hand over her chest to try and calm her heart and then went to answer it.

Detectives Elen Parry and Dan Blackwood were standing outside. They smiled at her, but Madeline could tell they were fake. They didn't care about her family like she did. There was no way that they could. Welcoming them into her home seemed like the worst decision she could make, and yet it wasn't really a choice. Turning them away would cement her guilt in the minds of the detectives. She knew letting them in would bring them closer to whatever evidence they didn't know about yet. She was sure there were tracks uncovered and clues in the open, but Madeline's mind hadn't been trained to spot them either as a police officer or a criminal.

She stepped aside and gestured towards the sofa. They went to sit down and Madeline put the kettle on without asking if they wanted a drink. They spoke to her – Madeline could hear them over the tinkering of spoons in mugs – but she never bothered to tune into the words. When she brought the coffees over on a tray and put them down on the table, both detectives shifted their bodies to angle themselves towards her. Madeline wasn't stupid: she knew how this worked now. Pulling her coffee off the tray, she held the mug with both hands by her chest like the smallest shield.

"Mrs Belvidere, we just have a couple of follow up questions for you," Detective Parry began.

"Then why didn't you call me to the station?" Madeline asked, immediately annoyed and wanting to show it.

"We thought you'd be more comfortable here."

"I didn't have to invite you in, you know. I could ask for a lawyer any time I want."

"Yes. You could."

"I'm trying to cooperate," Madeline said, her eyes darted back and forth between the two detectives. She wondered what Ned might say if he came home now.

"And we appreciate that. Look, Mrs Belvidere, if you're uncomfortable for any reason, we could take this back to the station and call you a lawyer, as you suggested..."

"Though we know you've done nothing wrong, so we can just hash this out over a coffee and leave you be," Detective Blackwood chipped in.

"Yes. I haven't done anything. I don't know anything. That's right," Madeline agreed, blowing on her coffee and daring to take a sip.

"Last time we spoke, you said Henry went to the beach

alone for a fishing trip, correct?" Detective Parry asked.

"No. I told you Ned said that."

"Either way, it wasn't true, was it?"

Madeline took a second sip of her coffee and looked at Detective Parry's face and then Detective Blackwood's, trying to appear calm as she cast her mind back to what she said previously. She shifted her weight in the chair she sat in, next to the sofa, and drew her eyebrows together.

"It was," she settled on, with a little nod to confirm.

"We have a photograph here of your son, Ned," Detective Parry said, producing a grainy, square image and sliding it across the coffee table to Madeline. "Can you confirm his identity here?" Madeline nodded. "It was captured from security footage at the beach. Is this the date and time Henry was there?"

"The date and time are correct," she said, crossing her legs and clutching her hands together around her mug.

"Then can you explain why we were told Henry was alone when Ned was clearly at the scene?" the detective pushed.

Madeline's mind whirred to life, trying to pick through everything she had said, everything Ned had said, and all the unknown things the police may have discovered in the time between.

"Henry was going on the fishing trip alone," Madeline explained slowly. "Which was true. Ned drove him there. A lift. He had to come back for work. He's our only source of income, you know. He was going to go back to pick up Henry at the end of the trip."

She knew that it didn't make sense. Why would Ned drop him off for a fishing trip with no luggage, no equipment, no place to stay, nothing? Why would he take him to the beach and not a hotel? If she could think through that, the police could. Christ, Kyle could think through that.

"And during all of this, where was the oxygen tank?" Detective Parry asked, casually picking up her coffee and taking a large gulp. When Madeline didn't respond, she prompted again: "please answer the question."

"I don't know," Madeline said at last.

Detective Parry nodded and glanced at her notes. "You said something interesting last time we spoke, Mrs Belvidere, which you also repeated today. You corrected me both times I asked if you said Henry went on a fishing trip. You made it very clear that Ned said that. It's stuck in my head. I'm curious why you keep making that distinction."

"I just want you to have to details down right. You know, to be more efficient and help Henry," she said.

"Right. But this trip was orchestrated by Ned?"

"No, it was Henry's idea."

"Was it also Henry's idea to go without his oxygen tank?" Detective Parry wasn't looking at her notes anymore. She was staring right at Madeline, who understood that she was being challenged.

"What are you implying, Detective?" she said.

"Did Henry knowingly go without his life support?"

Madeline stopped, her mouth popping open slightly. "Are you asking me if my husband intended to kill himself?"

"It's a line of inquiry that I have to pursue," Detective Parry said nonchalantly.

"Then perhaps you should pursue it with me in handcuffs because I've told you everything I know. The only way I'll go on is through a lawyer." Madeline stood up.

"If you need a lawyer to go on, then you haven't told me everything you know," Detective Parry said, rising to meet her.

"You need to leave or take me with you."

"Elen," Detective Blackwood whispered gently, "I think we should go."

Madeline made her way back to the door, holding it open for them. Detective Blackwood nodded to her on the way out and she heard him get into the car and start it up before Detective Parry had left. Parry turned around and called back to Madeline before she'd closed the door.

"Mrs Belvidere," she said, softer somehow.

"What?"

"I love my mum. She took such good care of me when I was a little girl. Even when I was a big girl and supposed to be living a life of my own. She has dementia and isn't the same now, but I still feel safe around her."

"What's your point?" Madeline snapped.

"A mother's love can do wonderful things. It is the strongest form of protection a person can have. But when it's misplaced, your protection can do more harm than good. Please think about that and get in touch if you have more information for us."

Before Madeline could think about how to acknowledge her unsolicited advice, Detective Parry had already walked away. Madeline closed the door with a click and went to collect the mugs from the living area. She put the sofa cushions back, stacked the magazines neatly again, and brought the glass on the dining table back to the sink with her. She did the washing up and wiped down the table, before sitting down on the corner of the sofa.

Had she said anything wrong? She felt like she had done better this time than in previous interviews. The picture of Ned from the security camera lodged itself in her mind. He looked so angry. He was furious in it, as though he was being forced to do something he really didn't want to do, when it was his idea all along. In fact, she had been sitting in this exact spot when Ned came in to tell her his plan.

A couple of months ago, right before Christmas, Henry, Lacey, and Kyle had all gone to bed, but Madeline couldn't sleep. She sat with her feet up, staring out of the window behind the sofa. It was completely dark out, and Madeline couldn't see anything through the glass, only her reflection staring back at her. She was exhausted, but couldn't rest, and forlorn, but couldn't cry.

Ned came home from a night-shift and they both jumped

when they saw each other; he mustn't have been expecting anyone to be awake at four in the morning and Madeline had no idea what time it was at all. He took a letter out of his pocket and handed it to his mother, before going into the bathroom. While he was gone, Madeline flicked on the lamp next to her and read the contents of the letter. It was everything she had expected. There was nothing left in the bank. Ned's pay cheques vanished the second he got them. They couldn't go on much longer.

When Ned came out of the bathroom, he sat on the sofa opposite his mother. He took the letter back and folded it again, slipping it into his pocket. Madeline turned to face him and noticed every detail on his face, lit up by the lamp. He glowed and yet she found him ugly. A dark seed had been planted in him when Karen died. It sat in the pit of his stomach, burrowing down into the lining and germinating there, feeding on the acid inside him. The branches grew where his veins should have been and the leaves irritated him beneath the skin. It grew from seed, to sapling, to tree. Now it was visible through his mouth; when he spoke Madeline could see the pain in his throat.

"We can't afford to carry on the way we are," he said.

"I know," she nodded, sadly.

"Mum, I've got two kids. I have to feed them. Pay the bills. Put clothes on their backs."

"And you do that." She reached out and patted his knee, then left her hand there to comfort him.

"But I can't forever. Not like this."

"What are we meant to do, Ned? We don't have a choice."

"We do. There's always a choice," he said darkly, and Madeline withdrew her hand, not knowing where this conversation was leading, but confident that she didn't want to follow.

Ned was looking at the floor, but his eyes flicked up to pierce hers when he next spoke. The lamp made his pupils glow amber until he transformed into a wolf before her. His hair was thick and straight. Teeth glinted in the open scowl of his mouth. Madeline wanted to look away from him, but couldn't. Ned's stare bore into her until she sweated.

"I need to take Dad away," he said.

"What?" Madeline's arms fell limply to her sides.

"It's the only way."

"Ned!"

"Shh! You'll wake everyone up," he said, rushing closer to her and gripping her shoulders in his massive hands.

"And where would you take him? We can't afford a care home. He doesn't need to be in a care home," she hissed.

"I'll figure something out. You know he's only got a year or two left at best. We're struggling now."

"I don't like this. We're not doing it. I'll call the police."

"Really? You would do that? You would do that to Lacey and Kyle? Your only living grandchildren?" he growled.

Madeline stood up and began to walk towards the bedroom, but Ned grabbed her arm. His grip was cold and sharp like an icicle; each finger almost cut into her. He pulled her back to him with such ease that she suddenly became conscious of how little she weighed. Now that they were turned away from the lamp, his eyes were as black as the window Madeline had been staring out of before he came in to see her. She couldn't see anything in them but her reflection that caught the light and shone as orange as fire. She was hot and cold at the same time.

"Do not tell anyone."

His voice was quiet and slow, but each word cut sharp through the air and stabbed at her. She saw herself flinch in his eyes. He didn't hit her. He did nothing but hold her arm and whisper. It was in the bluff of his gentleness that she saw danger.

Madeline thought about that night as she watched Detectives Parry and Blackwood drive away. There was no way she could have fully comprehended what Ned really meant at the time, and yet she had also made no move to do more. None of it had felt real to her. They hadn't been conversations people actually had. She had been too frightened to face her suspicions and just let everything unravel. By the time she had wrapped her mind around how serious, how real, it all was, she had already kissed Henry goodbye. Every waking minute she begged him to return to her, but if he didn't...if he didn't then at least she could try not to lose her boy too.

She went into each bedroom and gathered up all the laundry, taking it into the bathroom to load into the washing machine. She had to hold onto the top of it to lower herself to the floor. The door stuck a little, needing a forceful yank to open it. There was something in the back. Madeline reached into the gaping mouth of the washing machine and picked it up. She pulled it out and saw that it was one of Henry's socks. It was definitely his because Ned only wore plain black socks. This one was stripey and multi-coloured – a part of Henry's silent rebellion against the plainness of old age. Madeline sniffed it and breathed in the lavender from the washing powder. She began to weep then, in a way which she hadn't done before.

Rocking back and forth on the floor, sitting in the pile of dirty clothes, Madeline clutched the only clean item to her chest. This sock had tread where her husband had. It had quite literally followed his footsteps. She felt like it was closer to him in some ways than she was, because the promise she'd made to stay by his side had been broken a long time ago. The phone rang and for a moment she considered leaving it to sit with the sock for a while longer. On the fourth ring she huffed and hauled herself to her feet, folding the sock up and placing it into her pocket. She went to pick the phone up from where she'd left it on the coffee table. What happened next terrified and excited her.

"Mrs Belvidere?" the voice on the phone said. "You're needed at the hospital as soon as possible. It's your husband. Henry is awake."

HENRY

This **was not** the world that Henry remembered. The front door to the cottage was old, but he felt like he'd never seen it before. The paint flaked off like scales of icing and he placed one on his tongue. It was as bitter as vanilla, sweet as Viennetta, and cracked in his saliva. Spitting onto the deck below, he used his foot to spread it around, varnishing the splinters that prickled up like the nail clippings of trees. Madeline put her arm around his shoulders and used her spare hand to open the door, guiding him through it. Henry had visualised this moment so many times in his coma. Even waking up in his hospital bed a few days ago, he had pictured himself walking back into his home with his wife. Finally, the day had come when he was discharged, but it wasn't like what he had imagined.

It was a slow awakening, like a newborn baby. He had begun to move a little; first his fingers had twitched and then his eyes had rolled around more under their lids. His lips had spasmed at the corners as he had shaken off the last few seconds of his dream. Then his eyes had opened. Just a crack initially, but gradually they had blinked until they were wide open. Even after he had been able to look around, he hadn't quite been able to see. The white walls of the room had made the light bounce around, hitting every surface and propelling into the squint of his gaze. Everything he had looked at was new, the bed and the table to the left of it, with the window on the far wall overlooking the grey car park. The TV above the chair in the corner had hung like a black gaping hole. He had remembered what it did and that he had liked television, even though he hadn't owned one, but watching it had seemed unbearable. There had been no electricity at the beach.

Madeline took Henry to the sofa and helped him sit down. She went over to the kettle to make him a coffee and he watched her. He knew he liked coffee and that it had to be black. He smiled faintly to her, but his face felt slow and the gesture passed through her as though he'd never made it. She looked older than he remembered, and he felt cold as all the blood drained from his head.

"H-how long?" he asked.

"Two weeks. Around about," Madeline said, busying herself in the kitchen.

"I'm sorry."

"What about?"

"For being gone so long."

"You don't have to apologise. You didn't leave."

"I tried not to," Henry said and then, softly, "I tried to see your face."

Madeline nodded with her back still to him. She brought the coffee over and passed it to him. The cup was hot and Henry jerked back, spilling some of it onto himself. He didn't wince, but stared down at the pool soaking into his jeans and shook his head. The wet patch began to take the shape of a lion's head – wild-maned with teeth sharp – but when he blinked it looked ordinary again. As much as he stared, he couldn't make the stain appear to him as a lion again. Madeline reached over and placed her hands over his, which were still gripping the cup even though it hurt. She guided them down to the table and peeled his fingers off the mug and folded them into his lap, after inspecting them to make sure they weren't burned.

"Y-you'll have to forgive me," Henry said.

"For what?"

"I haven't had coffee in what feels like such a long time."

Outside, a car pulled up to the cottage and Henry heard three doors slam as the passengers got out. It felt like an hour went by before they came through the front door. He could hear the tap in the kitchen sink leak as water beaded up and hurtled down to the drain, centimetres and somehow metres below. Everything was bigger now. This world was louder. Voices that had been faint in his ears now felt like they were coming from inside him. The handle on the door turned and he heard it creak, cursing himself for not remember to oil it before his trip. There were a lot of things he hadn't done. Lacey and Kyle crashed in and rushed over to Henry. Kyle pulled himself up onto Henry's lap while Lacey cuddled up to his chest. He pulled them both so close that he thought he might press them into himself. They were a part of him.

"Grandpa!" Kyle shrieked.

"Hey, young man. How are you?" Henry said, scootching Kyle away from the wet coffee on his jeans.

"I'm okay. I missed you. Where did you go?"

"What did Grandma tell you?" Henry looked at Madeline, who looked away.

"That you were sick and would come home when you were better."said Kyle.

"Yeah, that's what happened. I wasn't very well and spent some time with a doctor. They've sorted me out now though, see?" He tickled Kyle.

"Grandpa?" Lacey said, still leaning against him.

"What is it, light of my life?"

"Where *did* you go?"

"You know where I was, darling. I was in the hospital getting better."

"No. I mean when you were asleep. In the coma," she said, whispering her next question as though the answer frightened her. "Where did you go?"

"What's a coma?" Kyle interrupted.

"It's like a long sleep," Henry replied before turning to Lacey. "I didn't go anywhere. I may have dreamed, but I was always right here, waiting to come home."

That was when Ned came through the door. Henry helped Kyle off his lap onto the sofa and stood up. He was still shaky on his feet after going without walking for a couple of weeks. Madeline lifted her hands to support him, but he waved her away. Henry walked around the edge of the coffee table and over to his son, until there was only a metre between them. They studied each other without speaking.

Ned was no different than how Henry remembered him. His hair stuck up from where he'd raked his hands through it – the only betrayal of his anxiety. His eyes were frozen and hard, staring straight through Henry until his father shuffled his weight from foot-to-foot. Henry didn't know why he was suddenly so worried. He cocked his head to one side and tried to remember. He knew there was definitely something wrong, something that he should know about Ned, but as much as he strained his mind, no memory came to him. All Henry knew was that he didn't trust his son.

"Dad," Ned spoke at last.

"Ned."

"Are you...are you okay now?" His son was being uncharacteristically cautious.

"Yes."

"Do you remember what happened?"

"...no," Henry answered, narrowing his eyes.

Ned sighed and his shoulders seemed to fall lower than before, as if he was now relaxed. Madeline came up behind Henry and slipped her hand into his, pulling him around and into a tight hug. Henry buried his nose into her hair until it tickled, but he made no move to scratch it. Letting go of his wife seemed impossible. She smelled exactly how he'd remembered her – sharp and sweet. Family. He felt her neck tense and swallow as she withdrew her arms from his shoulders. Seeing his family was all well and good, but he wanted to talk to Madeline privately. They had so much to catch up on, but he had to wait until night to discuss everything.

Eventually, night came. Henry and Madeline lay in bed together, side by side and unmoving. There was no knowing where to begin. It wasn't as if they could start where they left off, because Henry had no idea where that was anymore. It couldn't have been before the coma. Yes, it was the last time he'd spoken to her, but it wasn't the last time she'd spoken to him. He remembered that she was with him occasionally in his coma. Her voice would drift down through the sky. What was it she said to him? He couldn't carry the words with him into consciousness. They had been forgotten too.

"Tomorrow we'll have to go to the police station," Madeline said.

"What for?" He wriggled his toes underneath the duvet.

"The investigation. We have to go back in, apparently."

"Investigation?"

"Mmm." She shrugged. "Anyway, we don't have to go until Lacey and Kyle get out of school, so you'll have the day to relax, I suppose."

"What are you doing tomorrow?"

"Same as ever. A few errands."

"Could I come with you?" he asked.

"If you want."

"I don't want to be apart from you."

Madeline turned and looked at Henry. He reached over and laid his hand on hers, then they turned back to the window opposite, which they stared out of as they lay together. Her hand was cold and still at first, but began to warm under his until she interlocked their fingers. They stayed like this until Henry couldn't feel which fingers belonged to him and which were his wife's.

"What did you dream about?" she asked.

"What do you mean?"

"You told Lacey that you dreamed. That you didn't go anywhere. I want to know what happened."

"I-I can't remember." He brushed the question away as he stroked her fingers.

"You must remember some things."

"I don't think I do."

"No, you must," she persisted.

"Madeline, I —"

"Henry, you must."

Henry looked at his wife and saw that she was beginning to cry. That was when he understood. He took her face in his hands. Her tears dripped down her nose and trickled up his arms. He kissed her. At first in that gentle way that meant they'd accepted how old they had grown. Their lips pressed together, met with the solidity of their marriage, and then parted again as their age tremoured up their hands and made them shake. Then he kissed her again. It was a kiss to turn back the clocks. One that sent them reeling back in time to the very first. Henry saw the stars come out in the darkness of their bedroom and pulled her close, his heart drumming through his chest into her ear as they rested in each other's arms.

"There was nothing, at first," Henry began, trying to recall everything as best he could. "I only know that there was nothing because when I came into my dream, it felt like time had passed. I don't think I started dreaming right away. But I don't have any way of proving it. Dreams are supposed to happen so quickly. How can we prove that we ever really had them at all? I felt like I was really there. I didn't even know I was dreaming, I —"

"This is too fast, my love. Slow down. Begin at the beginning," she said, patting his chest.

"I was on a beach. It was huge. A beach that contained all beaches. Just massive. Every grain of sand felt like an obstacle. I didn't know where I was. I thought I was lost. I *was* lost, but only inside myself. I had no idea it was a dream at first. I-I remember walking…lots of walking…my god I couldn't breathe. I had no oxygen and felt like I was dying, but I wouldn't die." He reached for her hand again and stilled it with his own.

"And then what?"

"…your voice. It was your voice. It came out of nowhere. I ran…I didn't know I could, but I did. You weren't there. Madeline, you weren't there."

"I was. In your heart." She pulled herself against him as tightly as she could, and he kissed the top of her head.

"Of course, but…it's not the same. I don't think I can explain it. My heart couldn't contain you. It refused to hold you. The part of you I kept in myself wasn't enough. I needed all of you, only the version of you that exists in your body. You weren't there. Not the you I needed. But I didn't stop looking."

It pained him to recall what it was like wandering the long shores of his mind's isolation without her. For two weeks, she was right next to him but out of reach, whispering to him but couldn't converse. It was the furthest from her he'd ever been, even during the time before they met, when he didn't know she existed at all. At least then he was moving towards her. On the beach, they ran parallel to one another, with no meeting point in sight. It didn't matter how clear the horizon was, he couldn't see anything. And then the weather began to –

"Ah! That's right! I remember a storm!" he exclaimed, another piece of his memory settling into place.

"A storm?"

"It was so hot on the beach, but it turned. Even the sun disappeared," he said.

Madeline's head felt heavy on his shoulder and her arm

across his chest compressed him.

"I wanted to scream. To yell and shriek against the thunder." He sat up. "Sometimes all you have is a scream, and I didn't even have that. Not in that place. In that coma."

"If you're getting upset, we can stop." She sat up next to him.

"Don't I owe it to you to explain what was happening to me?"

"No. We don't have to talk about it."

"Remembering is…hard. The world has gone black around the edges."

"Can I tell you what it was like for me? Here without you?" Madeline asked.

"Of course."

She helped prop him up against the pillows so that he would be able to lean against something as she spoke. While they repositioned, still together but no longer interlocked, Henry noticed a streak of blood on the white sheets, but didn't say anything.

"I'd never felt my age before," she began. "I always feel like I'm just as I was when I was sixteen. Nothing in my head has changed since then. And you…I still see you exactly as I did the day we met. You don't look a day over seventeen. But then I saw you in the hospital bed, and your hand was so cold. I felt old. For the first time in my life, I felt my age. We're so close to dying. And I know it's awful and we're not to think like that, but how can I not? I realised in one day that we weren't teenagers. I don't know where my life went. Where we went.

"I missed everything about you. Everything you ever did that hurt me. I missed the arguments, Henry. How you'd look like you were on fire with rage and we'd scream, we'd burn up with our anger. But that was passion. Next thing I know you're lying in that bed unconscious. My god, I thought, Henry is old and he's going to die. That part of me is going to die. I know that was selfish. But I am selfish. I'm sixteen. Henry, I'm sixteen."

Henry pulled the covers up over her and let his wife shake. Her breath sounded caught in her throat as she tried to find the strength to draw in air between her sobs. There was nothing he could say to comfort Madeline and he knew it. In many ways, coming back to her might have made things worse. These were the sobs of a widow. She cried as though she was already grieving, and he had returned to undo her progress.

He looked out of the window again. Even though it was night he could see the scenery because the bedroom was dark and the moon was bright. The light caught the tops of the trees and Henry remembered the trees at the beach, and how they had reminded him of the ones from home.

"There's something else," he whispered gently, not wanting to make things worse, but needing to tell her everything now. "Not everything at the beach was unfamiliar. There was this oasis of trees in the middle. It was more of an island, really. I'm pretty sure it was an island because I never found anything that could constitute as mainland. But these trees...they were like the trees here. All except one. It was the tree from our garden at our old house. The one we carved our initials in. Do you remember the one?"

Madeline nodded.

"I had it with me on the beach. I found it in the storm when I was looking for shelter. I added an L and a K for Lacey and Kyle...actually...no...I remember Lacey's voice. She came to see me that day too. Something about her English class..."

"Yes!" Madeline said, her tears clearing a little. "You'll be so proud of her. She's in the advanced class now and seeing this really nice boy, Ezra, who has been helping her with the books like you did for her. I...I wanted to help her more. I just don't know how."

Henry frowned. When he brought up the tree, he meant

to take the conversation in a more comforting direction, but he remembered what Lacey told him. "She said she thought you were with me."

"What?"

"She said you changed. Like you'd left. And she thought your mind had gone to wherever mine was."

"Maybe it had," Madeline said, but he could tell from her tone that she was saying it to herself.

Henry kissed the top of her head and let her settle down to sleep. The moon burst through the window and Henry got up to shut the curtains. He didn't like to sleep with the curtains closed, but tonight he didn't want to see the world. He only wanted to see Madeline. As reached the window, he looked out. It was only a blink. It appeared in a flash. Henry swore that, underneath the nearest tree, he saw a figure raise an axe to swing at the trunk. The metal hit the wood with a crack. He shook his head and looked again, the figure was gone.

LACEY

Lacey tucked Ezra's copy of *Of Mice and Men* under her arm and walked towards the benches by the Science Block to meet him for lunch. She wanted to wear her favourite jacket that day, because she knew she'd be seeing him, but something wasn't right when she put it on in the morning. She did all the buttons up and looked at herself in the bathroom mirror, but it felt wrong. Had she put on weight? Why couldn't she breathe? No, today she'd wear a loose waterproof and think nothing more of it – as if she had a choice. Fortunately, the weather was beginning to turn a little, and Wales was warming up again. Lacey loved the days when it felt like the world was just beginning to come back to life. It felt like the way it did right before a storm, when the clouds sucked all the humidity out of the air.

When Lacey saw Ezra rummaging through his bag, she half-considered doubling back and hiding, pretending that she'd forgotten or got busy or…something. She'd always been a terrible liar. It wasn't just accepted that they would hang out together anymore, but expected; it was firmly established that they'd be spending their lunches together for the foreseeable future. Why, then, couldn't Lacey quell the feeling of her guts worming around whenever she looked at him? Would they go away if she knew what their relationship really was?

Anna called it the 'DTR talk'. Lacey felt a pang of guilt inside her when she considered how little time she'd spent with her best friend since being transferred out of Mr Golding's English class. Before she could change her mind, she took out her phone and messaged Anna: *meet me after school?* Quick as lightning came the reply as a single, thumbs up emoji. Yes. Lacey could explain herself then, and maybe ask some more questions about this 'DTR' and what it even meant.

Ezra zipped his bag closed and walked over to meet Lacey. She handed the book back to him with a half-smile.

"How was it?" he asked.

"I see what you mean. It's bittersweet."

"Bittersweet? Like you?" he laughed.

"Huh?"

"You're sweet, Lace. But we both know you'd beat me in a fight."

"And don't you forget it, or I'll go all Lennie on you," she teased, elbowing him gently.

"Damn, alright. Lennie Belvidere. I like it. But, if I'm George, I'm sorry but I'll ultimately win this."

"I don't know if I'd say George won exactly…"

"Fair point," Ezra said, putting his arm around Lacey's shoulders. "Right, Lennie, where are we eating?"

"Cafeteria?"

"Yawn. Could go out?"

"Where? I haven't left school for lunch before," she said, knowing that it was perfectly acceptable for Year 10s to leave school grounds for lunch, but never having done so once.

"I know a place."

He took his arm from her shoulders and Lacey felt cold where it had been. He tucked the book into the back pocket of his trousers rather than opening his bag. There were a couple of reasons why Lacey had never left school for lunch before. Anna was a vegan and always brought her own lunch from home, so there was never any point in going out. Lacey also knew that, unlike many of the other students, she couldn't afford to keep it up if she took a liking to it. With Ezra, she'd walk across the entire town and back just talking, and she knew she'd be blissfully content in doing so, no lunch necessary.

"What'll today's topic of conversation be?" Ezra asked as he held the school gate open for her.

"Do we need one?"

"Of course! How else can we get to the deep stuff?"

"Does it have to get deep?"

"What else would be the point?" he asked, slipping a hand underneath the strap of her bag and lifting it off her shoulder and on to his own. Before she could say anything, he prompted again. "I think I've decided. Today, I want to talk about…beautiful things."

"What?"

"You said when we went to Cegin that you haven't heard a guy call things beautiful before. That I was feminine. So let's talk about that. It's been on my mind since you said it," he shrugged, or at least he tried to but forgot he had a bag on each shoulder and smiled at himself.

"Out of everything we discussed, why did that stick in your head?" Lacey was a little taken aback.

"I'm not exactly a poster-boy for testosterone. At least, not in the stereotypical sense."

When Lacey opened her mouth to protest, he held up his hands. "Don't worry, I know. And I like it that way. I just want to know why you thought I should be."

"…the way you talk sometimes…it's like you're so much older," she said after thinking for a few moments.

"Am I confusing you?"

"Not really."

"Then I'll keep talking like this. And you can tell me what things you find beautiful."

"I don't know where to start," Lacey sighed. When Ezra got locked into a subject, he could be hard to shake off. Not that she wanted to shake him off... Lacey didn't know what she wanted.

"Alright, what do you find ugly?" he tried again. "It can be anything. A behaviour. A place. A thought. Anything."

"...burritos."

"That's the best you can do?" he gawped.

"Shit, Ezra, I don't know what you want me to say! I've never talked about anything like this before," she snapped. "It's so...odd. I don't understand it. I don't understand myself. So there. Burritos are ugly."

Lacey took her bag off his shoulder and put it across her body, so he couldn't take it from her again. She started to walk more quickly, forcing him to stride to keep up.

"I was endeavouring to understand you better, but I don't think I will. And I like that. It's a challenge," he panted.

"I'm not your challenge."

"I didn't mean it like that."

"Can we have a normal conversation?" Lacey asked. "I love talking about books and everything, but not right now. Let's just have lunch and be normal."

"Normal...okay." He fell silent. His pace went slightly out of sync with her and he began to fall behind.

"That wasn't supposed to kill the conversation," Lacey muttered.

"No! It hasn't. I'm just thinking."

They walked the rest of the way in silence. Every time Lacey thought of something she could say, she looked at Ezra and the thought immediately dropped out of her head. What had she said wrong? Had she said anything wrong at all? She didn't want to talk about anything grand. All these big ideas that made the world seem like a huge place were downright sickening. She thought about her grandpa then, who she'd been trying to force out of her head all day, and watched him shuffle back into her mind.

She knew what she found beautiful. As soon as Ezra asked it was the first thing to pop into her head. Grandma. There was no doubt in Lacey's mind that her grandmother was the most beautiful thing in the world to her, but she'd never share that with anyone. That was just for her to know and her alone. Even now, when she saw her grandmother age more rapidly in the last two weeks than any other time in her life, she still found that there was something precious about her. The thought of Grandma changing, of being as corruptible as everyone else, stuck in Lacey's head like thorns.

"Why do you talk like that?" she said, suddenly coming out of her thoughts.

They were standing outside a fish and chip shop. She stopped walking and faced him instead of going in.

"Like what?" he asked, but she could tell he already knew what she meant.

"Like you're in a John Green novel."

"What do you mean?"

"Nothing matters. That's the real truth of it. We're all just making it up as we go until one day we'll be adults and graduate with a first class degree in make believe. Anything else is just pretentious," she said, finally finding her words.

"I hate that word, Lace," he said quietly, but she could tell by the red of his cheeks that he was getting upset.

"You would. Because it's what you are. I don't give a shit about being deep all the time. It's fake. It's not raw. Not like real life. So you can pretend all you want to care about beautiful things, but I don't. Not really. Not when I think about it. I couldn't care less about beautiful shit. Stop trying to make this world any more meaningful than how it is now. Nothing means a bloody thing. Nothing."

Ezra looked as if if was the first time anyone had ever told him that the world wasn't as beautiful as he thought it was, and they fell into silence as they entered the chip shop. Lacey wasn't hungry anymore, but there wasn't anything else to do now but get their lunch. She almost figured out how to reach over and take his hand when they were waiting for the food to be made, but at the last minute, she forgot and couldn't do it. The man behind to counter passed them each a Styrofoam container with a regular portion of chips inside – Ezra's with gravy and Lacey's with extra vinegar. They took them outside and began the long walk back, eating as they went.

"Listen, Lace," he said at last, "I believe in fate. Maybe it has to do with how I was brought up. When my dad walked out on all of us, it felt like the worst day of my life. But slowly that day stopped feeling so crappy. The further away from it I got, the better that day seemed. I reached this point a few months ago, when I actually looked back on his leaving and smiled. It had been a good day. It hurt like nothing else in this world, but it was for the best. My mum and sisters are happy. They're strong. I'm better for it.

"So maybe I talk weird sometimes. So what? Who gives a shit? I'm making a point, aren't I? My life feels like it's split down into pieces, but I'm embracing it. That's the only way I know how to grow. I compartmentalise until I'm ready to deal with something, and then I let it out of its box and see it for what it is. Maybe I come off as repressed and pretentious, but it doesn't bother me."

"What do you mean 'compartmentalise?'" Lacey asked.

"It's something my therapist says a lot. I file my problems into mental boxes. Trap them there until I'm ready to deal with them. There's nothing wrong with doing that, as long as you deal with them at some point. It's like bottling up emotions temporarily, knowing that you'll take off the lid when the time is right. The trick is not being chicken shit about opening up when the time comes. That's the hard part."

"How do you know when the time is right to face stuff?"

"You just sort of feel it. You know. There's this moment of nothingness and a surge deep down. A call to action. Almost like when you finally stop feeling something there is a chance to choose what to feel next. We rarely get to choose our feelings. When everything is quiet and I feel like I might be turning numb, that's when I choose to think about the things I keep in bottles."

Lacey nodded like she understood. She reckoned Ezra got way more of this from his therapist than he was letting on, because he was becoming increasingly more difficult to follow. She wondered if she could be good at compartmentalising her thoughts, but decided that she wouldn't in the end. Her mind was too much like confetti; once it went off, it burst with colours and mess, and there was no way of putting it all back the way it was before. Something about the idea irked her. There was a coolness to living like that which revealed some inert apathy within anybody who could have that much control over their own thoughts and feelings. Ezra struck her as the sort of person who cared a lot about many things, and yet his ability to organise his whole life into a metaphorical filing cabinet seemed to show a side to him that she didn't know at all.

"Ezra," she said. "Do you remember when we were talking about *Jekyll and Hyde*, and you said everybody has two sides to them? Are these your two sides? One who is passionate about almost everything, and the other who can squirrel away all their emotions?"

He finished his last bite of chips and gravy and went over to the nearest bin to throw the box away. Lacey struggled to eat as she walked and, as if noticing, he led her to a low wall near a square of grass. They sat together and the stone was cold on the backs of her legs, but she was relieved to have a moment of stillness.

"I've never thought about it like that," he said after a pause. "Maybe. But that makes it seem like controlling my emotions is a bad thing. Hyper-rational. It's not. If it wasn't for that part of me, everything about my mind would go unchecked. My anger. My fears."

"Are you scared of a lot of things?" Lacey asked.

"No. Not a lot. But the few things that frighten me are more than enough. Like my sisters. I want them to always be okay. It freaks me out to think that something bad could ever happen to them, and worse still is the fact that I know bad things will happen. That's just life. What about you?"

Lacey said she was thinking to buy herself time, but the truth was that she knew exactly what she was afraid of and that it also happened to be the thing she found most beautiful. Out of nowhere, she had the urge to tell Ezra everything. She put the rest of her food to one side, uneaten and cold.

"My grandma. That's what is beautiful to me," she replied.

"But we changed topic. We were talking about our fears."

"Ezra, I think something is wrong with my family."

Without hesitation, he put his hand on hers and swivelled around, no longer sitting on the wall but crouching in front of her. She carried on talking.

"There are a lot of different things. Too many for me to compartmentalise like you. Everything bleeds into each other and gets all murky and mixed up. I think my grandpa's in danger," she said, and then immediately looked around to make sure they were really alone.

"Danger? Why? What does that have to do with your grandma?" Ezra was now gripping her hand properly, holding it between his and warming it.

"I think my family did something to him. My dad…he's not a good person. He's mean. And I know he hates Grandpa." She'd never said the words out loud before. They stung her ears and rattled around inside her mouth, sharp and hard like loose teeth.

"Would he hurt him?"

"I think he already has. I want to ask my grandma about

it, but she's changed. She's different. The kind of different that only comes from dealing with something heavy. I think she knows."

The truth of it hit her in that moment, and she couldn't hold her tears any longer. Ezra stood up and pulled her onto her feet, before wrapping his arms around her and pulling her close. He kissed her forehead and even in the middle of this black abyss, she still felt something inside her call for more of him.

"Look, I don't know the specifics, but I know you love your family," he whispered into her ear. "You're thoughtful and clever. But I can only offer you advice based on what I'd do." When Lacey nodded, he continued, "I'd talk to her, Lace. If you think she's the most beautiful thing in this world, then you must love her very much. I can tell by the way your face changes when you talk about her that she loves you too. Your whole face lifts up. So you need to talk to her. Letting your mind run wild will only drive you crazy."

She knew he was right. When was she going to bring this up? After school, they'd have to go down to the police station to talk to Detective Parry again. She didn't want to voice her fears to the police officer. What if she was wrong and got someone she loved in trouble? As much as Lacey loved her grandma, it was her grandpa who had suffered. It dawned on her then; he did go somewhere. He had dreams. Lacey needed to know what they were and what he remembered. She couldn't help but feel that she was in the dark. There were two sides to everybody, and she was only just beginning to see her family's other side. Lacey could tell already that they weren't the people she thought they were.

ELEN

Elen knocked on the door to her parents' house and held her breath. She shouldn't be there – she knew that. It was her lunch break and there wasn't enough time to explain everything to her family. Telling them all that was on her mind or in her heart and then listening to her father do the same would take hours. Then she'd spend time trying to make her mother remember her, fail, and pull herself together before she left. Elen had forty-five minutes. A little time seemed better than none at all, in the end.

She was here for a kiss on the cheek. It was all she thought about since the other day when she told Marcus about her mother. As the front door opened, her heart began to sink. She wouldn't get a kiss today or any other day.

Her father, Osian Parry, stood in the doorway. He shuffled back a step when he saw Elen out of surprise. In the seconds before they spoke, she studied his face. It seemed unchanged over the almost three decades that Elen had been alive, although she knew that wasn't the case. He must have aged dramatically between the ages of twenty-eight to sixty-two, but she couldn't remember. His hair was completely grey and she knew it used to be brown, but there was never a day in her life when she noticed it changing. Even now, as she looked at him, he only seemed more tired than usual.

"Hey, Dad."

"My god, El! Come in, come in. What are you doing here? It's so good to see you. Did you get my emails?" Osian said, ushering her inside with a flurry of questions and flapping hands.

When she sat down on the sofa in the living room, she chose her regular spot and sunk into the familiar shape of her imprint in the cushions. She had spent many nights here as she grew up, cuddled up to the arm of the worn sofa which her parents could never afford to replace. The lamp on the side table next to it emitted a warm glow that cast orange against the bookshelves above it. Elen wondered how many of those books she had read. After school she would have dropped her bag by the window, headed to the kitchen to get a glass of fruit juice from the fridge, and gone to that sofa corner. She'd rest her knees on the arm as she reached up to pull a book down in a cloud of dust. It didn't matter what the book had been or the character it had followed, so long as it had taken her mind off herself. The words had drifted up to her from the ageing pages and had felt warm in her head, while the juice had trickled cold down her throat. The two sensations had mingled into bliss as she had let herself become swallowed by the sofa, becoming enveloped by a world that hadn't been hers.

Elen remembered one evening when she had been reading a book after school – the title of which evaded her now – and voices had drifted to her from the kitchen.

Her dad's voice: "Beverley, what are doing?"

Her mum's: "Oh, Osian. You'll be late for work."

"What do you mean? I've been to work."

"I'm making breakfast."

"No, Bev, you're making dinner."

"Dinner?"

"Yeah…is that pancake mix?"

"For breakfast."

"No…no…Bev…"

Elen had drifted further into the freedom of her book. For a moment, she had stopped hearing her parents' words and only heard the sound of their voices. There had been a break in the sound that had come as an absent note of sadness through the hallway and into the living room where Elen had huddled. They had come into the room then, her father's arm around her mother's shoulders.

He had guided her into the chair opposite Elen, where her mother had liked to sit in the mornings and do crosswords with her coffee. Beverley had looked over to her daughter, momentarily confused, and then turned her attention out the window. In silence, they had each continued to get lost in a world beyond their home.

After Elen had left home and started university, she had stopped reading for fun altogether. It hadn't been until some years later that she had realised it was nothing more than rudimentary escapism and, once she had "escaped," she no longer felt the need to let herself be absorbed in fiction. Her life had become centred entirely on the real world and the evils within it.

She hoped that her lunch break would be enough time to talk to her father, who seemed more flustered than usual. From her spot on the sofa she observed her surroundings. The room was almost exactly the way it had always been, right down to the books on the shelf which only she had ever bothered to read. The only difference was that a voile was hung in the window so that nobody could see into the house from the street. It made it a little harder to look out, which no doubt irritated her mother.

"I can't stay for long," Elen said. "It's my lunch hour."

"Lunch? You must be hungry then," Osian said, hovering next to her, but not sitting.

"I'm okay."

"Don't be ridiculous. We've got potato salad – your favourite."

"…I suppose I am a little hungry."

Her father grinned and hurried to the kitchen, returning with a plate heaped with everything he could find in the fridge that seemed to go together. Elen moved to stand up and head to the dining room, but he waved her back down onto the sofa.

"You eat here. It's far comfier. Just be careful not to drop anything," he said, handing her the plate, along with a knife and fork.

"Yes. Thanks, Dad."

Elen picked up a boiled egg and bit the end off as he watched her. She could tell by the way he had swatted her back down that her mother was in the dining room. It wasn't that Elen didn't want to see her, but more that she didn't know how. Before she left, she'd have to face her. Elen was here for a reason and she knew it. As if sensing her thoughts, her father asked after her work.

"It's good, mostly," she said. "I want to talk to you about something to do with work, actually. It's really been bothering me. I'm not allowed to discuss case details with anyone, so I've kept most of my thoughts all to myself. But I need to talk through it with someone I trust to try and figure out what's wrong. I don't know why I feel this way or where to even begin."

"Begin at the beginning, cariad."

"This stays between us, Dad?"

"It won't leave this room. What's going on?"

Elen pinned the knife and fork down with a thumb so they wouldn't slide off the plate as she leaned forwards.

"There's this man," she explained. "His name is Henry. He's only a few years older than you. I think his family hurt him. That's the part that's bothering me. He was comatose. I went to see him and he looked so weak. Not human at all. He looked like an old oil painting. Both shiny and sallow."

"What is it about him that upsets you?"

She wasn't sure how to say the next part, so she just let it out and trusted that her father would understand.

"He reminds me of Mum. He's woken up now and been released from hospital. Physically everything is fine, but he can't remember what happened to him, apparently. Just little flashes, but he gets them mixed up with his dreams. His mind is so fragile and he may have gone back to the people that did that to him."

"Can't you make an arrest?" Osian sounded concerned.

"Not yet. There isn't enough to go on if we want to secure a conviction. We're almost there, I can feel it. It's so close. Meanwhile he's in that house with them. It's not even a house. It's barely a cottage. They all live in this shack together in the middle of nowhere." She shook her head.

Osian raised a hand and nodded – his signal that a cup of tea was needed for this conversation. He went to the kitchen and Elen heard familiar sounds: tap, kettle clicked on, cupboard, mugs, cupboard, drawer, teaspoon, drawer, kettle clicked off, tins, water, tink tink tink... He came back in holding two mugs of tea and put them on a side table, on two coasters.

"Okay. That's better," he said. "Who is his family?" he continued the conversation without missing a beat.

"He's got two grandchildren. Lacey and Kyle. They're both sweet enough, but I'm certain they don't know anything. He has his wife Madeline. She's...I don't know what to make of her. I'm not sure how much of a hand she had in what happened. There's something behind her eyes...a sort of fear...or dread. She knows something, but I can't say what. I only hope she learns to put the others before her son."

"And this son, does he live there too?" Osian asked.

"Yeah. There's something wrong with him, Dad. He seems so normal on the outside, but then you stare at him for a little too long and his eyes snap to yours, burrow right down to the back of your skull, the pit in your head. He knows you then. Everything about you. It feels like you're being preyed on. Like he could jump from his seat and rip....I'm sorry, Dad. This is too much," she said, stopping abruptly and returning to her food to ease the intensity back out of the conversation.

"You're alright, El. He really scares you, huh?"

"I'd never admit that to anyone –"

"I'm not anyone," Osian said.

"Yeah...yes, he scares me. I think he tried to kill his father. There's something different about him. I don't want him to walk. I don't want to even give him the chance."

Her father nodded and leaned back in his seat, drumming his fingers on the side table as he thought. Elen had seen that look before, the night Andrew Brace broke up with her and she'd come over to be with her parents. That night she had felt like a child again. It had been before her mother got really bad, when she could still be comforting and warm to Elen. Her father had watched as his two loves held each other, but Elen could tell he had only been thinking of violence.

Osian Parry was a small, gentle man. He was soft-spoken and delicate. He always said he had a long fuse, but once someone had used it all up, he'd explode without remorse. His fuse had burned up that night. Their eyes met for a moment over her mother's shoulder and they exchanged their thoughts in silence.

I'll go over there, Elen. I'll give him a piece of my mind.

Dad, please. Leave it.

I mean it, El. I'll kill him.

No...it's done.

I –

It's over.

He had nodded and went to the kitchen where, in between her sobs and her mother's shushing, Elen had heard the crack of a beer can opening. Now, as she described Ned Belvidere to her father, Osian had that same fire behind his eyes. He fumbled around on the side table for his cup of tea, all the while staring straight ahead, and took a short sip. When he put it back down, the thud of the ceramic against the soft, wooden coaster seemed to trigger him to refocus his attention on Elen.

"I know what kind of man you're describing," he said. "An anti-man. Around the edges he looks like a person, but inside he is hollow. There is a gap in him. If you put a man like that under too much pressure, he'll crack. He's empty inside. There's nothing for him to use to push back. Some men are hollow out of grief and loss. Some are hollow because there is no kindness left inside them. You need to figure out which kind of hollow he is to find out what will put pressure on him. Once you've done that, he'll cave. Don't worry, cariad, I know you'll crack him. You'll get him."

Elen was about to ask whether he had ever met anyone like this, but just as she began to, her mother came into the room. They stared at each other without speaking. Elen never spoke first; she didn't know which role she'd have to play with each visit. Osian didn't want to speak – it was clear from the way he pressed his lips together – but he stood up anyway.

"Beverley? Do you need anything?" he asked.

"I heard you talking. Who's this woman?"

Before Osian could reply, Elen cut in, "My name is Elen. I'm a detective."

"A woman detective? How progressive..." she said, and Osian shook his head.

"Yes, mu – Mrs Parry."

"Is there something wrong? Has something happened?"

Beverley asked.

"I came to see you."

"What for?"

"She's just making sure everything is alright here," Osian said. "The neighbourhood. Our home. Why don't you two talk while I make you a cup of tea, dear?" he said to his wife.

"She has a plate. She's eating?" Beverley asked, incredulous.

"Welsh hospitality, my love," he said, before going to the kitchen.

Beverley made her way slowly to her chair and lowered herself into it, never taking her eyes off Elen. When she was satisfied that Elen was safe to be around, she turned her attention to the window. She drew back upon seeing the voile for both the first and fiftieth time, then lifted it aside with a finger, peering around the edge to observe the street beyond the glass. Then she let it go, the voile gliding back to the pane of glass like a veil.

"This is a good neighbourhood. We don't have problems around here," she said to Elen.

"I'm glad to hear it. I want you to be safe."

Beverley raised her eyebrows.

"On behalf of the police department," Elen added, hurriedly.

"I appreciate your vigilance. It's high time we had a police force get to know the people it protects. I really believe that. I think..." Beverley trailed off and her face went blank.

"Yes?" Elen prompted, gently.

"I'm sorry, what was I saying?"

"The police should get to know the locals."

"Ah. Yes, that's what I think."

Osian came back into the room carrying a third cup of tea. Elen knew that her mother's was decaffeinated and that she mustn't say anything about it. He went to stand behind Beverley and rested one hand on her shoulder. Elen thought they looked like a photograph. They were perfectly posed and happy. On the surface, this moment was ordinary.

"Well, I should get going," Elen said after checking her watch.

"I'll walk you to your car," Osian said.

Beverley frowned, but remained silent. She reached down the side of her chair for the newspaper and flipped to the crossword but, upon seeing it already filled out, ripped it in half and hurled it across the room. Osian looked pleadingly at Elen, who nodded. She understood that her father couldn't come out with her now. She smiled at him, nodded, and left. On the way back to her car, she could feel herself being watched. When she turned back to look at the house, the voile obscured everything.

Using the speaker phone in her car, she called Dan at the station as she drove back to him. Her mind mulled over everything that her father had told her. The fact the Ned was hollow may not be the most significant detail. It was why he was hollow. Perhaps this would lead to motive, and the pressure Elen needed to crack him.

"Dan?"

"Hey, Elen, how were the parents?" he said. His voice was slightly muffled and Elen could tell that he was eating his lunch.

"Good. Both good. Mum seemed to be having an alright day. But Dad brought up something important. I need you to do me a favour."

"Name it."

"Find everything you can on Ned Belvidere. Birth certificates, job applications, mentions in his high school newspaper…everything. I'll be back in about fifteen to lend a hand. I've got an idea." She drummed her hands on the steering wheel at a red light until Dan told her to stop, because it was drumming right down his ear.

"Care to enlighten me?" he said after.

"What if the information we need to get a confession has nothing to do with what happened at the beach? What if it's further back? Something is very wrong with that family and it existed long before whatever the hell happened to Henry."

"On it."

She heard the crunch of Dan biting into what she presumed was an apple as she hung up, wondering what it was that could make a man completely empty. Shouldn't her father be losing his mind now too? He was watching the woman he'd given his life to disappear from him, and he could do nothing to stop it. Marcus was enduring a similar pain with his sister, who suffered with cancer. Every time he saw her, he watched the only person in this world that shared his blood fade away from him. Yet every day Marcus got up and did his job. Her father woke up and made her mother breakfast whether she remembered him or not. How could they remain so steadfastly dutiful? Then there were others who lost themselves within their losses. How could she tell the difference?

Elen decided that there must have been an indicator, early on, which revealed the path Ned was going to take. Not everything could be boiled down to one moment. Not all actions could be justified or excused on the basis of a collection of unfortunate minutes. Still, she couldn't help but wonder that there must have been an undeniable, powerful instance that shaped Ned Belvidere, but left his soul unformed. When she looked at him and felt his gaze bore into her, she saw that he existed in a colourless world, one of shade and coldness. She dare not meet those eyes again and yet, in her mind, she would see them. There had to be a point in his life that did this to him – a specific shadow that had fallen over him.

A dread crept over her then when she thought of meeting him later that day. The Belvideres were due at the station for 4 pm that afternoon. Would she have enough time to find out anything valuable about him? As a detective she knew better than anyone that no person was ever completely innocent. There wasn't a single person capable of being accountable for their actions who hadn't transgressed in some way – even her. What kind of hollow would Elen become, if something traumatic ever happened to her? Would she be able to remain good and focused like her father and Marcus? It was equally possible that she would shut down. Elen thought about herself that night Andrew broke up with her, when she had last been cradled by her mother. She had been so young and broken. She had been lucky to have her mother then, when she really needed her.

That was when Elen thought of Lacey Belvidere, motherless and with no father to be found inside Ned. How was she coping? One of the greatest dangers of hollowness was the inconceivable and highly likely way that it could be passed on. Trauma created trauma. Abruptly, it dawned on Elen. Amid her thoughts of her mother and Lacey, she phoned Dan back. She was only five minutes away from the station now, but it couldn't wait for a second.

"Elen? What's wrong?" he sighed.

"Nothing's wrong. I had an idea. Find out everything you can on Ned's wife. Karen. Karen Belvidere."

It was the one incident that would have affected the entire family, but Elen had been so wrapped up in the now that she hadn't looked at the emotional contexts in which the actions of the Belvideres took place. As Elen pulled into her parking space at the police station, she closed her eyes for a few seconds. She hoped she'd be able to find a moment's peace before heading inside but, against the backs of her own eyelids, she saw Ned staring at her.

MADELINE

Madeline woke up in her husband's arms. He had seen something through the window before bed which frightened him, but refused to say what it was. She had no way of knowing precisely what apparition seemed to haunt her husband's gaze, but she felt as though she knew. It was Henry who had no idea. He couldn't remember what happened to him, but Madeline did. She understood everything fully, but was bound to silence.

She slowly and carefully lifted Henry's arm off her and laid it at his side, then slipped out of bed as quietly and gently as she could. When she looked down on him after she stood up, she had to clamp a hand over her mouth to stop herself from crying out. He looked just as he did in the hospital, asleep but not resting, alive but not living. She was certain that this secret would kill her. He turned in his sleep and his movement startled her. Madeline slipped into her dressing gown and hurried out of the room before she burst into tears.

She closed the door behind her with a soft click and turned to find Ned sitting at the dining table. When Madeline looked at her son, her whole body felt like it was shrinking. She was a child again, with no knowledge about how to raise another person. Like she told Henry last night, she didn't feel like she'd aged a day since she was sixteen. Ned looked up at his mother and she saw her little boy once more. He hadn't aged either. As Madeline went to make breakfast, she felt herself being watched.

"How is he?" Ned asked.

"He's good," she said, getting down four bowls. "A bit shaken up, I think. Obviously it's a very difficult time for him." She remembered she needed a fifth bowl.

"Obviously."

"He keeps seeing things that aren't real."

"What do you mean?"

"Last night," Madeline began, already regretting that she had told him, "he said he saw something out of the window."

"Did he say who it was?"

"No. Do you want coffee?" Madeline asked, making one when Ned nodded.

It hadn't gone over her head that Ned asked 'who' the thing outside the window was. Even Henry just said it was something and didn't specify that it was a person. She brought the drink over to her son and put it down in front of him, just as Henry came out of their bedroom. Henry didn't make eye contact with anyone as he shuffled to the bathroom. Madeline and Ned didn't speak while they waited for him to come back. The cottage that had once felt too small was now a mile wide. Henry walked back in and rubbed his eyes when he finally looked at Madeline, as though his wife was blinding. She made him a coffee too and they all sat around the dining room table.

"Mum said you saw something last night," Ned said, finally breaking the silence. "What was it?"

Henry's forehead wrinkled the way it always did when he was about to lie. When he first told Madeline about the movement outside the window, she only believed him because of those wrinkles that split across his face when he tried to pretend he hadn't seen anything after all. The doctor said that it might take some time for Henry to re-adjust and this made sense to Madeline, but she wasn't sure how his 'adjustments' would manifest themselves. She had no idea that they could mean hallucinations.

"It was nothing," Henry said.

"Bullshit," Ned hissed as ice flashed behind his eyes.

Madeline remembered the moment she first feared her son.

It was the day of Karen's funeral and Ned crouched next to her fresh grave, where his wife was now resting. Madeline remembered that her favourite flowers were morning glories, even though they were nothing special. Karen had said that the way they popped up in the garden, even when she hadn't remembered planting them, always made her smile. They were deep blue with yellow centres. When Lacey was a child, Karen had told her that they looked like the sun in the sky on a clear day, and that was because they were jealous of the beauty and stole a little from the skies for themselves. For her funeral, Madeline and Henry had spent thirty minutes in the garden collecting all the morning glories they could find.

Ned had his palm spread flat over the ground and his chest heaved as if it was filling with air only to collapse in on itself. His face was red, but this time it wasn't just from the whisky he'd thrown down his throat for courage. He looked like there was a pressure building inside him that was so intense that he would erupt if he didn't focus on tightening every single muscle in his body. The almonds of his eyes were stark against the rough hue of his skin, like petals in lava. Madeline glanced down at the flower petals in the basket on her arm and bit her lip.

The hem of her dress flicked up and must have caught Ned's peripheral vision. When their eyes met, Madeline nearly dropped her basket. There was so much hatred boiling inside him and Madeline knew she had failed. There was nothing she could do to protect her son. She trod carefully around the graves that would be Karen's neighbours through eternity. Her footsteps were awkward and she hesitated before each one, constantly surprised at how her shoes sank into the mossy earth. Something about the softness of the ground made her feel sick. Madeline laid her one free hand over her stomach to steady herself.

"Ned?" she said.

He didn't reply. Instead, he looked away from her and back to Karen's headstone. His pupils darted back and forth over the words so much that Madeline thought he might wear down the granite. The epitaph was from a song that Madeline only knew from when Karen would sing it in the garden, pulling weeds underneath the oak tree. *I was grounded while you filled the skies.*

"Her favourite song," Ned said.

"What's it called?"

"'The Whole of the Moon'." Ned's lips replicated a smile as best they could. "It came on in this pub we were at when we were staying in London. Our first trip."

"I remember you saving up for that."

"Two jobs. Eight months. She was so happy."

Ned took his hand off the disturbed ground and stared at the impression of his fingers in the dirt. As if it had somehow offended him, he brushed over the handprint to scatter it. Lifting a finger covered in soil he traced the letters of her name on the headstone. Karen Ann Belvidere. Madeline frowned and stepped closer on the nauseating, spongy graveyard.

"It was this little pub outside the city centre. Damned if I remember what it was called, but we were so hungry that we didn't even check. Just smelled something delicious and followed our noses inside. We sat at a table next to the window. When the clouds lifted her hair took in the sun…just breathed the light in like it was a part of her. The song came on while we waited for our food. I could see it,

Mum. I saw the notes catch her ear and fill her head."

He took his hand away from her headstone and stood up. Madeline came to stand next to him, wanting to take his hand and press it to her cheek the way she did when he was a child, but knowing it would do nothing. She could only stare at him, watching the scene play behind his eyes as he remembered.

"She saw things I never did, Mum. It was like the world opened up to her in ways it wouldn't for me. I think I could have been jealous, but she never made me feel like there was anything wrong with me. But I know there is. I know there is."

"Ned? You aren't making any sense..." Madeline decided to touch his arm, but he pulled away.

"I felt like I was a good person just from being around her. And now she's...the music stopped. She took the music with her."

She couldn't tell her son that she was afraid. That's not what mothers did. Her own mother must have worried herself sick when Madeline had come home from school in tears from being bullied and chased, but she had never said a word. Madeline stood side-by-side with Ned, staring straight ahead. He swayed a little before stopping and shaking his head, as if he was trying to find the song and failed. They didn't speak again for a few minutes and, during that time, Madeline thought about what Ned had told her. *She never made me feel like there was anything wrong with me. But I know there is.*

Madeline plunged a hand into the basket of petals and kept her fingers straight as she wriggled them, letting them brush through their tips like blue velvet. She knew that her son was forever changed now that Karen was gone. She took a fistful of the petals and scattered them over the grave. Some of them got caught in the breeze on the way down, fluttering and landing in the soil like butterflies. Before she could take any more, Ned seized the basket and flung it a few graves over, until it landed and spilled its floral insides onto a stranger's grave.

"Ned!" Madeline exclaimed.

"She doesn't need them," he said, and dropped to his knees again to disperse them from her grave the way he had brushed away his own handprint. "She doesn't need anything to show that we love her. We don't have to prove anything."

"This isn't about proving something. These were her favour —"

"I know what her favourite flower was."

"Then you should let her have them."

"No!" Ned shouted. "You don't get to tell me what I should and shouldn't do. Not for her!"

"What is this about?"

"You know."

She did know. She thought back to Karen's last day, when the whole family had been with her in the hospital. Part of Madeline wished that Karen had been suffering from some sort of disease, that her life would come undone slowly like a complicated knot, until the last strands peacefully unravelled as she slept. Death hadn't come this way. It had come in the squeal of brakes on Ffordd Pentre Du. It had come in the sour stench of rubber burning on tarmac. It had come in the space of a final, staggered breath that had fallen between Karen and the rest of her life like the petals on her grave.

"I can't believe you defended him," Ned whispered.

He looked up at his mother again, and she shook. Venom snaked in the red veins of his eyes and they turned to the darkest black. His upper lip curled back over his pointed, white teeth. Madeline clutched her hands to her chest and felt her heartbeat rise. The grief Ned felt was becoming something else and it was overtaking him.

He never lost that venomous glare. Now as Madeline evaded

her sons questions about Henry's hallucinations, he stared icily at her until she shivered. His sipped the coffee while it was still too hot to drink and didn't flinch or complain even though it must have burned his tongue. She turned her back to him to make snacks for Lacey and Kyle to take to school, but immediately felt vulnerable when she couldn't see him anymore. The hairs on her neck crept up as light as whispers and her legs felt numb. As hard as she tried to stay out of the middle of Ned and Henry, she was always inevitably dragged back. There was nothing she could do to step out of the crossfire these days. Not since Ned had taken Henry away. As Madeline chopped apples for her grandchildren and remembered Karen, she knew that her son wouldn't never leave this alone. After all, it was Henry's fault that his wife was dead.

HENRY

"**Mum said you** saw something last night," Ned said. "What was it?"

Henry pretended to be confused. He lifted his coffee to his lips and felt the steam rise up. It was a shame it was so hot – a drink was the perfect way to buy time when Henry was unsure how to answer a question.

"It was nothing," Henry said at last, hoping that Ned would dismiss the topic altogether.

"Bullshit."

Henry looked up at his wife who was standing next to him and she raised her eyebrows as if to say: *don't fight him on this. You know he's right. Just leave it be.* Worry flicked across her face as she looked at their son, and Henry wished he knew what she was thinking. Yes, he could still read the little tells on her face and much of their unspoken language had remained intact, but there was something new inside Madeline that Henry could not touch. She came to him in waves; sometimes she let her emotions crash over him like she did last night. Other times, he barely rode the crest of her thoughts, sitting like white foam on the top of her heart and never seeing anything underneath the surface. Today he was on the crests.

Madeline gave one last concerned look over Ned before

turning to slice up apples for their grandchildren to take to school. Henry blew on his coffee and watched the steam billow away from him as he recalled what he saw the night before. He swore that there had been a figure outside, but there couldn't have been. It didn't make sense for a person to be lurking about behind the cottage and besides, they had vanished before Henry could really process what he had seen. The figure definitely had an axe and had been about to swing at the tree opposite the window before Henry had blinked the apparition away.

"Right. Well. Time for work," Ned said, downing the last of his coffee and standing up, the chair legs screeching against the kitchen tiles.

Henry watched his son lift his rucksack onto his shoulder. He was standing in front of the window and the light transformed him into a silhouette. That was when Henry saw the figure again and remembered where he recognised it. The strange shadow lurking in the night was with him in his coma. As Ned raised his arms to pull his bag on, Henry saw the axe in his hands. Each dark finger rolled around the handle and his head turned to face his father. Henry shook his head as Ned made his way out of the cottage. He heard the car door shut and the engine start.

"It was Ned," Henry said at last, when he was sure the car had driven away.

"What was?" Madeline asked, without turning around.

"Last night."

"You mean outside? Don't be ridiculous. He was asleep last night."

"No, I know. It wasn't really him. It was only what I saw."

Madeline kept her back to Henry, but he heard her put the knife down hard on the counter. She leaned forwards and he could tell that she was putting all of her weight onto her hands, holding herself up. She dropped her head so her neck sunk down lower than her shoulders. Something was pressing on her mind. Henry wasn't sure what it was, so he carried on explaining himself.

"I think I saw Ned in my dream."

"You had a dream last night?" Madeline asked flatly.

"Not last night. My coma. I'm struggling to remember exactly what it was, but I think I saw him there. A shadow with an axe."

"If he was just a shadow, how do you know it was Ned?" Madeline opened the cupboard to get some bags for the apple slices.

"His face. There was a flash…it must have been when it was storming. I saw him again last night through the window."

"But you were awake last night."

"I know."

"Look, Henry," Madeline said, finally turning around, "I don't know what you want me to say."

"Don't you believe me?" Henry looked at her face and saw that it was blank.

"If you say it happened, then I believe you."

"But you're upset."

"I'm not upset." Madeline's face was still unemotional.

"You are. There's nothing to you right now. I've annoyed you. What is it?"

"Nothing," Madeline started to say, but Henry shot her a look that begged for the truth. "You saw his face."

"Yes?"

"And not mine? I'm sorry. It's selfish. After all you've been through. But you never dreamed about me?"

She began dumping the apple slices into the bags before tying them shut violently. Grabbing Lacey and Kyle's schoolbags off the hooks by the door, she shoved the snacks into the front pockets. Her movements were jerky and abrupt. Henry didn't have any of the right words. There was nothing he could say to reassure her, but he would try his best.

"The reason you weren't there was because it was a dark

place. You're my absolute joy. There was no space for you in that nightmare. It wasn't like going on vacation. I was trapped. You were – are – my freedom. How could I crave you if you were there?" he said.

Madeline nodded, seemingly satisfied with this answer.

"Do you think I'm crazy?" he asked.

"No. Of course I don't. But…why Ned?"

"I'm not sure. It feels important, but I don't know yet."

Henry watched as his wife let out a deep sigh. He hadn't noticed that she had been holding her breath. She nodded and went to wake up Lacey and Kyle. Henry watched her go into their grandchildren's bedroom. As she turned to leave the kitchen, her bathrobe came undone a little to show the bright pink pyjamas Lacey had got her. They had a pattern of white high heels printed across them in alternating styles and angles. He smiled to himself at how ill-suited they were for her. She did everything she could to please her family.

He went to their bedroom to get dressed. It still didn't feel like his home. The quilt on the bed wasn't the one he remembered. It felt like he had walked through a mirror into Wonderland. Everything seemed ordinary on the surface, but it was in the details that this place was unwelcoming. There used to be a photograph of him from Ned's graduation on Madeline's bedside table. Where had it gone? He looked around the room and couldn't see it. Had she hated seeing his smile so much? Going over to the table and opening the drawer, Henry covered his mouth with his hand when he saw the picture frame.

His own face smiled up at him from behind the glass. It was taken before anything unforgivable happened to the Belvideres. Ned hadn't met Karen. They still had their old house. Their future was undetermined as far as they knew. Henry picked up the photograph and examined it more closely.

Madeline was always meticulous with the housework. Every Saturday she had her routine. Henry would often wake up to the sounds of her moving around the bedroom. When he turned over, she'd be standing there with a cloth, dusting the bedside table and all the knick-knacks she kept on it, including the photograph. From the looks of it now, it hadn't been wiped down since before Henry was hospitalised.

He took it with him over to the window, opening the curtains. There was nobody outside. There never was. Holding the photo up so the morning sun caught the glass he frowned as he examined the smudges. There wasn't any dust, which meant it had been kept in the drawer for a while, just as he suspected. There were spots dotted all over it that streaked down in lines. It took Henry a couple of seconds to realise that they were tears. There were fingerprints all around the edges of the glass. He could photo frame his wife in bed, wearing those ridiculous pyjamas and gripping this picture between her shaking hands, crying onto his smile from decades ago. That was when he saw one fingerprint in the middle of the photo over his face. Had she been blocking him out or trying to touch him?

Henry heard the floorboards outside the room squeak. He knew she'd be coming in here next to get changed. Dashing over to the bedside table, he put the picture back in the drawer and shut it. Finding some clothes in the wardrobe that looked like his, he got dressed. He couldn't remember owning them as he did up the buttons on the blue shirt. Did he buy this? Everything seemed to be so inconsequential. There was nothing he wanted apart from his family, but something lingered in the space between them. *Why Ned?* Madeline had asked.

Truthfully, Henry couldn't answer. It was hard to explain. He knew that he knew, he just didn't know what that was yet. There was absolutely no other way to phrase it, and Madeline couldn't possibly understand. It wasn't her fault. How could he explain to her that the answers to all their questions were lost somewhere inside his head? When she came into the bedroom, he tried his best to read her mind, failing just as he expected he would.

"Madeline?" he asked.

"Yes?"

"What are you thinking?"

She looked at him and nibbled on her bottom lip the way she always did when she was trying to dance around a question.

"I thought today we'd go to the shops. Get some stuff in. We're out of almost everything; it's ridiculous. Then I wanted to spend some time in the garden, before we have to go to the police station," she said.

Henry knew she was answering a different question to the one he had asked, but he didn't point it out. Instead, he nodded and fumbled around in the drawer under the bed to pull out a pair of shoes. He watched the tide of his wife's mind pull away from him, but didn't complain. After all, he couldn't demand that she give him all of herself when he couldn't do the same for her.

Henry wheezed a little and Madeline went to his side of the bed to his oxygen tank, which she wheeled over to him. She helped him fit the tube into his nostrils and pulled the elastic straps around his ears. Her face was a different picture up close. He could see every blemish, each wrinkle, and he loved all of her. Henry knew that no matter what had happened, she would take care of him, just as she always had.

"I'm looking forwards to meeting Detective Parry," he said.

"Why's that?"

"Maybe she'll be able to tell me more about what happened."

"Oh. Yes. Maybe."

Madeline stood up so abruptly that she nearly tripped over Henry's tank. She smiled at him, but picked at the skin around her thumbs with her fingernails. He thought about the picture of him tucked into the drawer. He had become her secret. She'd cried over him, mourned him, and now he was back. Henry wondered if part of her didn't want him back, or if she had already shut him away in a drawer in her mind.

ELEN

Elen **drummed her** fingers on the desk as she watched the last few minutes go by before her interview with the Belvideres. It would be a long evening and she had to make sure she did this right. Her father had called Ned an 'anti-man.' Something a long time ago had taken all the humanity out of him. Thanks to Dan's research that afternoon, Elen finally knew what that was.

She stared at the news articles that Dan had found online and had printed off for her. As was typical of him, he'd categorised them all by date and fitted them neatly into a folder with the case number on the front. He was taking the last deep swallow of coffee before putting the empty mug down on a coaster. He pushed it a millimetre to the left until it was perfectly centred and then smiled absently. His soft brown eyes turned hard as he read over the notes on his computer. As 4 pm hit, an alarm went off on his watch. He stood up abruptly, pushed his chair under his desk, and switched off his computer monitor. Reaching into a desk drawer, he popped a mint into his mouth and slipped a spare pen into his breast pocket. When Dan saw Elen looking at him, he smiled. Holding out a hand for the file – which Elen passed to him without a word – he straightened his tie with the other hand.

"Are you ready for this?" he asked.

"Yeah. I think we've finally got something that will crack one of them. And now we can talk to Henry properly… A lot of good can come from this."

Dan nodded and held the office door open for her as they made their way down the corridor to the interrogation room. They were under strict orders from Marcus to avoid saying 'interrogation' at all costs though. These were only 'interviews' to 'follow up,' and more police jargon that danced around what they really meant. Even so, there were some things that Elen had to face head on.

"Dan? I just…I just wanted to say that…what I mean is—"

"Spit it out, El. Don't have all day."

There were a lot of people who found Dan rude. Some people saw him as a freak. He was too fussy with where his belongings went and had to be punctual for everything, right down to the minute. He spoke plainly and honestly. For some, these were off putting qualities, but Elen found them reassuring. There was so much in her life that involved lying and euphemisms. What Elen needed in a partner was someone unafraid of the truth and a person who prided himself on every minor detail.

"Thank you," she said.

"What for?"

"I know you've got other things on your plate besides this case. And I know you don't understand why I've become so attached to it. I don't think anyone gets that. Not really. But you've helped me anyway. You've stuck by me and backed me up. I'm grateful for that. We know better than anyone that people rarely say what they mean, but I have to say it now. Thank you."

Dan looked at her and, as she spoke, confusion flickered across his face. They reached the end of the corridor where they turned onto another one. Elen stopped walking when she saw the Belvidere family sitting on chairs outside the interview room. She stood still in the corner with Dan looking at them all waiting.

"I'm just doing my job," he said.

"Yeah. But it's more than that. You've been a good friend to me."

"Well, you know..." Dan trailed off and looked down, seemingly unsure of how to deal with anything really heartfelt.

Elen nodded. She did know. Looking past Dan at the family she was about to crack apart, Elen let out a deep breath. As if sensing her thoughts, Ned's head snapped up and he locked eyes with her. She stepped back involuntarily and swore she caught a smile on his lips. Clenching her fists, she marched towards the Belvideres with Dan next to her, matching every stride down the long corridor. When they all stood face-to-face, Elen looked at Henry for the first time since he'd woken up.

He looked like a different man. The one from the hospital had been close to death. He had been still and his arms had been packed with tubes. This one was still attached to an oxygen tank, but his cheeks were pink and he moved with blood and life. She held the door to the interrogation room open for him and his wife got up to help him, but Dan quickly waved her away. The way she stared after Elen made her shiver, but Elen was saving her for last. Madeline knew exactly what was going on here. Elen might need Henry and Ned to fill in the story, but Madeline was the key. She would tie it all together. Elen knew it.

The interrogation room was normally bare, but they had tried to make it as comfortable as possible. The walls were grey and the floor tiles were a similar shade. In the centre was a metal table and matching chairs, and they were all bolted to the floor. There wasn't supposed to be anything stimulating in sight, but Dan had made arrangements to have cushions put on all the chairs and for a jug of water with some glasses to be set on a tray on the table.

Elen and Dan sat across the table from Henry. Dan took out a notebook and pen, crossed his legs, and sat back in his chair. The entire conversation was going to be recorded and there was a security camera in the corner, but Dan preferred to take his own notes too. He said he liked to observe the smallest, human details with his own eyes.

"We're recording this conversation. Can you confirm you understand this?" Elen asked.

"Yes."

"This means we require an audible answer to every question. Understood?"

"Yes."

"Please state your full name and age."

"Henry Dylan Belvidere. Sixty seven."

Ordinarily, Elen found that people glanced at the recorder with apprehension when the interview started, but Henry leaned forwards and looked directly at her. He didn't even bother regarding Dan, whose presence sometimes made people nervous. This made Elen feel as though she was being interrogated somehow.

"I recognise your voice," Henry said.

"You do?"

"You came to see me in the hospital. I don't remember exactly what you said. My mind was fuzzy during that time. But I recall that you had a kind voice. I was right."

"Thanks," Elen paused and shifted in her seat. "Listen, Mr Belvidere –"

"You can call me Henry. This whole thing will be less frightening if you call me Henry."

"Henry…you're frightened? Why?"

"I'm not sure," Henry said, sitting back a little. "I've been having these bad dreams. But I don't know if it matters."

"It might. Let's start at the beginning. Do you remember how you got to the beach?"

"I think…I think Ned was taking me fishing. We used to do things like that together."

"You think? Do you not remember?" Elen watched Henry frown as he tried to sort through his muddled memories. "It's okay, Henry. Here," she said, pouring him a glass of water and passing it over to him.

"Thank you. It was a trip we'd talked about taking for a little while. One last time before I got really bad," he said, tapping the oxygen tank with a hand, "but I don't remember actually going there. Though I suppose I must have done if that was where I was found."

"So you remember nothing from that day?"

"No. I'm sorry."

"What about from the coma? You mentioned dreams? Anything from before you woke up?"

Henry lifted the glass of water to his lips and his hands shook. A little splashed up around the curve of the glass and landed on his face, between his nose and upper lip. With the back of his hand, Henry wiped the water away and put the glass back down. Dan eyeballed the water dribbling down the side of the coaster-less glass to the table and shifted with obvious discomfort.

"I– I keep seeing a man with an axe," he said, stammering a little. "In my coma, I dreamed about a man with an axe chopping down a tree. It was a special tree. One from a house I used to live in. I thought I saw him again last night. He was going to take down the tree by my bedroom window. When I blinked he was gone, so I must have been dreaming, although I swore I was awake."

"Did you recognise him?"

Henry bit his lip and breathed in as much air as he could. Elen leaned forwards and placed her hand on the table in front of Henry. It was a technique she had learned a long time ago, and used many times when people were on the verge of becoming upset. She recognised the twitches in the face, the dropping of the gaze, and reached out. It was a way of holding a person's hand without touching them. Sometimes it helped to just see someone else moving close to comfort them. Henry angled himself to be nearer to her again, as if he also wanted answers.

"Yes. My son," he said at last, taking another mouthful of water from the glass.

"You've been dreaming about Ned taking down trees?" When Henry nodded, Elen opened one of the folders that contained photographs from the scene of the incident and removed one, passing it over to him. "Do you know this place?"

Elen didn't look at the photograph. It was one she had seen before many times. She spent her time studying Henry's face as he looked at it. She knew every detail of the picture, from the bench Henry sat on during the storm to the placements of the branches on the tree above it.

"…yes. I'm not sure from where though."

"That was where you were found. The day you went to the beach a storm blew in. A particularly nasty storm. The general theory is that you went to that bench underneath the tree to shelter from the rain. A branch broke off in the wind and hit you on the head. That was how you ended up in the coma."

Henry nodded. Elen knew he understood the words, but not how everything connected just yet. Getting someone to remember things they had forgotten was an arduous process, one that she had rehearsed many times with her mother who sat in her chair by the window and existed in another time and place than Elen, who had to jolt her back to being here and now.

"We couldn't find your oxygen tank," she continued. "We scoured the area for it. There was also no sign of any fishing equipment. You weren't dressed for the weather. No bags with you at all. Ned was nowhere in sight. Do you ever wonder if your dreams are connected to these events in more ways than you realise?"

"Dream analysis? Not very by-the-book, is it?" Henry smiled faintly.

"Perhaps not on the surface. But my job is in the details. Every last one of them," Elen smiled back, before seriousness descended onto her face. "It was a tree branch that hit you in the head in real life. It's Ned tearing down trees that haunt your dreams."

"What are you getting at?"

"Is there any reason why Ned would want to hurt you?" Elen asked, already knowing the answer.

Henry folded his arms and Elen knew she was losing him. This family was starting to drive her mad. How could they stick so close together when it was obvious something was seriously wrong? She looked over at Dan, who tightened his lips in his classic *don't push it* look. Elen raised an eyebrow to say back: *I've got this.*

"You have your language too," Henry said. "Madeline and I do. That way of speaking without words. It shows closeness. You think you're the only people with questions? You don't think I've got a hundred of my own? If you know something I don't, just tell me, because I'm sick of being in the dark. I spent a fortnight trapped in my own mind. I'd hate to spend more time caught in others."

"Can you go get Ned for me?" Elen asked Dan, without taking her eyes off Henry.

"Elen…what?" Dan whispered.

"Please. This concerns them both now. I think Henry has told us all he knows for the time being and we need to speak to Ned next. But Henry wants answers too, right? I don't see the harm in letting him listen."

Dan shook his head. She knew that he understood exactly what she was planning on doing, but there was no way he could deny this request without Henry getting upset. She'd designed it so that this seemed to still be all about helping Henry, even though it was rapidly becoming about catching Ned out. Elen was certain that Henry's dreams were linked to the truth. It might not be scientific or objective, but there were too many similarities for it to be completely meaningless.

Without any further protest Dan left and returned a few moments later with Ned. The room immediately felt colder when Ned walked in. Henry pulled his oxygen tank away from the fourth chair so that Ned could sit down. Dan settled himself back next to Elen and reopened his notebook on a fresh page, taking down notes without hesitation. No doubt he was recording Ned's clothes, demeanour, and body language before he even spoke.

Elen watched Ned glance down at the photograph she'd shown to Henry, but saw no traces of recognition on his face, even though they had the security footage that placed him thirty metres from that spot. He smiled with his mouth, but his eyes were dead and glassy. He was the last one to sit down and the first one to speak. His voice cut through the room like a razor; it was delicate and precise, dissecting the emotions in the room as though he wanted to study each one individually and at his leisure.

"Detective Parry. A pleasure once again," he said, holding out his hand.

"Mr Belvidere," Elen said, ignoring the offer of a handshake.

Unlike his father, Ned didn't give her a more familiar name to use, and he wrinkled his nose at her refusal to shake his hand. Perhaps he didn't mean to give so much of himself away this quickly, but Elen knew how much he valued respect now. This was a small personal tick, but could prove crucial in extracting the truth from him later on.

"Naturally, we have to record this conversation for our records. Is this acceptable to you?" Elen asked, aware of Dan's raised eyebrows as she began to speak more formally.

"Yes. That's fine."

"So we'll require audible answers only, please."

"Of course," Ned said, looking over at Henry with a blank expression. "Does my father have to be here for this? You had a private chat with him. Don't I get any privacy?"

"Your privacy is of the utmost importance to us, I can assure you. However, so is your father's wellbeing. I'm sure you know far more than I do about how confusing this has been for him."

"And me," Ned cut in.

"Yes. And you. We just want you all to get the answers you're after. That's what you want, isn't it? What's best for your family?"

Elen smiled, knowing that she had him in the palm of her hand. Ned's nostrils flared. It was so quick that any normal person would never have noticed it, but she did, and she knew Dan would have as well. The cameras and the voice recorder couldn't pick up the tiny flecks of rage that spasmed across his face in flashes. Ned dropped his angry visage as quick as he had revealed it and agreed.

"I was wondering if you could explain something to me," Elen began. "You and your mother both stated on multiple occasions that Henry went on this trip alone. To fish, right?"

"That's right," Ned said.

"Could you take a look at this photo?" Elen said, pulling a picture out of the file and sliding it over the table to Ned.

He was in the photograph paying for parking at the beach. Ned sat back and rubbed his eyes before taking a second look, and then he laughed. Elen knew that she had something.

"That's me," he said.

"And where are you?"

"Looks like the car park where I dropped my dad off."

"So he didn't go on this trip alone?"

Henry looked at Ned with confusion. Elen had seen that look before on many people's faces. The widened eyes, slightly parted lips, and lifeless hands were what a real epiphany looked like. She wanted to reach out to Henry again, but this time take his hand and hold it properly. It seemed right to hold onto him the way she did when her mother was on the cusp of losing her memory. She knew Ned sensed her bond with his father. Ned leaned so far forwards that his chest was pressed flat against the edge of the table.

"He did. I dropped him off. The trip was his, but I had to take him there, of course," Ned said.

"Of course. And what about his oxygen tank? His luggage? Fishing equipment? Hotels?"

"Dad said he'd sorted all the arrangements. As for everything else, I couldn't tell you. I dropped him off and that was it. Honestly, Dad, what are you like?"

Elen could tell that Henry had no idea what was true and what wasn't, but she was certain Ned was using his lapse in memory as a way to dance around the truth. It was time for Elen to increase the pressure.

"Well, we couldn't find any trace of anything. Just Henry by himself."

"I don't know what to tell you."

"Still, you must be so happy to have him back at home."

"Delighted."

"Especially after you've dealt with so much loss already," Elen said.

Ned froze in his seat and stared at her. There was always a fear with interrogation and questioning that the person being questioned could end it at any point. They could only be held for so long. They could ask for a lawyer whenever they wanted. Unless they were being charged, they couldn't be kept. Ned had no obligation to answer anything. Elen didn't fear these outcomes though. The way Ned raised his chin when he was provoked told her he was proud. She saw his hubris burning inside him. This was a man who believed he could get out of any mess he wanted by his own brains alone. They had entered into a game of chess now. Each move counted and neither would call the match off until there was a clear winner.

ELEN

Ned looked over the printout and for a moment, Elen thought she caught whispers of horror cross his face. It was a news article from a few years ago with a bold headline that was slightly smudged from it being snatched out of the printer. It stated, unemotionally: LOCAL WOMAN DIES IN CRASH. Ned pressed his hands together and held them to his lips. It would have looked like a prayer on anyone else, but not on Ned. His eyes were vacuous, devoid of all colour. They were black holes set in the space of his mind, behind which dwelled the singularity of his grief – the point from which all his pain imploded. They flickered over the words on the page and as though pulling them apart, sucking them out of time.

Elen had already read it. She had memorised every sentence accidentally as she had poured over it, unsure of exactly how she would use it, but knowing that this would be how she cracked Ned.

"What's this got to do with anything?" he said, his voice not as sharp as it had been before.

"You loved Karen, didn't you?"

Ned didn't say anything. He sat back and folded his arms.

"I've seen her grave, you know," Elen said.

He banged the flats of his palms on the table. Henry jumped and Ned's head snapped around. He locked his stare on his father. Elen knew she had him.

"You have no right to go there," Ned said.

"It's a public space. *I was grounded while you filled the skies*," she said, quoting Karen's epitaph. "It's a lovely song. I think you're the only person I've met who knows it."

"If you think you can create some sort of affinity with me, you're mistaken," he whispered, as if lowering his volume would help him control his emotions.

"She used to sing it in the garden," Henry said.

"Shut up, Dad."

"She did. Terrible singer, but then again, I didn't think much about the song. She made it sound fantastic though."

"Shut up," Ned hissed. "You don't get to talk about her."

"Why's that?" Elen asked. "Could it be something to do with this?"

She pointed to a highlighted paragraph that put Henry in the driver's seat when Karen was killed. Ned stared at Elen so intensely that she thought she could feel his eyes in the back of her skull. Henry leaned over to read the article. Without breaking his gaze at Elen, Ned pushed the piece of paper over to Henry's side of the table. Elen was first to look away, only so she could study Henry's face as he explored the contents of the newspaper article.

At first there was a look of surprise, but it gradually resolved into one of grief. He laid a hand on his oxygen tank and struggled to breathe, but it was from the act of processing this horror more than his condition.

"You already knew this, Henry," Elen said.

"I did. But —"

"But you've been so preoccupied with yourself to think about her. The entire family has," Ned said.

"It was years ago, son."

"No. To me it's every day."

Elen was shocked to see genuine sadness in Ned. His

bottom lip quivered, and he squeezed his eyes shut. The intimidation game was over. Ned didn't appear able to look at the

world right now. She felt numb then. Her father had given her the perspective she needed to crack Ned – the anti-man – but she didn't think she'd feel so guilty about it. Karen's death was the key, but it was also the most painful experience of this man's life. Whether he felt remorse now or not, he used to be whole. He used to love.

"What happened, Mr Belvidere?" she asked Ned.

"You know what happened. You read the article."

"I do and I did. But that doesn't cover everything, does it? It doesn't tell me what happened to you. That's what this is about isn't it?"

"Everyone has forgotten."

"And you could never forget her. She was perfect. She filled your skies."

"She was. She was perfect."

"And your father is the last person who should be forgetting."

"Yes!" Ned shouted and Elen knew she had him.

"Why?"

"Because...because..."

"Why, Ned?"

"Because it's his fault!" Ned screamed.

Silence fell around them so hard they felt it break on their shoulders as it crashed down. Henry covered his face with his hands and rocked himself back and forth. Dan stood up and went around the table to put his arm around Henry, who seemed simultaneously younger and older in the face of this revelation. They stood up together and Dan gestured with his head that Elen should follow. The three of them left Ned in tears in the interrogation room, banging his head softly on the metal tabletop.

Dan sent Henry down to the seating area where his wife and grandchildren were, before turning back to Elen. He rubbed his right hand that was obviously cramping from frantically taking notes for forty-five minutes.

"I hope you know what you're doing, El. I trust you, but you have to be careful. These are people's lives," he said.

"I know. Believe me, I understand that. But it's clear now that Ned is harbouring real anger towards his father. We have that down now. It's concrete. Undeniable."

"Even so, perhaps you should take a break for now."

"Right, I'll tell you what I need to do. You go in there and retake his statement on everything that's happened. Go over all of it in detail. We've brought this emotion out of him. If he's forced to relive it in this state of mind...I think he'll crack."

"Elen," Dan said, raking his hands through his hair, "I don't know if –"

"I'm the lead on this one, Dan. Do it."

"Fine. And what'll you do?"

"I'm going to talk to his mother."

"Just...be nice, Elen. We have to do our jobs, yes, but we can do them with a little tact."

If she wasn't elated from reaching an emotional breakthrough with Ned, that comment might have annoyed her, but Elen only smiled and carried on down the corridor towards the family. Madeline folded her arms when she saw Elen coming, closing herself off as much as she could.

"Mrs Belvidere, could you please come with me? I want to have a quick chat with you," Elen said as cordially as she could manage.

Madeline followed her without a word. Elen knew that Henry must have said something to her while they were waiting. It couldn't have been much – there wasn't enough time for everything – but Karen must have come up. Elen led her up to the conference room. There would be no line of questions. They sat next to each other by the large wooden table. Elen saw Madeline tapping her feet, but the sound of it was muffled by the thick navy carpet. She had cups of tea brought in for them on a tray with milk and sugar. Madeline stared at the drinks as though they were a trap.

They looked at each other over the corner of the table. While she left Ned to stew in his nerves, it was time to unravel Madeline. If she got everything she could out of the family – enough to make Ned believe they had turned against him at least – then she would have the best possible chance at cracking him. She was so close now. Elen knew beyond doubt that Madeline was at the centre of this, but she wasn't confused like her husband. She wasn't calculating like her son. Madeline ran on love. She had chosen to protect her family and stuck with it. Her faith in love was unshakeable.

"Henry seems to be doing well," Elen began, conversationally. "You've done so much for him. It really shows."

Madeline nodded but stayed silent.

"Of course, you'll be aware of his dreams. Those nightmares about that figure."

Another nod.

"Must be difficult knowing what to say about all that."

Madeline sighed and took a sip of tea.

"I'm sure the loss of Karen makes it even harder for you all."

"What?" Madeline finally said.

"Well, it's obvious, isn't it? Ned blames Henry so much for that. Doesn't seem like he'll ever forgive him."

"That wasn't Henry's fault."

Madeline was being split in half. Elen could see the pain in her eyes as she found herself caught up between her husband and her son. She played with the hem of her shirt, tugging at a loose thread. Madeline wrapped it around her forefinger and pulled it, trying to snap it off, but only managing to cut off the circulation to her fingertip, turning the skin white and bloodless.

"Can I tell you a story?" Elen asked, waiting for the third

nod before continuing. "A few years back there was this man walking his dog along the beach. The same beach Henry was at. It was the summer. So hot the sun could boil your skin off. A few yards ahead of him these kids were walking barefoot. One of them tripped over a rock. Hurt his foot. In anger, he picked up the rock, chucked it, and off they went thinking nothing more of it.

"The dog saw the rock and perked his ears up. Everything is a game to a dog. That's why people love them so much. He pulled his owner over to it. The man picked the rock up and held it in the sunlight. That was when he realised – this was no ordinary rock. It was a lump of ambergris."

"What's that?" Madeline asked, speaking at last.

"To put it crudely: whale vomit. But, to be more specific, it's a very special material. Uses include making wonderful perfumes, ironically enough. Something that should be disgusting can be used for something beautiful. Which is sort of the point. It's worth an insane amount of money. More than you'd ever know. This man and his dog, well, they took the lump home, didn't they? Made around 70k on it, in the end. Crazy.

"And that's just it. Whale vomit. Something that shouldn't be worth a damn to anyone: this ugly, old, white lump, tossed aside on a beach like it means absolutely nothing. And yet, as fate would have it, it turned out to be far more valuable, more precious, than anyone realised."

Madeline looked at her hands going limp in her lap. For a few minutes she didn't move. Her face fell and she appeared almost comatose herself. It was hard to tell if her eyes were even open because she was looking so far down to the floor between her feet. Abruptly, her arm shot out and she grabbed the tea, gulping it down. It was like she wished it was something else, as though the faster she drank it, the closer it was to alcohol.

"Is that what you think happened then?" she said.

"You tell me."

"Do you think you're clever? Coming up with some metaphor to describe my husband. Whale vomit, is he? Do you think I just threw him away, is that it?"

"Madeline –"

"Mrs Belvidere."

"Mrs Belvidere, I only meant to suggest that whatever happened to your husband must have made you realise how precious he is to you. More so than before."

Madeline stood up and walked over to the window, wrapping her arms around herself. She stood so close to the glass that her breath steamed up the area in front of her. Leaning forwards, she pressed her head against the condensation and shut her eyes. Elen walked over to her. They stood side-by-side looking out of the window together.

The view from the conference room wasn't an impressive one. They could see the car park and the road, but that was it. Everywhere they looked was grey. Marcus walked out of a side door and rested up against the wall, lighting up a cigarette. Elen couldn't help but look at him.

"Who's he?" Madeline asked, softly.

"My boss. And a friend. He's had it rough lately."

"He's handsome. My Henry was such a handsome young man. That's how I see him today."

"Look, I'm sorry if I offended you before, Mrs Belvidere, I just –"

"You didn't offend me. The idea did. The very thought that I could ever not see how precious Henry was to me. That was what offended me," she said, looking at Elen again. "When I look at Henry, he's still the man I married. But it's the same with Ned. I see him, and he's the baby I gave birth to."

"It must be hard to stand in the middle of them," Elen said.

Madeline laughed quietly and nodded. Elen knew that Madeline understood she meant, but neither one elaborated on the specifics. The space that the two women had between them was starting to disappear. In another world, Elen thought that she could have been in this family. At this thought, she wanted to throw herself into Madeline's arms. Elen was immediately embarrassed by her imagination and looked away from her, trying to conjure up images of her own mother – of Beverley Parry before she lost herself.

"I'm sorry, I didn't mean to laugh," Madeline said, misreading Elen's shame as disdain. "It's only that it was a bit of an understatement. It has been hard."

"Perhaps…perhaps you could tell me about Karen?"

"She was special. I was happy to have her as my daughter-in-law. I don't have a single bad thing to say about her. Nobody does. Least of all our Ned."

"And the accident?"

"Ned hasn't been the same since then," she said. "Sorry, could I have some water?"

Elen went over to the water cooler in the corner and filled up a paper cup. She put it on the table and sat down, encouraging Madeline to do the same. Her walk over to the chair was slow, like she was somewhere else suddenly. She looked around the room as though there were no walls, no ceiling. She lifted the cup to her mouth and sipped daintily.

"Can you tell me what happened?" Elen asked, giving away no sign that she already knew the details.

"Henry was driving. They were heading along Ffordd Pentre Du back home. Henry was struggling to breathe. He looked down for a second. One second. A car came around the corner. It was nothing more than an accident, really. Henry had been having health problems. Another complication before he was finally diagnosed with emphysema. It was such a tragic time for it. Ned never stopped blaming him. I can see it every time he looks at his father. He detests everything about him."

Tears welled up in Madeline's eyes and dripped down her nose. Her shoulders rolled back as if a huge weight had finally been lifted from them. Elen reached across the table and laid her hand in front of Madeline, palm down, just like she had done with Henry. However, unlike Henry, Madeline seized it between her own hands and clasped Elen tightly.

"But Ned knows it wasn't Henry's fault, right? They investigated it at the time. Open and shut accident," Elen said.

"He must know. Deep down, I'm sure he does. But even so, Ned needs someone to blame. He will never survive his grief without a target. Henry made sense to him. I know he's wrong for it. I can't talk him down from his rage. So the whole family just rides it out. His happiness was taken from him, so now none of us get any."

"Madeline," Elen said unable to stop herself, but she wasn't corrected back to a cold *Mrs Belvidere*. "Has Ned ever tried to move on? Or find happiness in something else?"

"No. God, no, how could he? Just after receiving so much joy and being instantly robbed of it?"

"Wait. What do you mean, 'receiving so much joy?'"

Madeline dropped Elen's hand like it had become red hot and it hit the table with a thud. They both jumped at the sound, unaware of how transfixed they had become in the story. Madeline laid a hand over her stomach and Elen sat back. That was all she needed to see. She knew.

"Karen was pregnant, wasn't she?" Elen asked.

"Yes," Madeline nodded, starting to choke on the beginnings of tears. "Their third. Henry was driving her home from a hospital appointment. Ned will never forgive him. Not ever."

This was it. Now Elen knew the full story. This was the final piece of the puzzle of Ned Belvidere and it was all Elen needed to work a confession out of him. It was the last thing she wanted though. This situation was less black and white than Elen realised. The only way to get through this would be to hold onto the image of Henry, discarded on a beach like he meant nothing. 'An eye for an eye' had no place in Elen's ethos. Human lives couldn't be traded and now she had a job to do.

NED

As Ned sat in the interrogation room, he wondered what would have happened if Galen had been born. When he was brave or drunk enough to face the thought of his unborn son, he let him creep into his mind and play there. Galen Elis Belvidere. The name was always on his lips – a whisper away from being spoken. Ned turned to the one-way window which appeared to him like a mirror and looked at himself. Galen materialised in his arms as he folded them across this stomach. This is how small he would have been the day of his birth and how little he stayed in Ned's mind, even though he had actually no bigger than an onion when Karen died. At least, that was what they had read online, which had led to endless jokes about their perfect onion baby.

They had chosen the name a few weeks into the pregnancy. They had picked one for a boy and one for a girl, because they still had some waiting to do before they found out the sex. With Lacey they had spent several months deciding what to call her and Kyle had been 'Baby Boy Belvidere' for four days after the birth, but with Galen they had known immediately. Ned bounced his empty arms gently up and down and stared at the news article in front of him. Karen had been on her way to tell Ned the news. They were going to have a son. Ned stood up and began to pace around the interrogation room. How different would his life have been if she had made it home that day?

Ned sat at the table staring at the mess Lacey had left before getting a lift from a friend's mother to school. Kyle sat next to him with paper and crayons, scribbling excitedly and singing to himself without using any real words. Sighing, Ned got up and collected the plates, bringing them to the sink to wash up. He ran the water from the tap until it was so hot that steam rose in clouds and made the view through the window in front of him look misty. The tree in the garden with blossoming with delicate pink flowers and morning glories bowed daintily in the grass. He turned off the water and began to scrub the plates clean.

"Daddy!" Kyle squealed, and Ned turning around to see him holding up his finished drawing, puffing his chest out with pride. "I did it!"

"Yes, you did. That's a great picture, mate."

"Thanks," said Kyle, dropping everything and running into the living room.

Ned smiled after him, letting the murky water be sucked down the drain and wiping down the wet countertop. He went over to the table and picked up Kyle's drawing, furrowing his brow as he tried to figure out what it was supposed to depict. His son didn't have the art skills that Lacey had. Kyle had taken longer to learn to read and write too. In fact, Kyle had taken longer to do just about everything than his sister did, but he had a sweetness to him that was more than enough. Ned took the picture to the fridge, pinning it up with two of the alphabet magnets – a K and a B for Kyle's initials – and remembered the day he was most proud of his son.

Kyle had just met this new boy at the day nursery. When Ned had gone in to pick him up, he had been pulled aside by their teacher into a little office next to the playroom. He had found it ridiculous that he should refer to this person as a teacher – all the children had done all day was play and nap, but he had held his tongue. The office was a joke too; it had hardly been a place for business with the daffodil yellow beanbags in the corner and the cartoon posters all over the walls. The teacher had been very young, easily fifteen years Ned's junior, but had seemed friendly enough. She had sat on one side of the desk and gestured to Ned to sit opposite her.

"I just wanted to let you know what Kyle did today," she had begun.

Ned had been terrified immediately. No parent wanted to hear those words. It was far better to receive no news whatsoever. All Ned had wished for since he became a parent was for each day to pass uneventfully. That's why they had settled on 'Galen' as a name in the end. It was supposed to mean 'calm.' There was nothing better than a calm and quiet life. Ned had fidgeted in the chair and clasped his hands together.

"We had a new boy join the class today. Rhys. Nice, but a little withdrawn. Kyle won't be bringing his bear home today because he gave it to Rhys and wouldn't take it back. Almost threw a tantrum when we tried to get Rhys to return it. Apparently, Rhys was frightened to go to sleep at nap time because he has bad dreams, and the bear...what does Kyle call him..."

"Bernie," Ned had filled in the blank for her.

"Yes, Bernie. According to Kyle, Bernie fights off bad dreams. It did the trick. But I wanted to let you know how good that was and why Bernie isn't with Kyle at the moment."

This had been something all good parents should hope for when it comes to their children. If they started their lives out sharing and protecting people, surely they would continue to live productive and caring lives. As Ned stared across the kitchen at Kyle's drawing on the fridge, he began to see the vague resemblance of figures in the scribbles. He squinted and tilted his head until he could half make out the outline of a man in the middle and maybe a child at his side. A father and son. Ned's pride was cut short again by a knock at the front door. When he went to go see who it was, two fingers slid through the letterbox and a voice said: "Ned? Babe, it's me. Forgot my key again, didn't I?"

He opened the door to find Karen standing there next to the pram in which Galen sat, looking around wide-eyed at the world around him. She stood there in a sundress that clung a little to her body. The last remnants of her baby bump were still visible, but it was beautiful. It was proof of what she could do that he could not. It was evidence of their children's lives. She knew this and never made any attempt to hide her changing body from the world. The dress was blue with white daisies printed over it to match the flower she'd tucked behind her ear. Ned reached out to touch the petals and she smiled.

"From the park. Galen liked the flowers. He's happy today," she said.

She pushed the pram into the hallway and Ned unbuckled his son, lifting him up into the air and bringing him down to his chest. Galen rested his head on Ned's shoulder and wisps of his dark hair tickled Ned's neck. Karen folded up the pram and put it away in the storage cupboard under the stairs.

When Lacey came home from school, the five of them piled onto the sofa and put the television on. Lacey curled up next to Karen and Kyle snuggled in the crook of Ned's arm. Between them, Galen drifted off to sleep, warmed by the skin of his parents on either side. Ned looked down at him and felt safe. Galen would grow up surrounded by a family who would do everything they could to protect and care for him.

Ned beat his hands on top of the metal table in the interrogation room and howled. It sounded like his voice was trying to strangle him from within his throat. He knew he was being watched. They would see and hear everything, but his façade was slipping away. The words of the news article in front of him spun around in his mind. LOCAL WOMAN DIES IN CRASH. LOCAL WOMAN DIED IN CRASH. WOMAN DIED IN ACCIDENT. SHE DIED BY ACCIDENT. SHE DIED ON PURPOSE. KAREN DIED. KAREN DIED. KAREN DIED. KAREN DIED. KAREN DIED.

Detective Parry walked back in while Ned was slumped forwards, his forehead resting on the cool metal surface in front of him. He didn't need to look up to know it was her. He recognised the sound of her boots on the floor: hard and sharp steps that felt like they were stomping inside his skull. It was obvious she was staring at him. Who wouldn't stare at a grown man sat face down at a table?

"Mr Belvidere?" she asked after a few moments.

He detested her voice. It burrowed its way inside his brain and squirmed around there. It was a little nasally, the kind that cut through all the other sounds around it. If she was talking in a crowd of twenty people, her voice would be the only one that stood out. It was vile. It burst through all his thoughts, and all he wanted to do was picture Galen.

"I've been a good dad," he said.

"And your mother believes you've been a good son too. You have, haven't you?"

"Yes. I have."

"I think we should talk about your father." Her voice stabbed him. She was going to talk about Henry anyway, whether Ned wanted to or not and he knew it. "You blame him for what happened, don't you?"

Ned sat up and wiped his tears and damp cheeks with his sleeve. She had come in alone this time. The thin man with the notebook wasn't there and Ned supposed he was probably watching through the glass. His note-taking was meticulous and unstoppable. Ned couldn't imagine the other detective not watching the rest of the interview. That's what Detective Parry called it: an 'interview,' but it wasn't. This was an interrogation and Ned realised that. There was something smug about her. The softness of her lips and the hardness of her eyes was an expression he was able to recognise, as it was one he wore himself every day. She had everything she needed, but betrayed nothing until she was ready. Ned found himself admiring her for a moment, before remembering that he hated her.

"Of course I blame him. Silly old man has gone senile. How else do you explain what happened to him?" Ned said, knowing exactly what the detective was getting at.

"No. Not the beach. Karen. You blame him for what happened to Karen," she paused but Ned stayed silent. "It's not surprising. Especially given the circumstances."

She knows, Ned thought to himself.

"Your mother said something very interesting. Did you know that when she looks at you, she still sees her baby? The one she gave birth to? I thought that was very sweet."

Where is this going?

"I wonder if that's how you see Lacey and Kyle? Like your babies? Must be just awful then, to see them like that while having lost one as well."

This bitch...

"Your mother said his name was going to be Galen. A gorgeous name. Well-chosen. 'Robbed of joy' was how she described you after the incident."

Ned considered how much damage he could do if he jumped over the table right now and balled up his fists. How dare she say the name of his unborn child? She was using his pain against him and for that he wanted to hurt her. Ned pictured how quickly her lips would turn purple and welt up if he smacked her in that irritating little mouth.

"Henry didn't just take away Karen or Galen. How could

you love your other children when they reminded you of what you'd lost? And your father...must have been infuriating to see him every day when Karen would never come home. Your mother loves him so much. She loves all of you. That's what makes her so aggravating, isn't it? How could she defend the man who did this over you? Isn't it a clear choice? You must be going crazy, Mr Belvidere. Just crazy –"

"Stop talking," Ned warned.

She did as he asked for a moment. Her eyes appeared to warm to him as they watched each other, picking up on every twitch and tick of the other person. Detective Parry leaned back in her chair and brought her hands together, entwining the fingers of her left hand with those of her right. She brushed her thumbs over each other, and Ned fixated on them. He thought about how they were the perfect size to wrap his own hand around. They looked milky, soft, and so easy to snap out of place.

"I know I'm right. That's why you did it. You took Henry away and left him there. He was supposed to die. You wanted him to die," she began again.

"No."

"Yes. Yes, of course you did. His mistake ripped your world into pieces so small that they couldn't be put back together, and they didn't mean anything apart. But you never wanted to hurt him, did you, Ned?"

His ear pricked up at the sound of his first name. There was no judgement in her voice anymore. She was trying to soothe him. Slowly, she placed a hand on the lip of the table in front of her.

"No. I never wanted that," he said.

"I know you didn't. He hurt you, but it was all emotional. He was going to suffer, but it would be a result of confusion and longing, just like you. No torture. No physical pain. Just him missing his family until he slipped away. That's all you wanted, wasn't it? To let him slip away and take your grief with him."

She slid her hand over to him slowly and left it in front of
him, palm down on the metal. Ned stared at her hand and
studied the lines on it. There was a freckle below her middle
fingernail, and she was wearing a watch with a silver face
and leather strap. Karen used to have one similar to it. Ned
kept it in a box underneath his bed, vowing never to look at
it again. It's face was smashed from the car crash. The
hands were frozen at the time it happened.

"I'm here to help you," she whispered, "but I need you to
tell me what happened."

Ned placed his hand on the news article and pushed it
over to Detective Parry. She looked down at it, unsure of
what to do with it at first, before picking it up and slipping
it back into the folder.

"What else do you have in there?" he asked, nodding at
the folder.

"Photographs mostly. And a report," she said.

"What's the report for?"

"It's from Lacey's school. About possible neglect."

He looked back to the glass of the one-way window in the
interrogation room and tried to picture Galen in his arms
again like he had done earlier, but he wouldn't come to him.
Ned rubbed his forehead and felt the wrinkles and lines that
had split his skin since Karen died.

"Would you like to read it?" she asked.

"No. But you could...you could tell me what it says."

"Of course," she said, pulling the paper out of the folder.

"Thank you, Detective."

"My name is Elen," she said, pausing to refresh her
memory with the report before continuing. "It's from her
P.E. teacher. About Lacey's weight. She's losing a lot, you
know."

Ned nodded and then shook his head. Elen opened her
mouth to carry on, but stopped and put the report away. She
leaned forwards then and met him halfway over the table

until he could see under the fluorescent lights that her hair was dyed and there wasn't a trace of make up on her face. Women never came so close to him anymore. She smelled like coconuts.

"I never saw her again," he whispered.

"You did. Every day. You saw her every minute you were with your family. Which is somehow worse, isn't it?"

"I don't know how to make anything better. There's no money. With Karen's income gone and Dad...he has life insurance, you know. I was just trying to work things out."

"Leaving Henry at the beach was never going to do that."

"No, it wasn't."

"You did leave him there, didn't you?"

Elen put her hand back in front of him and he looked at the watch. He reached out and put his finger over the glass, stroking the edges of the circle. He had traced the cracks in Karen's with his finger. He had the pattern memorised perfectly – the slightly off-centre hole and the concentric circles around the outside, cut up with jagged lines that moved from the middle of the glass to the surrounding metal.

"Yes," Ned said. "I did."

"Tell me what happened. In your own words. Take your time."

That was exactly what Ned did. He relayed all the details to Elen about the crash and his feelings. He revisited the night he had decided to do it and begun making plans, right down to the bottom of every can or lager in the fridge. Ned went over the way he had treated Lacey and Madeline. All the words that needed to be said were said, until Ned had nothing left inside him to give the world. He held his arms across himself so that his elbows rested in each palm, and he caressed one like it was a baby's head.

"When I drove off, I saw him sitting on the bench staring out at the sea. That tree hung over him like the one my parents had in their old house. He carved our initials into it on my first day for school. HMN. He said it was our family tree – he used to think that was so funny. And then a branch snaps off this one that looks just like it and hits him. Sometimes I wonder if it was our tree, and whether that was my branch. But I don't know that it matters."

It didn't. Ned felt the weight that sat in place of his heart lift and give way to a rush of relief. It took another couple of hours to get his full statement down perfectly and for Detective Blackwood to come in and go over it, checking until it was consistent. The whole time, Ned looked down, seeing Galen resting in his arms, finally at peace. When it was all over, the handcuffs were snapped to Ned's wrists. Detective Parry had pulled his arms apart to bring them behind his back, and the apparition of Galen disintegrated as he became unborn once more.

LACEY

The drive home from the police station went on forever. Lacey and Kyle sat in the back with their grandparents in the front. On the way, their grandma had sat between them with Ned driving and Henry in the passenger seat. Now the space next to Lacey served as a reminder that their lives were changing forever. She turned herself away from the empty seat and looked out of the window. The car stopped as the row of traffic pulled up to a red light. They waited in front of a small house with a family in the front garden.

It was evening now and the last minutes of sunlight were disappearing fast behind the row of houses to the west. Lacey watched as a young girl sat cross-legged in the grass with three dolls around her, forming the circle of a secret meeting to which only her and her toys were privy. If Lacey had to estimate how old the child was, she'd say seven or eight, but Lacey was never any good at judging age. When she looked in the mirror herself, she couldn't believe that she was almost fifteen. It wasn't something she thought about often, but every now and then she would see a child who reminded her.

How much time was fourteen years? Lacey could measure

it by the years themselves, or by months, weeks, days, and even smaller scales of time, but it wasn't enough. She needed a way of quantifying her life that also captured how much she had lived, learned, and lost. What could over seven hundred Mondays tell her about what she was like? Was she a good person? Sometimes when she stood in front of her reflection, she'd paw at herself and wonder what made an adult a real grown up. She would tug the back of her shirt and ball the loose material into a fist so that the front of her top was taut against her skin. Even though she could see herself thinning out, she couldn't help but notice a softness to her body that betrayed her youth. She wasn't an adult yet and she knew it, but not in the same way as the little girl in front of the house.

The girl was the sort of child that was obviously going to grow into a beautiful young woman in a few years. She was tanned with rich blonde hair – a walking stereotype for a healthy young girl – and had a cherub quality about her. Lacey caught a glimpse of herself in the window and saw her narrow, pale features and stark black hair. Her grandparents always said she was beautiful, but weren't they obliged to say that? Whereas her dad... her dad. Lacey placed a hand on the empty seat next to her and wondered where he was. As she considered all the possibilities of what he was doing without them, a man walked out of the house and scooped the girl up into his arms.

He must have been her father, because when she squealed with delight they both smiled and looked identical. The car began to pull away before Lacey could examine his features any closer, and the two of them sped behind Lacey in a blur. She would never see them again. Lacey was sad about this and there was no other way to describe it. She had never met them and knew nothing about them, but as they disappeared, so too did Lacey's ability to answer the questions she had about them.

She fished around in her pocket for her earbuds, looking

for something to block the world out. As she pulled them out, she realised one earbud had fallen down and got caught through her belt loop. It didn't even cross her mind to take her time and thread the wire back through until it was free. Instead, she yanked it until the wire split all the way up the middle from where it parted to reach each earbud down to the jack on the end. Lacey stared at the divided earbuds as though she couldn't figure out what happened. They weren't broken – music would still play through them – and they could be stuck back together with glue or tape, but they weren't going to be the same as before. It was entirely her fault. She should have been more patient, more observant. Scrunching up the wires in her palm, she stuffed them back into her pocket, pleased to find the car turning onto gravel road that lead through the farm to the cottage.

The road was a mile long, but the length of it seemed to change with the weather. When Lacey and Kyle got the bus home from school, it stopped at the top of the gravel road. They walked the rest of the way back, quickly in the winter and sluggishly when it was hot. The weather was just beginning to turn now; the cold months were reaching their close and a little warmth was creeping back into the earth.

At school once, people were discussing their favourite season. When it was Lacey's turn to pick one, she couldn't. Welsh winters were too cold for her. The one time she forgot her gloves and the walk home when she got off the bus was painful. She could feel the wind biting the tips of her fingers and, when she finally reached the front door, it was a struggle to get her key to slip into the lock. Her hands were completely numb. There was something barren about rural Wales in winter too. Living on a farm was a good deal less idyllic when all the grass and trees were dead, and no crops would grow. Kyle would run through the hard and empty fields, hollering about the apocalypse. Winter definitely felt like the end.

Then there was the spring, which didn't feel much

different to the summer, it just rained a little more. Some kind of precipitation should feel refreshing, but often it came down warm and evaporated immediately, only to hang in the air around Lacey, making her skin cling to her clothes and her hair frizz. She could see the humidity in ripples across the sky, like the world had been submerged in an invisible ocean. Spring wasn't for her either.

When summer came, she couldn't move. It felt like the entire world was bleeding. Everywhere was so damp and sticky that the air itself developed a syrupy viscosity that soaked into every pore. Going outside was unbearable, even when it was only to sit down and try to remain immobile in a rare patch of shade. Lacey loathed the season so much that her grandmother had enforced the rule of 'The Green Hour,' which she had read about in one of her housekeeping magazines. Lacey didn't understand why Madeline read them; they were overflowing with female stereotypes and pictures of beautiful items the Belvideres couldn't even dream of affording. 'The Green Hour' only gave Lacey another reason to despise them. The concept was simple: force your children to spend at least an hour outside every day. The problem was that this was a blanket solution, and the long walk home from school or gym class didn't seem to count. Lacey used to sit in the shed to shade herself from the harsh sunlight, but the last time she had done that she had scared herself with her own imagination.

There was never anywhere to sit in the shed, so she always mounted the ride-on lawnmower that was parked in the middle. Most days this worked well enough, but there were times when her father would take it out to cut the grass and, when he drove back, he didn't park it in quite the same spot. If the mower was a couple of inches to the left, a stripe of white hot sun thrashed through a crack in the roof and whipped down into Lacey's eyes. It made it difficult to do anything, least of all read anything, which is what she often chose to do with her Green Hour. Madeline would lecture her, saying that holing up in some dark room with a book was completely missing the point, so Lacey had to smuggle her reading material out underneath her t-shirt. It was more fun that way, as though she was rebelling even if it was far-fetched to compare it to anything like a rebellion.

On this particular day, she sat with her legs dangling either side of the mower with a copy of *Dracula* in her lap. She was out later than usual because she had been putting off her Green Hour in the hopes that nobody would notice. Unfortunately, Madeline realised after dinner and made her go anyway, even though it was nearing half past eight in the evening. It was still light out – the sun wouldn't set properly for another hour, but as she sat reading, the world felt much darker than it was really. A breeze entered through the open door and picked up at her feet, scattering leaves that had died many years ago around the shed floor. They were so brown and crinkled that it was hard to tell what trees they once belonged to, and the sound they made as they scraped their crisp edges were reminiscent of nails tapping and dragging across wood. A jacket that hung on a hook above the workbench moved a little in the draught. The sleeves tingled with life above a screwdriver, as though it was reaching...

Lacey shook her head and focused on the words in front of her. Jonathan was leaning out the window and *there–* Dracula scurried up the side of the castle wall like a lizard. Lacey could see him and his eyes black with hunger, a reptilian tongue flicking out of his mouth to caress his lips and make them slick with saliva, better for seduction and violation. She pulled her shirt sleeves until the seams dug into her armpits and the white collar sat halfway up her neck. Outside, the trees whispered. Time passed. The sun now left a red trace across her bare thighs. She tugged at her shorts to try and make the discoloured light hit her clothes instead of her skin, but it only glowed more intensely, until it appeared embedded in her flesh. As she turned the page, the leaves crawled to her side. It was at that moment, without warning, that a raven flew into the shed. It flapped over Lacey's head and circled around, before perching itself on a beam above the door.

Dracula, Lacey thought, before feeling embarrassed that it had crossed her mind at all. Even so, there was something odd about it. The raven watched her, aware of every move Lacey made. She wanted to leave, but it was right above the exit and there was no other way out. As if it knew this, the bird inched closer towards her. It was out of the light and its body was so black that it was barely visible. It was a silhouette against the wooden panels – a shadow fading into the backdrop of every other shadow. The only parts she could make out were its glassy eyes and razor beak. Tearing her stare away from the raven long enough to check her watch, she saw that it was about time to go inside. She couldn't stay here waiting for it to go. It was a bird. That was all. She was bigger and scarier. She could leave if she wanted.

She knew she was thinking these things only to convince herself that she wasn't worried. It was an unnerving creature. Lacey swung her right leg back over the lawn mower to meet her left, and jumped onto the floor. The raven didn't flinch. She held the book up over her head and ducked slightly, before walking out the door. Just as she made it to the threshold, it took off. Flying only centimetres above her, the raven blew past and disappeared into the line of trees adjacent to them. She never saw it again, but always felt like it was watching her. Every time she saw a raven after that, it felt like the one from the shed, following her. It took her several more weeks to finish *Dracula*.

As the car pulled up the driveway to the cottage now, Lacey looked at the shed with the ride-on lawnmower inside. That was where she had to wait to go home and feel safe again.

All of a sudden, there was no place she would rather be than sitting there. Henry turned off the ignition and they all froze in their seats for a moment; none of them were sure what to do next. Kyle hopped out first. Lacey watched from the backseat as Henry reached a hand over to Madeline and placed it on her shoulder. She jumped like she didn't know he was there and he withdrew immediately. Henry opened the door and got out, pulling his oxygen tank with him. He struggled a little as it caught the lip of the door, which jolted Madeline back out of her daydream. She got out and helped him bring it down. As they turned to go inside, Madeline looked back to see Lacey, who wasn't getting out of the car. Madeline stopped walking and crossed her arms. Lacey could tell that she was going to stand there until she got out. Sighing, Lacey unbuckled her seatbelt and opened the door, slamming it behind her when her feet were firmly on the ground. Then she walked over to the deck and sat down to wait.

"Not coming inside?" Madeline asked her. Her voice shook and Lacey knew she was trying to be casual, but there was something she wasn't saying.

"I want to sit here," she replied.

"What for?"

"I don't know."

That was the truth. She didn't know what she was waiting for. When they were told her father wasn't coming back with them, nobody said why. Her grandparents were taken aside and spoken to by Detective Blackwood, but Lacey couldn't read their faces. Blackwood spoke and Lacey watched his lips move. They reminded her of Ezra. There was something about them that appeared to smile and pout at the same time. As he talked to her grandparents, they curved into kindness, resembled reassurance, but her grandmother's eyes widened and burned with sadness. What did this mean? Henry showed no expression, like he wasn't even there. He had that look on his face a lot lately, as though he was imagining some other place. There was a lot that Lacey wasn't being told.

"I'm not a child, you know," she said as Madeline began to walk inside.

"You're not an adult either."

"I didn't say I was. I just said I wasn't a kid."

Lacey watched her grandmother's chest heave as she turned and walked over to her, sitting down on the deck. The two of them stared out into the trees opposite. Lacey scanned the branches for the sign of a raven, but there was nothing there.

"There's something you're not telling me," Lacey said.

"You're not old enough to understand."

"No. That's you making assumptions. I understand plenty. I could understand anything if you explained it right. But that's the problem. You won't tell me anything."

"What do you want to know?"

Lacey tried to stretch her dangling legs down to touch the dirt beneath them, but she was too short. She still had growing left to do. Maybe she was too young. Almost fifteen didn't seem so bad though. She was starting to look like a woman. Her conversations with Ezra were grown up, weren't they? Things that used to embarrass her now enticed her. She thought about his lips again. Questions flooded her mind and drowned her. What was it like to kiss someone? What was love? Could she love someone who hurt her? Where was her father? She looked up at the sky and saw that the sun was fading. The colour of her father's black eyes was getting stronger as the sun disappeared. Her mother's favourite blue flowers were being set on fire in the atmosphere above her head. Where was her mother? Did she even have parents now?

"What happened to Dad?" she settled on, after her thoughts had stopped swirling so violently in her head.

"He has to go away for a while," Madeline said.

She looked at her grandmother and saw the lies trickle

down her cheeks. In the space of a few seconds, Lacey became a real adult. She put her arm around her grandmother and pulled her against her chest. Lacey couldn't make sense of her feelings. When she thought about how she had been kept in the dark about everything that had happened, a rage burned up her spine and projected itself into the sky around the farm. Then she felt her t-shirt dampen over her heart with her grandmother's tears, and she felt soft again.

"Your dad is a confused man," Madeline said when she caught her breath. "He doesn't know how to express his feelings. He used to be so emotional. Everything about him was so intense. When he lost your mum, that part of him burned out. He doesn't feel much anymore. A person can make terrible, terrible choices when they don't have a heart left."

"I don't understand."

"He made an awful choice and now he has to work through the consequences."

"Grandma," Lacey said, pushing her grandmother off her by her shoulders and holding her in the light. "Has...has Dad been..."

"Yes," Madeline said, already knowing the rest of the question. "He's been arrested."

Lacey didn't move even though she felt like she was collapsing. Her thoughts became dizzying and she pulled her grandmother back into her arms. If she was comforting someone, she had a purpose, a job to do, and she wouldn't vomit from the shock. Lacey squeezed her eyes shut as her mind spiralled to the worst excesses. She thought about the way he made her eat until she was sick and how he unpicked her insecurities for the world to see. Didn't she hate him? What were these tears for? The world felt colder with him gone, even though she shook with anxiety when he was here. What had he done? When she opened her eyes, her sight was drawn back to the trees. Immediately, she felt like she was being watched again. The raven was out there, haunting her.

MADELINE

Madeline drove without knowing her destination. The grandchildren were in bed and Henry was on the sofa, but she couldn't bear to sit with him. If she stopped moving, she would be accepting that there was nothing else that could be done. Sitting down with Henry meant that she was resigning herself to waiting for her son to come home and nothing else. She had to do more than wait. Her inaction was what had made the situation as bad as it was and she knew it. There were plenty of points when she could have done something differently, but would the outcome be different? Madeline doubted that she could have stopped Ned if she tried her hardest. His trouble began a long time ago, on the day he lost Karen. Madeline knew where she was going.

She pulled into the cemetery and drove down the road until she was as close as she could get. Something people never talked about, she noticed, was what it was like navigating a graveyard. There were no landmarks; nothing stood out to help her find her way around. She didn't even need to think about where to go. The car appeared to drive itself and stopped in just the right place every time. Her feet carried her through the grass, past the rows of headstones, until she arrived. Everything about walking to Karen was instinctual. No consideration or plan went into it. The map to this spot could be found in Madeline's palm print, along the veins around her heart, and in all the dips and movements of her brain. There was no forgetting the way to Karen's grave.

These days, she only came by twice a year – on Karen's birthday and the anniversary of her death. It was near to neither today and Madeline wished she had bought flowers like she normally did. Henry would come with her on each visit. Together they would pull out the weeds that grew in the grass that blanketed her resting place. They threw away the old flowers and replaced them, giving them fresh water and feed. Henry found the act of leaving flowers each time strange, especially as Madeline always paid extra for a nicer bouquet. She had explained to him that it was a sign they hadn't forgotten Karen, and Henry would always ask the same question: *a sign for who*? Madeline never told her husband that she believed Karen was still with them in spirit.

They had never been a religious couple. While they had both been raised Christians, something about the Church hadn't stuck with them as they worked on their life together. They tried to be good people and that was it. Henry never developed beyond his atheism and Ned followed suit. There was nothing wrong with that in the slightest, but as Madeline got older, it stopped being enough for her. The more years that passed, the more she wished she could believe in anything. After Karen died, the thought that someone so good could be gone forever had been too much to bear. She held a silent faith within herself that no one was ever truly gone. Her thoughts about Karen were directed to her and, though she never prayed aloud, she often found herself wishing for blessings. Her wishes weren't to a deity. It felt unlikely that someone all-powerful could begin to understand a creature as powerless as herself. Instead, she prayed to Karen. She asked her to watch the children, forgive Ned, and keep her company when she was alone. Whether Karen was really there or not, Madeline had nurtured a spiritual friend in her.

It made sense that she had come to the cemetery now, even though she wasn't thinking. She was only moving, following her footsteps to the grave of her only friend. When the words *Karen Ann Belvidere* were in sight, Madeline's mind switched itself back on and she began to breathe heavily. Ned never came to visit her. He hadn't been back here since the funeral. Madeline wondered if they buried part of her son with his wife that day. All his pain was replaced with ferocity. A man so frightened to feel couldn't open himself up to believe in anything or anyone but his own grit. Madeline knew that would never be enough. She didn't fight him on his choices, only wished secretly to Karen that he might someday grow out of them. When she reached Karen's grave she stood before the headstone for a while.

She wanted to say something. It seemed only right that now, when she needed someone the most, she could voice her secret prayers aloud. In many ways, this was what she feared most; saying her thoughts openly made them real. Her declarations would translate her worries into real fears that could not be unsaid.

"Karen," Madeline whispered, feeling self-conscious.

What could she say that would change the world? Did she possess the right words that could create a real revolution? She used to believe that her voice could make a difference. When she was a teenager, her and her friends had rallied to protest all sorts of nonsense. At fourteen, she hadn't believed that her voice didn't count. She remembered taking the bus down to London with Samantha Jones and Violet Williams who had both been older than her. They had sung as they went to join in with the latest wave of righteous indignation. Madeline couldn't remember every detail – it was all so long ago that the memories were turning hazy and yellow like the photographs she had from the time – but she could recall the feeling with such accuracy that she could trick herself into believing she was fourteen again.

Every chant had felt like part of the weather; they had filled the sky and had rained back down on them until they had become tangible in the air. Madeline had believed wholeheartedly that she was changing the world each day. The world had been brighter than it had ever been and she was at the centre of it. The feeling that she could leave a mark on this world was one that slipped away from her as the years passed. She barely recognised herself anymore. All the opportunities dried up for her and so she just accepted her fate without protest. She didn't believe in revolution these days.

"How are you?" she asked, as if this was a two-way conversation, a discussion like any other. She expected to feel Karen's reply in the breeze, spell out an answer in the motion of the clouds, but there wasn't anyone there. She tried to sort through the tangled sentences in her head, but three words echoed out clearer than the rest: "I need help."

Madeline lowered herself to her knees by Karen's side and stroked the words on her headstone as if her fingertips would find a new meaning in them that her eyes had overlooked. The first few drops of rain began to come down from the sky and Madeline slipped her jacket off. She draped it over the headstone as though the corners were shoulders that needed covering. She stroked her bare arms and stared as the hairs on them rose, unused to the sensation of being touched in the cold. Now all she had to do was learn how to talk.

"Nobody tells the truth," she said. "Did you ever know that? I feel like nobody has ever told me the truth. I was brought up a good Christian girl. I was raised to prioritise my love for God and my family. Nobody told me the love doesn't always last. That it isn't always enough. There's so much of it inside me, Karen. I love my husband. I love my son. I love my grandchildren. Why isn't it enough?"

It was almost dark and the gates would soon be locked. The rain came down a little harder, enough to brush her forearms with a coat that glittered when she turned them in the rising moonlight, like dew that froze on the grass. Madeline shivered, but didn't feel anything. This body was someone else's. These arms weren't hers. *You filled the skies*, the epitaph read, and Madeline tilted her head back to see the moon, full and suspended above her.

"I love you," Madeline whispered, letting the words drift up and hang with the vapour of her breath in the twilight. "Maybe I didn't say that enough, but it's all I can do to say it now. To the only other person who ever cared for Ned as much as I do. You really loved him, didn't you? Don't you?"

Her reply came in the splitting of the sky and rain began to pour down like every star was weeping onto the cemetery below. Madeline rubbed her arms and pulled the jacket further over the headstone to keep it dry, so she could still make out the words. She recalled Karen's smile that hadn't been perfect or celebrity-white. She had been full of life once. She would always be alive in those moments in the past where Madeline remembered her living.

"Do your worst," she said to the rain.

The weather obeyed her, soaking through her skin until she could feel the slickness of her bones. She was heavier as she absorbed the storm and became part of it, knowing that she could sink into the earth beside Karen and believe she was going home.

"You're right here. Right underneath me. But how far away are you really?" Madeline pressed a palm into the dirt and watched it creep over her fingers. Henry had told her when he had woken up that his vision felt black around the edges. As she watched her pale skin become engulfed in the soil, she saw what he meant. This earth represented death and it was falling all around her body.

"I have to talk to you. I don't believe in anything else, but you. Not anymore. I've done a horrible thing. I let Ned carry on with his recklessness. Karen…" she paused, "I'm afraid. I can't explain it. I'm scared. I should have stopped his bad behaviour the night we lost you. Right there and then I should have told him to cut it out, but I didn't. I was trying to understand him, to be fair, until I didn't know who he was anymore. Until he frightened me. Do you know what that's like? Were you ever scared of him?"

As she spoke, sensation returned to her body and Madeline realised that she was dangerously cold. Knowing she had to get to the car soon before the cemetery gates were locked, she tried to push herself to her feet. The ground beneath her had grown slippery and wet. Her knees buckled, unable to lift her up the way they used to do. One of her feet slid out from underneath her and she twisted her ankle, falling on her side into the dirt. Pain shot up her leg and radiated through her flesh and muscles, rolling over her limb. She reached down and grabbed her calf, knowing how brittle her bones were lately. She lay on her side, realising that she was right on top of Karen.

Madeline didn't move. Slowly and deliberately, she lowered a flushed cheek down to the grave and rested her face a few feet over Karen's. After a minute, she craned her neck up to see the headstone above her and for a second read her own name in the granite. Her chest heaved and she let out a sob that was soon lost in the sound of rain on graves. She had made a mistake by not being brave. Sometimes taking no action was the same as doing something unforgivable. Her love should have been enough to stand up to Ned and fight for her husband, but it wasn't. Her inaction was evil. This good Christian girl who had once believed in peace had grown into a bitter, doomed woman.

"My boy," was all she had left to say, so she said it over and over. "My boy, my boy, my boy…" she cried above her daughter-in-law, but nobody called back to her.

HENRY

Henry gasped when Madeline came into the bedroom. She was covered in dirt and shaking like a newborn baby. He pulled his nasal cannula from his nose without a thought and hurried to the chest of drawers to pull out a spare blanket. Draping it over her shoulders, he tried to rub warmth back into her arms and eased her down onto the edge of the bed. She was limping and needed help sitting down.

"Christ, Madeline. What happened to you? Where's your jacket?" he asked, but she didn't say anything. She turned to look out of the window and Henry followed her gaze out to the trees opposite where he once saw Ned's figure, armed with an axe. "You're thinking about him too," he said.

"Yes," she whispered.

"Where's your jacket?" he asked again.

"With Karen."

Henry nodded. She didn't have to say anything else. After everything that happened at the police station, it didn't surprise him in the slightest that she had gone to the cemetery when she ran out of the cottage. He knew she spoke to Karen sometimes. It was supposed to be a secret, but he overheard her in the garden on several occasions. He never told Madeline that he knew – that would surely embarrass her – so he kept it to himself and pretended to be none the wiser. The last time he caught her it was before the weather had turned cold, when she had been watering the vegetable patch in the garden. Walking around the edges with the hose, she had drawn dark lines of water over the rows of butternut squash, which had been all she seemed to be able to grow there.

A blackbird had flown down and sat on the grass nearby, tilting its head from side-to-side as it watched Madeline care for the plants. She had seen it and stopped, the two creatures watching each other and if they had been trying to understand what it was about themselves that had been worth looking at. She had smiled and nodded to the blackbird who sunned its feathers in the autumn light.

"Me too, Karen," Madeline had said, finishing off a conversation she had been having with herself.

Henry had been coming out of the cottage to see if she wanted something to drink when he had heard her. He had stopped in his tracks and had watched her move so lightly on her feet that she could have been dancing. These had been the moments he treasured, when he could watch her and see youth return to her footsteps. Those times were precious to him, gazing at his wife mesmerising him so many decades after the very first time she did. He had crept quietly back inside, leaving her for a couple more minutes to finish talking. It hadn't been his place to interrupt.

Madeline sat on the bed shivering underneath the blanket. Her eyes were wide and Henry knew she could see something through the window. Perhaps it was Ned as he had seen him. How long had their son been surrendering to his resentment? When was the first time they could have stopped this? He tried to pull his wife against him, but she resisted. Henry went to the bathroom and grabbed a flannel, which he dampened with warm water and brought back into the bedroom. Gently, he turned her face to his and wiped the dirt from it. Her eyes were as red as blood and Henry decided that he wasn't going to ask her what happened. She was home now. That was what mattered. As he finished cleaning her cheeks, he went to stand up and put the cloth in the bathroom, but she grabbed his wrist. She moved so quickly that it surprised Henry and he dropped the dirty flannel. It hit the floor boards with a wet splat.

"I have to tell you something," she said. "I knew."

Henry remembered their wedding reception. They had sat in the middle of a large, oblong table that faced the rest of the hall, but Henry had only looked at her. She had chosen a simple dress without a train or any detailing, but somehow it had made her look even more elegant. She had reminded Henry of the angel ornament that had sat on top of his childhood Christmas tree every year. The angel had worn a white, satin dress, and its curly blonde hair had been wrapped up in a bun to show a feminine and graceful neck. Madeline had on pearl earrings which the ornament hadn't had and her real body had only made her seem more angelic. He had held her hand at the table and refused to put it down, so he had to eat all his food only using his left hand, which ultimately had made a huge mess, but Madeline had laughed.

As he remembered that day, Henry realised how much he missed her laugh. It was a rare pleasure to hear it now. She knew. He barely had time to process his feelings towards Ned after all the revelations that had smothered him this evening and now his wife was piling onto it. There was so much he had to process and he wasn't sure if he could. He closed his eyes to go back to their wedding day and see her again the way he loved her. She had leaned over to feed him some of her chicken which she had known he wanted to try before he asked. She had smiled at him while he had made a show and dance about how delicious all the food she had picked out for the occasion tasted.

"I knew you'd like it," she had said.

She always knew. How could he have been home for two days now and not seen that she knew? Henry stood up and walked over to the window, leaning on the sill and staring out into the blackness. It was time to address what was really happening here. Henry needed answers.

"What do you mean you knew?" he said.

"Ned told me. I...I didn't stop him."

Henry didn't look at her. He looked up and imagined the full moon in the sky, and saw the apparition of her white dress again. Her voice behind him was broken and defeated. He wanted to turn around pull her to him the way that he had done for their first dance. He had wrapped his arms around her waist and rested his chin on her shoulder, feeling the skin of her neck against his cheek. She had smelled like roses and wine. Henry's arms shook like they wouldn't be able to hold his weight much longer. He forgot that he didn't have his oxygen tank. Breathing didn't seem to matter anymore.

"Why not?" he asked. All his questions were calculated.

"I was scared."

God, to reach out for her, to rock her in his arms and lie to her. He gritted his teeth and tested the friction of his feet on the floor. He was rooted and solid. He would not be swayed. *Don't think of her as your bride right now. Remember what happened. You're not on the beach anymore. Remember, Henry, you have to remember,* he told himself.

"Why are you telling me this now?" Henry asked

"Because I spoke to Karen."

"What?" Henry asked, dropping his guard and turning to look at her.

"I felt like I'd die if I didn't tell you."

She looked smaller as she drowned in the blanket, still unable to stop shaking from when the storm had penetrated her bones. This was a far cry from how they were at their wedding. As he watched the hollowness of her eyes follow every breath of air he wheezed for, he realised that he never saw his bride again after that day. A few hours after they were wed, they had begun the slow decline to this point. Their lives has always been heading this way, whether they fought it or not.

"Do you even know what I'm going through right now?" he asked, sick of twisting and contorting himself to avoid his own pain. "Do you have any idea what today has been like?"

"He's our son, Hen –"

"Does our son blame you for what happened to Karen and Galen? Does our son resent you enough to do something like this? Does he?"

"Henry –"

"You have no fucking idea what it's like in my head right now," Henry hissed.

Madeline shrunk back even further into the blanket until only her face was showing. It was round against the navy blue fleece and once again she was the perfect frame of the moon. Just like the sky, she was inescapable. Between his blinks he saw flashes of the beach and remembered her voice calling to him across dimensions. She lied to him even there; as he walked the line between worlds she harboured this darkness in her heart. He saw their tree there from the old house, where they carved their initials for Ned. They created a mark that would outlast them. Her M fit into his lips like a kiss that transcended his coma and his unconscious mind. Ned had come for it with his axe. Henry was near to death in that moment and still he pined for her, when she had helped bring him there.

"I'm trying to understand," she said, cutting his thoughts short.

"You can't."

"But I want to."

"And I've told you that you can't. How could you possibly?"

"Please, let me try," she begged, reaching for his wrist, but he yanked it away.

"After all you've done, I don't think so." His voice was quiet. Steady.

"Look, I was trying to protect this family."

"And how did that work out?"

"Henry –"

"Our son left me for dead!" Henry shouted, finally losing his patience.

They both stopped. It was the first time either of them had said the words aloud, but that was what had happened. There were no other words left to say to each other. Henry bit his tongue hard and felt blood swarm his mouth. It glistened red between his teeth and as he swallowed it he felt sick. He couldn't explain how he felt at all. Turning back to the window he saw Ned with the axe again. The shadow stood, facing his father and smiling. His teeth were bloody like his father's and his smile was wide like a wolf's. Henry shook and snarled, but Ned continued to glower at him before raising the axe and bringing it to his mouth. Ned stuck out his tongue and licked the blade that glinted in the bride-white moon. Unable to rip the vision from his mind Henry balled up his right hand into a fist and drove it through the window. Madeline yelped and the glass shattered. The cold night air rushed in and made the cuts on Henry's knuckles sting. He saw his reflection in the sharp shards of glass that still clung to the frame and saw blood drip from his lips and fingers. He was a life-sucking vampire, ready to be violent. He wanted revenge. Henry turned around to look at his wife.

He wasn't like that. As much as he craved to express himself in pain, he couldn't hurt anybody but himself. Madeline wrapped the blanket around herself tightly like it would shield her from him and Henry began to feel dizzy. He didn't think that she had been scared of him before, but as she trembled before him, Henry saw what she must have felt like around Ned. He couldn't bear to look at her anymore and went to the bedroom door. When he wrenched it open, Lacey was standing on the other side with her mouth open.

Henry knew that there was a special look that person wore when they were having a life-changing epiphany. Lacey's face had it now as he saw the truth spark and dance behind her eyes. She was realising something horrific, just as he had done today. Henry felt a sudden closeness to his granddaughter then. Granted, they had always shared a special relationship which was unlike any other pairing in the family, but as they looked at each other in the doorway, their love took a new shape. Both of them had their lives redefined today, in an amount of time too short to make any sense of it. While Henry wished his grandchildren didn't have to go through this, a small part of him was grateful that he wasn't alone anymore.

Lacey didn't appear to care for their new connection in that moment. Henry went to take a step towards her, but she backed away just as he had retracted from Madeline's touch moments before. The complications repulsed everyone, but Henry was also inextricably complex – to recede from them was to withdraw from who he was now. He looked into Lacey's eyes and they replayed everything that happened together. As they reached the end of their memories and met in the present moment, Lacey bolted. She turned and fled from Henry. He hurried after her, but she dashed like lightning from the cottage and out the front door.

"Lacey!" Henry shouted, but she didn't stop.

He wasn't fast enough. Henry doubled over wheezing and knew he had to go into the bedroom to get his oxygen tank. There was a few seconds then in which he considered trying to go after Lacey instead. The thought of going back into the bedroom with Madeline filled him with a despair he couldn't reconcile. Wouldn't it be better to die chasing someone he cared about than fighting a person who he didn't know anymore? Henry settled for fumbling around in the dark kitchen for his phone. He dialled Lacey's number and lay down on the sofa, staring up at the ceiling.

"I knew you'd have your phone," he wheezed when she picked up.

Lacey didn't say anything, but Henry could hear her breathing heavily from the running.

"You know I can't run after you, princess."

"…I know," came a whisper.

"Where did you run to?"

"I'm only down the road."

"Come home, Lacey."

"That place isn't my home."

Henry couldn't lie to her. She had been kept in the dark just as he had. Anymore secrets and she might never want to come back. Henry knew this because it was how he felt. It didn't feel like his home anymore either, but there was nothing to be done tonight.

"Please wake up and shout at me," he said.

"What?"

"That's what you told me, isn't it? When you came to visit me in the hospital. I remember. You said you wanted me to wake up, even if it was only to shout. Well, I'm awake now, princess. But I'm not going to shout at you."

For a few moments Henry didn't hear anything. He had never heard what the colour black sounded like before, but now he knew. It sounded like someone he loved on the phone, refusing to speak to him. Black sounded like a boundary. It was static. Lacey sniffed sharply, and Henry took it as a sign to carry on.

"If I scared you, then I'm sorry. I scared myself."

"You didn't scare me, Grandpa. Everyone else did."

"Tell me about it. I'm being open with you. But I need you to do the same with me. Just like we've always done, right?"

That did it. Lacey sighed deeply and the spilled everything that made up who she was in that moment into Henry's ear. Something about the distance and darkness seemed to make it easier to tell him her thoughts.

"I don't understand how they could do something like that. And to try and blame it on you because of what happened to Mum. It's not an excuse. They made her seem tainted. Like her memory is cursed. And it's not like I don't hurt from losing her just like the rest of you. She was my Mum. Galen was my brother. But everyone treats me like I was too young or stupid to understand what that meant. What it still means."

This time, it was Henry's turn to remain silent. He listened to the blackness and to his granddaughter's heart breaking a few metres down the road. Clasping his chest and craving oxygen, he stayed where he was, unable to tear himself from the phone long enough to go into the bedroom and breathe. His hand was badly swollen from punching through the window. He felt the ridges of his knuckles disappear with the fingers of his free hand and picked away at the drying blood.

"I held Grandma," she said. "I comforted her a few hours ago. But she wasn't crying because she was sad. She was crying because she felt sorry for herself and wasn't brave enough to tell the truth. How can I forgive someone who won't be honest with me?"

As Henry continued to listen, he wondered if he could ever forgive his wife. What was right? She told him the truth in the end, but Henry didn't owe her for it. She wasn't the angel on top of his Christmas tree. The woman he had married didn't live here anymore. He thought about the Madeline he remembered as he reflected on the moon and felt scabs grow over his cuts, while he struggled to breathe and at last knew the sound of black.

LACEY

Lacey sat on the empty football pitch at school and warmed herself in the sun. Spring was finally beginning to break through the winter. Everywhere Lacey looked, the world was blooming. Birds she couldn't identify perched on the goalposts and glowered down at her as the haunting feeling crept back into her body. She leaned back on her hands and stretched her legs out in front of her, shaking her hair loose over her shoulders, dismissing that unsettling sensation she was all too used to having these days. Clovers sprouted in the grass around her and tickled her legs which were bare from the hem of her shorts to the tops of her socks. The pitch was strictly off limits except for P.E. class, but as long as she stayed sitting by the wall of the Science building, no one would be able to see her.

Somewhere in the distance behind, she heard the bell ring for the end of class, but she didn't move. It was time to make her way to Advanced English and Ezra would be there waiting for her, but Lacey wasn't sure if she could see him at the moment. In fact, she had been actively avoiding him for the last couple of weeks. When she thought about him now, a sickly feeling bubbled in her stomach and she couldn't help but feel embarrassed by her attraction. She was fifteen now, but her age didn't measure her maturity and she knew it. It was hard to know if she was more or less intelligent than others her age, and whether that even mattered when it came to precociousness. Grabbing a tuft of grass in her hand, she ripped the blades up from the soil and smoothed them out in her palm. Selecting three of roughly equal length, she threw the rest away. Lacey tied the ends together carefully so as not to tear the grass, and then began plaiting them until she had a little braid pressed into the centre of her hand.

She stared at the plait until her eyes unfocused and it began to look like a fuzzy, green caterpillar. Her grandmother had taught her how to do this when she was so young that she couldn't remember the first time they had done it, but now whenever Lacey sat outside in a field it was second nature to rip out some pieces and entwine them. When she began to do it with her hair as a smarter alternative to a ponytail, she found herself thinking of Madeline every time without fail. It was like her grandmother was standing next to her telling her what to do and Lacey could pretend they were together. If she ever got lonely, Lacey could plait her hair and feel warm and loved again. She stared at the grass in her palm and scrunched up her nose. Lacey pinched each end of the braid between a thumb and forefinger, and pulled until it ripped it half. It tightened under the strain at first, as the pressure brought the individual blades closer together, but they only appeared stronger. In reality, they were so taut that ripping apart was the only logical outcome.

Reaching into her bag, she pulled out her copy of *Flowers for Algernon* which she had to read for class. Even though she knew she was going to skip the lesson the day the book was assigned, she read it anyway. She wasn't ditching class for the usual reasons. She'd done the work and enjoyed it, it was her favourite class, and there was nobody there with whom she had a problem. It was only that she didn't want to see Ezra. Technically, that wasn't necessarily true. It wasn't so much that she didn't want to see him, but rather that she didn't know how. He would have more questions than ever and all she wanted to do was be happy with him. How could she pretend everything was alright when it wasn't? Soon, he'd have the truth from her and then even he would look at her in that confused and pitying way that people seemed to stare at Lacey with now. The detectives at the station, before Lacey even knew what happened, pulled their brows together and offered the same flat smile. Her teachers gave her a reassuring pat on the shoulder and tipped their heads to the side. The only person who didn't look at Lacey like they felt sorry for her was her grandfather. Henry always gave her honest expressions to match his words.

She flipped through the pages again, fanning herself with the text. Stroking the covers, she traces the embossing with her fingers and let her eyes catch words as she flicked through the work again. Something about the story of a happy but ignorant person becoming a miserable genius and then reverting back made Lacey think of herself. She had once come from a place of luxurious unknowing, where the world was full of opportunity. She had loved herself then, before she knew anything. When Lacey had begun to learn about the world — see her father for what he was, her grandmother's weakness, her grandfather's pain — she started to hate herself. She didn't fit in the world the way she thought she had done before. Lacey felt just like Charlie Gordon, and she was scared to go back to the way things were. Granted, there was no way she could lose the part of herself she had gained through this ordeal. Lacey had been irrevocably changed, but perhaps not for the better.

Lacey looked up at the birds on the goalposts. They sang down to her alone across the empty football pitch. Winter was quickly becoming a memory, but her discontent was steadfast. Two weeks had passed since her father's arrest, but it was hard to say how she felt about it. Some nights, when she woke up and looked over to Kyle asleep in the bed next to hers, she remembered Ned happily. Her favourite memory of them was when he had picked her up from a play rehearsal at school and for a moment, she had almost loved where she lived.

Dad had never come to collect her at the high school before. When he showed up in his car, Lacey couldn't help but grin. Inside, it was so roomy that she could stretch her legs out on the passenger side and lay her feet flat on the part of the foot well that sloped up to meet the back of the glove-box. It was a second hand car and still smelled like cigarettes, but Lacey didn't mind. Ned slid a CD into the player and drummed his hands on the steering wheel to music Lacey didn't recognise, but liked because it made her father dance.

"How was the rehearsal?" he asked.

"Good. Still need to get my last few lines down."

They fell back into silence in a way that was natural to them. It was dark out and the orange lights on the streets cast a fiery glow across the pavements and framed shadows in the dark, blacker than the sky which still clung to the remaining traces of blue. Stars came out to stare and wink at them as they hurtled through the dusk towards the cottage. The outline of Bannau Brycheiniog rose through the haze of trees and wrapped themselves in the thick night air.

"It's nice here," Ned said.

Lacey looked over to him in surprise; she had never heard him speak so softly or tenderly before. His eyes that were normally harsh and stark were gentle, flickering over the landscape as though they were caressing the horizon. She was caught offguard and nodded.

"Do you like it here?" he asked her.

"Sometimes."

"What do you mean?"

"A lot of times I hate it. The weather. The isolation. I don't have a lot of friends. But then sometimes it's like you say. Nice."

Ned had stopped tapping his hands to the rhythm of the music. She could see he was frowning because the light caught his face in new ways; it got lost in the dips of his forehead and under his pout, but highlighted and bounced off his cheeks.

"You don't need friends," was all he said.

As Lacey sat on the football pitch, she wondered if her father had been right. Did she need friends? Did she need Ezra? Then she remembered the other times with her father – the times when the night wasn't around them, but inside them. *Nobody likes a tubby girl. Ezra wouldn't want a fat girlfriend.* She looked down at her legs and prodded them with a finger. She pinched herself and twisted so she could turn to look at her bum. For two weeks, she hadn't been afraid of what her father might say or do and even though Lacey knew it was a good change, she missed him. She forgot she was still pinching herself as she thought about him. Why did she still love him? Her thumb and fingers began to dig into her thigh and tears glazed her eyes. *Hate him,* she ordered herself. *Hate him. Please.* She couldn't bring herself into a rage. *Why don't I hate him? He's evil. Look what he did. Hate him.* Lacey gritted her teeth and closed her eyes, trying to push some contempt out of herself, but there was nothing. She looked down and saw the broken plait of grass next to *Flowers for Algernon*. The only thing that Lacey felt was alone as she lost her place in the world.

Snatching her bag up and digging around, she pulled out her phone. Her hands were shaking as she pressed the right combination of keys to message Ezra: *meet me on the football pitch.* Her skin had turned crimson where she was pinching it and if it bruised, Lacey wouldn't be surprised. She tucked her book back into her bag and sat forwards, crossing her legs and holding her head in her hands. It wasn't clear how long she sat like that, but soon she heard footsteps coming up to her. Lacey didn't look up. The steps stopped and the person sat down next to her without speaking. After a minute, Lacey lifted her head to see who it was. Ezra was sat in the same position as her, staring at the birds.

"I have to tell you something," Lacey said at last.

"About what happened to your grandpa," he said.

She nodded, half-impressed that he connected the dots so quickly. Ezra continued to look away from her and she knew it was to keep his face blank while she spoke.

"I was right. My dad did do something."

"What did he do?"

"He took my grandpa to the beach. He left him there without his oxygen tank. He...he wanted him to die."

Lacey bit her lip. Ezra looked at her then and she didn't see the pity she feared on his face. It was empathy and real kindness. He shuffled closer to her and put his arm on her knee.

"I keep trying to hate him. For what he's done to Grandpa. For how he's treated me and Kyle. But I can't. What's wrong with me? Why do I miss him?"

"Because you're a good person, Lacey."

"I don't believe good people exist."

"What do you mean?"

"My grandma. She knew. She knew this whole time," she said, and then began to weep.

Ezra put his arm around Lacey and pulled her against him, holding her while she shook. Her cries were stifled at first, but soon they tore out of her throat so loudly that it crossed her mind that someone might hear and come to get them off the field. Ezra must have known this too, because he held her tighter and let her cry into his shirt.

"Oh, Lace. I wish you had told me sooner," he said and he rocked her in his arms.

"I'm sorry, I'm sorry…"

"No! Don't apologise, that's not what I… I just meant I want to help you."

"What good would it do? My family is all ripped up."

"What's happening?"

Lacey pulled back from him and wiped her tears and nose with the back of her hand, wishing desperately for a tissue. She looked out across the pitch. Everything looked so open and bright. It was nothing like her bedroom, which felt small and dark. It wasn't her home anymore.

Henry had thought about moving out and into emergency housing for a while, taking Lacey and Kyle with him. She would have gone with him without a second thought, but a dark truth dawned on them. It was likely that Henry wouldn't live until Lacey turned eighteen and they needed someone to take care of them. Madeline was the only person left. Lacey told herself she would prefer foster care, but this wouldn't have been best for Kyle. They would continue to live in the cottage together, Madeline moving into Ned's bedroom, and try to keep going as long as they could. As Lacey sat and looked at the world around her, it was clear that it was all beyond her reach.

"Nothing. Everything is the same. And yet it's changed forever," she said.

Ezra nodded as though he understood, and perhaps a part of him did. He took her arm and placed her hand in his so he could rub it soothingly. They looked at each other. Ezra gave her a soft smile and wiped the rest of her tears from her cheeks. Lacey looked at his lips and felt a surge to kiss them. Then they turned away from each other and looked back out across the field. Lacey was young, clever, and brave. If she felt like there was no where she belonged, she would make her own place, but not today. Today she would let herself be weak. There would be time for romance. She would learn to love her body and herself. A day would arrive when she would be able to kiss him. It wasn't today. A bird flew down from the goalposts and landed in front of them. Lacey saw that it was a raven and smiled. She might well have been haunted, but she knew enough to not try to change the events of a life that had passed on. Today had been written, but tomorrow would always be hers.

ELEN

Marcus drove for about fifteen more minutes along the motorway and pulled off at the second exit. When he'd reached the destination, he parked the car and they both got out. Elen looked around with a mixture of awe and confusion. They were at a war memorial.

"What are we doing here?" she asked.

"I'll show you."

Marcus led Elen towards the memorial. It was a large, open tunnel. The walls on either side were covered in the names of fallen soldiers organised by the county in Wales from which they came. The roof was supported by a series of thick, regal columns in the centre. The tunnel was open on both ends so that daylight could run straight through it. When dusk approached, as it did now, small lights on the wall came on and channelled people's gazes along the names to the other side. At the far end, there was a statue of a soldier saluting, and a bench circled it so that anybody who needed a moment's reflection could have it.

"This is my favourite place," Marcus said.

He walked off a little way ahead and Elen watched him move. He wasn't as ragged as he had been a few weeks ago.

When she spoke to him, there was less urgency in his voice. They didn't talk much about his sister who was still deep in her battle with cancer, but from the way he carried himself now it was clear that he had made some small peace with the news. His shirt was still coming untucked a little in the back, but this struck Elen as a part of his personality more than a sign of distress; Marcus had always been somewhat rough around the edges.

She followed his eyes zeroing in on a name along the left wall. Elen could tell by the way he looked that it was a specific name. He knew exactly where it was and his eyes were drawn straight to it, as if out of habit. Marcus raised an arm and ran a thumb fondly over the letters. Elen came quietly after him and waiting for him to speak.

"Sometimes I feel like I'm going to wear down the engraving from touching it so much," he said.

"Who is it?"

"My great-grandfather."

Elen read the name *Aled Gawain Pugh* and stood next to Marcus in silence. He smiled as he stared at the letters and continued talking without tearing his gaze away from them.

"I used to hear stories about him from my grandparents growing up. I almost felt like I knew the guy," he said.

Marcus ran his thumb over the name once last time before leading Elen to the statue. They sat down together on the circular bench. The seat was cold underneath her. She could see the moon hanging in a velvety firmament which seemed closer than it had ever been. For a moment, the muscles in her arms twitched as though she were about to reach out and try to touch it, to run her thumb across the sky and feel the bumps and ridges of the stars the way Marcus stroked his great-grandfather's name.

"How is your sister doing?" she asked.

"Strong-willed as ever. She's a fighter. They always say that though, right? It's hard sometimes, but she's managing. I...I come up here every now and then – when it's a hard day – and talk to my great-granddad. He never answers me, but I don't think that's the point. Sometimes just showing up and talking is more important."

Elen knew he meant that in more contexts than just his family. There was another motive for bringing her up here and she could sense it. That was one of the most frustrating parts about working in law enforcement; she could sense when someone was lying or meant something else. Elen was trained to be suspicious and she knew a conceit when she heard one.

"You've been different since you solved the Belvidere case, El," he said.

"I have?"

"You seem more distant. Always looking up at the sky and not focusing on what's going on around you."

"Are you talking to me as Chief Inspector Richardson or Marcus?"

"As Marcus. As someone who cares about you."

He stood up and walked out of the tunnel. There was a grassy area enclosed by a waist-high metal fence. Underneath there was a rapid drop down to the motorway they had just been driving on. Marcus went to the fence and leaned on it with his elbows, looking out to the land before him. Elen sat on the bench a little longer watching him. His head moved around as he took in all the sights, before dropping to look down. After a moment passed without him moving, Elen went over to him.

They stood looking out at the lights of cars coming into view and then exiting it one by one. Each represented a human being who they had been charged with protecting. Elen knew Marcus was right. She hadn't been the same since the case closed. The truth was, she missed Henry. The emotional connection she made to him didn't make any sense. It was entirely irrational and poor Mr Belvidere had no idea she valued him as anything more than a victim, but she did. He had embodied her feelings about her mother for the past couple of months and now he was gone, she felt the void of her mother's mind growing underneath her.

"Henry…he was like my mum. But without being her," she said.

"Maybe you need to see her then."

"I don't think that's a good idea."

"Do you know how often I come up here?" Marcus said, and Elen shook her head, so he continued. "Every fortnight, on average. Every week if I have the time. And do you think my great-granddad has ever said anything back to me? Sometimes…sometimes I sit at that statue and beg for a sign. I never get one. But the act of coming here, of showing up and trying, that makes all the difference."

She nodded and he didn't say anything else. When he took her home, he put the radio on and sang to her the entire way until she was laughing an ugly laugh which made her snort and giggle. He stopped the car outside her house and she unbuckled her seatbelt, hopping out and fumbling around in her bag for her house keys. Marcus waited until she'd opened her door before driving off. She turned and looked back over her shoulder, waving at him one last time before shutting the door and locking it.

Sitting on the stairs, she pried her boots off her feet and rubbed her toes. Padding barefoot up to the bedroom, she smiled to find her cat, Dennis, curled up asleep on the bed. She pulled her clothes off and dropped them onto the floor even though the laundry basket was only two metres away, then went into the bathroom and turned on the shower.

The hot water crashed onto her body and steam filled up the room. Clasping the shower curtain to her body she leaned out of the shower to open the window and let some of the hot air out. When she was finished, she wrapped a towel around herself and went back to the bedroom where she dried off and pulled on her pyjamas, slinging the towel over the drying rack in the hallway. Dennis stretched and rolled onto his back. She turned off the light and got into bed.

Dennis crawled up beside her and hopped onto her stomach, where he curled back up and carried on sleeping. Elen stroked him absent-mindedly, feeling far too awake to sleep yet.

"How was your day, Den Den?" she whispered. "Mine was good. I have a new friend. You'll like Marcus. He's weird and stressed, which means he could do with some cat cuddles. I'll teach him where you like to be scratched, like here," she said, scratching behind Dennis's ears until he began purring and rubbing his head against her hand. "There you go, boy."

She put her hands by her sides and pushed herself so she was half-sitting, then wriggled the pillow enough to help prop her up. Marcus's words continued to replay in her mind on repeat. Perhaps it would help to see her family more regularly. She couldn't find the comfort she wanted in her mother, but she wasn't going to find it anywhere else either.

"Do you think I'm a bad person?" she asked Dennis. "Do I neglect people?"

Elen pictured her mother in her chair by the window. She wouldn't be there forever. Was she a bad daughter? A person could be a loyal friend, a good detective, a reliable homeowner, but none of it qualified as a good moral standing if she hurt people. How much had she hurt her father? Was it solely her responsibility to find out and fix everything?

"People are confusing, Den Den. Cats are so much easier."

As if on cue, Dennis decided enough was enough and grabbed Elen's hand between his front paws, digging his claws in and kicking her with his back feet. He scratched right the way up her arm and it stung.

"Ow, you little shit!" Elen jumped and Dennis rolled off her, dropping onto the bed and falling asleep as though it hadn't meant anything at all.

She cradled her sore hand with her other arm and looked over to the clock on the bedside table. It was only ten, but she didn't have anything else to do besides go to bed. Her eye caught the phone next to her clock and the urge to phone her father surged through her body. It was too late in the day for that. Before she got too nervous and changed her mind, she picked up the phone and opened her text conversation with her father.

Thinking of coming over after work tomorrow. Let me know if that works for you. I'll bring dinner with me! x

She couldn't change anything she had done but, as she lay there in the dark watching how much of her life had faded from view already, she knew she had to cherish the present. Marcus was right. She didn't need an answer or that connection back. She just had to voice her feelings for her own sake. Henry Belvidere had shown her that. He had his voice taken from him and had fought for it back. Life was messy and nobody fell on the side of good or bad – people existed in a foggy, murky place in between, where they all fought to feel their way through the mist. Elen could do it alone, or she could hold onto as many people as she could. She made her choice.

MADELINE

In the end there was nothing at all, not even a scream. Madeline lay in Ned's bed on her back with her arms stretched out each side. Her belongings were in a pile at the end of the bed and the room was exactly as her son had left it. She had been sleeping in here for two weeks since the night Henry broke the window. Madeline looked around the bedroom trying to shake off the confusion that she still felt when she woke up in the night. She expected to open her eyes to see her bedside table and more than once she had reached over to open the drawer, only to find it wasn't there. Madeline knew what she was looking for; her favourite picture of Henry used to only be an arm's length away. Now it was somewhere on the floor in her pile of clothes, wrapped up in a blouse to protect it. While she often wanted to look at the picture, she never rifled through her belongings to find it.

There was something about the night that made her want to see Henry's face. She found herself missing her old bedroom, even though it used to be a porch. It was a small space with large windows and a door across the longest wall. Madeline found that she had spent most nights before Henry woke up sitting on the edge of the bed, staring out across the fields opposite wondering if this world still had a place for her. The room had felt smaller with each sun set and Madeline had begun to feel like she was trapped in a glass box – a relic in a display cabinet, there to showcase history more than to serve a purpose.

There were times now when the thought of being in Ned's room grew to be too much and she had to go outside, leaving the cottage entirely to find herself in the night air. Owls let haunting notes linger in the trees. Crickets chirped and rubbed together. The distant glow of orange stars reaching the ends of their lives hung in the air, warming the sky above the cold outline of mountains. Madeline's sole hope used to be that she could burn beautifully as her life came to a close, but now she didn't care how she burned as long as she did.

Most nights, there were plenty of stars to be admired from the deck of the cottage. There was a secret, guilty pleasure to be taken from watching the world when it was empty. As her family slept in their beds and she wandered out into the darkness, she was able to recognise Earth as a planet. In her daily life, there was no time to appreciate that she was the most pathetic speck in an intricate painting of the universe. When she was alone, she could look at the stars no longer polluted by light, feel the wind whisper into the grass on the fields, and hear the sounds of animals she couldn't dream of noticing when the sun was up. It was almost perverse, like she was watching the world undress before her eyes. Everything was naked when she was outside alone; Wales put on a show for her, teased Madeline with its nudity. *Look at me*, the landscape called. *I have oceans of wet, mountains of body, valleys of depth and longing... nobody else is looking but you, Madeline. Only you can see me this way, in this moment. Don't you love me? Don't you want to live?*

She turned over and fumbled around for Ned's alarm clock to see what time it was, having no reaction at all upon seeing that she was wide awake at two in the morning. It was one of those nights when she had to get out of the cottage. She pulled a pair of shoes out from underneath the bed and slipped them on, and then went to Ned's drawers to pull out one of his hoodies. Madeline pulled it on over her head and grabbed her keys. Sneaking out of the bedroom to the living space, she made her way to the front door. As she reached Henry's bedroom which she used to share, she stopped and stared at the closed door for a moment. What could she say to him if she was on the other side? It was no use saying she was sorry or trying to explain her actions any more. The truth was that she loved Ned and Henry. Continuing out the front door, she locked up after herself and began to walk towards Beatrice Wallace's empty house down the gravel road.

Small stones crunched and ground under her shoes like teeth gnashing together as she walked along, determined to keep going until she couldn't any more. There used to be a time when she was nervous about going out in the dark by herself, especially when she was out in the countryside as she was now. The world didn't seem so frightening after everything Madeline had experienced, which only made her realise she knew a good deal less than she thought she did about life. If anything, her ignorance made her see the world as though she was looking at it through a pair of polarised sunglasses; the earth burned hot and bright underneath her feet, but everything above her faded into a tinted haze.

When she reached the house, Madeline turned and walked around it into the garden. There was a small gap in the fence on the left that led into an open field on a hill. She just about managed to squeeze through and picked her way across the uneven ground on the other side until she was up the slight incline and onto the grass. Her heart was crashing against her chest and her body clamoured for air and a break, but Madeline kept pushing forwards. Nothing short of death could make her stop. When she reached the top of the hill, she kept going until she was as close to the centre of the field as possible. There, she collapsed onto the ground and sprawled out. She lifted Ned's hoodie up over her mouth and nose and breathed in his scent, closing her eyes and visualising the last time she saw him.

She was the only one who visited him while he was remanded in custody. The two of them sat across from the table in the visitation room in silence for some time. Ned stared down at the floor while Madeline examined him, looking for signs of distress and trying to collate all her thoughts into meaningful sentences. His usually clean-shaven face was breaking out in grey stubble and dark circles painted the skin underneath his eyes.

"All I want is for you to be home," she said.

Ned looked up at her and, when their eyes met, Madeline saw that she would never have her wish. He was being kept here while he awaited trial because it was ruled unsafe to send him back into the house with Henry should Ned be guilty of his crimes. The words 'attempted murder' were tetric and left Madeline's tongue feeling raw. This was her boy.

"I think you love me," Madeline said.

"I do."

She believed him. He hadn't mentioned a word about her knowledge of the situation to the police at all. Neither had Henry, but she knew in the case of the latter, it was a practical decision more than anything to do with their marriage. Ned leaned forwards so his chest was pressed up against the edge of the table. Then he placed his palms flat on the table in front of him and stared at them like they belonged to someone else.

"It was wrong. All wrong. None of it makes any sense. I just want to know why, Ned," she said.

"Karen —"

"No. Not Karen. Why was this your only choice?"

He stared at her and she lost herself in his eyes. She remembered the first time they looked up at her. In the hospital, she had been sore and bleeding, her body burning with battle, her throat raw and thirsty from screaming, but he watched her until she couldn't feel anything. Madeline had held Ned in her arms and they had been covered in each other, but she had become clean and weightless. The eyes had been the colour of the darkest night, deep and full of a rich history that Madeline could only have dreamed of exploring. The whites of his eyes had beached the black sands and she had found the horizon gazing back at her. Now they glanced at her from a couple of feet away, but she couldn't stroke his cheek or cradle him anymore. All she could do was watch those eyes and continue her quest to decipher what lay behind them, understanding then that she would never know.

"I knew once. It was all about her. And Galen. My son I never got to meet. But I was killing their memories. I don't know anymore," he said. "I don't think I had a reason. Not a real one. Is that possible?"

Madeline knew that was true. During the investigation, Detective Parry kept trying to break everything down into one concise and comprehensible motive, but life was never as black and white as the police wanted her to believe. She existed in the grey area in between. It was a misty place full of confusion and doubt. Her horrors lived there, but so did her love. There was no time left for reasons or excuses. They couldn't go back.

"I think you had reasons, but perhaps you don't know what they are," she said. "Something made you do this. But you don't have to know what it was."

"That's so typical of you."

"What is?"

"You always do this," Ned said. "You try to justify everything. Even having no justification becomes some kind of reasoning for you. I just couldn't handle it. That's the bottom line. I couldn't hack it anymore. Is that what you want to hear?"

"Want to hear?" Madeline was incredulous. "I don't want to hear any of this."

She reached up and rubbed her temples, trying to stop the headache she could feel coming on. Ned pushed one of his hands forwards across the table, over to hers. Madeline looked at it for a beat and then allowed her own hand to find its way over to him.

"I don't want to see the end of us," she whispered.

"What?"

"God, Ned, I love this family. I love Henry. I love you. I love Lacey and Kyle and Karen... I have so many people who I care about and you're all pulling off in different directions. I don't want to choose one over the other. I want you all. I don't want to see the time when I could have my family together end."

Ned nodded, withdrawing his hand and Madeline knew that their time together had already come to a close. She got up to leave and Ned rose with her, stepping in her way as she moved to walk out of the door. Then, without speaking, he stepped forwards and put his arms around her, pulling her into a hug. Her arms hung limp at her sides while she realised what was happening. When her body caught up to her mind, she lifted her arms and wrapped them around her son. He was so much taller than she was, but she laid her hands on his back and pressed him against her the way she had done when he was a boy.

"I will always love you," she said.

Two weeks later, out on the field at half past two in the morning, Madeline breathed in the sweet scent of washing powder and deodorant from Ned's hoodie. She opened her eyes and stared up at the sky. The stars were bright above her and sparkled like sequins against a dark ocean into which Madeline wished she could cast herself.

"Karen," she whispered. "Are you there?"

Madeline held her breath, half-expecting a voice to echo down to her from above, saying *yes. I've always been here. I'm permanent.*

"You filled the skies, right? Like it says on your headstone? Ned said you saw the whole of the moon, like the song. Did you see everything? The truth? You loved my son. You saw something good in him when others didn't. Am I missing something? Am I only waning when you were full? I have so many questions, Karen."

She laid there for a while longer in case an answer came to her, whether it was from an ethereal voice or a sudden thought inside her head, but nothing happened. It was hard to say how much time had passed while she looked up at the stars, but it had been long enough that Madeline began to forget she was lying on solid ground and started to feel like she was part of the sky. A chill spread through her body and tingled across her skin. She sat up, using her hands to push herself with a little struggle.

As Madeline hauled herself to her feet, she looked at the trees nearby. They were the first row of the woods that rose in the fields and went all the way up the slopes of the hillside until they bled into the mountains themselves. They called out to her. Taking one last glance at the sky, Madeline staggered over to the trees. As she came to the first one, she placed a hand on the trunk and felt the armour of the bark scratch at her fingertips. From the edge of the field, she could barely see through the trees. It was as though the world ended there. If she kept walking, she would drop off the Earth altogether. Madeline knew she couldn't stay out all night. Venturing forwards, she made up her mind and stepped into the woods. It was time to go home.

Publisher Biography

Barnard Publishing Ltd. was established in 2022 by Becca Barnard after finishing her Masters, with the goal of offering publishing services in North Wales where there is a significant lack. She hopes one day to join forces with her father's company, Barnard Engineering, to create Barnard Corp., and together rule the universe.

Author Biography

Briony Collins is a writer based in North Wales, where she also owns and runs the publishing company Atomic Bohemian. She is the winner of the 2016 Exeter Novel Prize, runner up of the 2022 Danby Prize, and a winner of the 2024 Black Bough Manuscript Competition.

Briony takes an active role in supporting writers in Wales as an educator, mentor, and editor. She has served on the *Poetry Wales* Sub-committee and has collaborated with Black Bough Poetry to create more opportunities for writers living in Wales and beyond. She is also a Fellow of the Higher Education Academy.

When she isn't working, Briony is curled up on the sofa watching terrible horror films with her husband, Tom, and their two guinea pigs, Brady and Delia.

www.brionycollins.co.uk

Trigger Warnings:

- eating disorder
- forced eating/emetophobia
- coma/hospital scenes
- child loss
- domestic abuse
- attempted senicide
- loss of a loved one/grief
- mention of possible attempted suicide
- mention of terminal illness, mention of dementia
- police procedure